THE *Beauty* OF A BEAST

WITH
BELLE AND THE DRAGON

BY
TONY MYERS

 www.trafford.com

North America & international
toll-free: 1 888 232 4444 (USA & Canada)
fax: 812 355 4082

ACKNOWLEDGMENTS

I would like to start by saying thank you to my wife Charity for proofreading the manuscript. Thank you for your patience in working through my book. I love you so much. In regard to editing, I also want to say thank you to Stephen for "coming out of retirement" to edit the manuscript. I know you spent many hours on it, and for that I am extremely grateful.

To the fans of Singleton and Stealing the Magic, I must say that your emails, comments, and words of encouragement were extremely motivating in my ambition to write another book. Your support kept me writing on the hard days. Thank you so much! I take all your encouragement to heart.

I also want to thank Mitch and the whole crew at the Waterloo Chick-fil-a. You guys provided a wonderful atmosphere for writing this book. The service is always friendly, and the food is always tasty. Keep up the good work, my friends.

Our small group also deserves a large amount of gratitude for their encouragement and support. Thank you guys especially for the 5-hour energy drink that pushed me to the finish line.

My family is wonderful. I want to thank both my immediate and extended family. I appreciate all the excitement and interest in the book. You are always supportive of me as an author and for that I'm so grateful. I especially want to mention Charity, Hannah Beth, Anthony and Elliot. I love you guys so much!

Lastly, I would like to give my love and gratitude to God. I once was blind, but now I see. I'm so thankful for the Amazing Grace that is found in your Son. He is the one who saved me... opened my eyes. To Him be all glory, honor, and praise!

To my wife, Charity,
לִבִּי
ἀγάπη μου

Thankful for this journey we have
together. We were meant to be.

∽❧∾

Belle and the Dragon

A short prequel

1

$\mathcal{B}$elle awoke and sat up in her bed. She was breathing heavily. It was early, still dark out. Her dreams had awakened her again. This was a common occurrence. She wiped the sweat from her forehead and looked around the room. Looking to her right, she could see rain beating against the window.

Pulling the covers off, she quickly slid out of bed and walked toward the window. She looked out to the mountains in the distance, admiring them from afar. Belle enjoyed being in a room far above the tree line. For as long as she could remember, she had lived in this tower. It was the highest spot in the castle. Being the only daughter of the king definitely came with its perks. Everyone in the villages greatly admired King Sebastian's twenty-year-old beautiful daughter, and this quiet tower provided the great peace she needed in her world of fame.

She tried to think of her dream. She so deeply wished she could remember it. Only bits and pieces would come to her. *What was it?* she thought to herself. It was a strange feeling. Intuitively Belle knew this was the same recurring dream she was having every week. The strange thing, too, was that something was not right with the dream. She just couldn't place what it was, but she knew something was wrong. A piece of it was troubling. The desire to remember was growing every week. She would have given a lot of gold to help figure out the nature of her dream.

The lightning continued to strike in the distance. She wondered if she could go back to sleep. She walked back to her bed and climbed under the covers. She looked over at the lantern on the table beside her bed. Her medicine was sitting next to the lantern. The nursemaid must have come in and left it while she was sleeping. Picking up the small cup, Belle drank it down quickly. It tasted terrible, but she had become immune to the taste a long time ago.

For as long as she could remember she had taken medicine. The nursemaid would routinely bring it in at night, and she would take it first thing when she woke up. Belle wasn't totally sure what it was for, but her father always said it was for her demeanor and anxiety. Many times she had asked her father if she would ever be cured. He would always tell her that their doctors could retest in a few years and see if it was helping. She knew it would never happen.

Belle gathered her brown hair in a ponytail and tied it back. She readjusted her pillow before lying down. Shutting her eyes, she tried to relax. She could hear more than just the rain on the window pane. At first she thought it was her imagination, but after a while she knew that it wasn't. She heard voices coming from downstairs.

What's going on? she thought to herself. *It's too early for Father to be engaging in matters of business.* She quickly got back out of bed and headed for the door. Turning the handle, she opened the door slowly. The voices became louder. She could hear shouting and arguing.

Belle quickly walked to her bed and grabbed the lantern. Lighting the lantern, she walked back toward the opened door. She slowly crept down the spiral steps of the tower. The voices grew louder with every step. Her father's voice was clear, but many of the other voices she did not immediately recognize.

Reaching the bottom, she peeked around the corner into the meeting room. She could see a large round table and her father, the king, on one end arguing his point. He was dressed in a dark red robe with his crown sitting on the table. His long curly, brown hair could be clearly seen. His advisor, Hector de Serpent, was close to his side, gritting his teeth angrily as a few strands of dark black hair covered his face. On the other side of the table were about a dozen fully-armed knights, who were ready for battle. It looked as if her father, King Sebastian, was angrily arguing and pleading with them. Belle tried to listen in on what was he was saying but struggled to grasp the full context of their conversation. Across the table from the king, the chief knight of the realm, Michael, was arguing on behalf of his men. Belle couldn't hear him very clearly but could tell he was trying to make a case against what King Sebastian was saying.

Belle knew that Michael de Bolbec was the only person in the whole kingdom who could argue with the king in such a fiery tone. He had proven himself in various battles in defense of the kingdom and had accomplished much, even at the age of 25. He was strong, brave and handsome and, though it was never said, Belle knew that her father was trying to groom him to one day be her husband. It seemed that everyone in the kingdom knew of this fact, which always made conversation with Michael a little awkward.

"Listen, I'm not into the game of appeasement," Michael said, jamming his index finger on the table. His voice was strong and could be recognized anywhere. "This creature has oppressed us long enough. I say it's time to strike and time to strike hard."

The King shook his head, "Michael, what are you talking about? He has left us in peace for years. The people barely remember the last victim."

Michael hit the table hard with his fist. His blond hair partially covered his face as he shouted angrily, "Peace, you think this is peace? The people live in fear of him. He sits there day after day on our border, waiting for someone from our land to come close."

"Hold your tongue, Michael!" Hector responded, pausing a moment to lick his lips. His voice reminded Michael of what a human snake would sound like. "You ought to know better than to talk to the king in this way. You ought to be bowing before him, not talking to him in his manner." Hector quickly pulled a dagger from his side. Michael remained unfazed, not in the least bit scared of Hector.

"Quiet down, Hector. I can handle this," King Sebastian spoke. Hector lowered his dagger, giving Michael an angry look. Belle despised Hector. He always dressed himself in dark green clothing and seemed to linger in the shadows. She often objected to the advice and opinions he seemed to plant in her father's mind. She wished he would listen to her warnings, but it was always to no avail.

"Ok, listen, King," Michael said, brushing his hair out of his eyes. "This creature needs to be shown strength. I'm not sure if my men and I will be able to quietly hunt him down and destroy him, but I'd say at least let's come to him with swords drawn ready to fight. Some of these creatures are conscious enough to detect emotions like fear and courage. Let's show him the latter. Let's show him the strength of the kingdom."

Though no one directly said it, Belle knew the creature they were referring to... a dragon; a cave dwelling dragon that caused the people of Mendolon to live in fear. On his own, he had created a forbidden territory east of the kingdom that the people stayed away from. His cave sat in the middle of this ten-mile territory. The townspeople refused to enter the area. In the past some of the new travelers to the kingdom thought the dragon was a myth, but five years ago any talk of a myth was put to silence. A merchant was eaten when he tried to take a shortcut by journeying through the area. His bones were later found at the edge of the territory. The dragon left them as a warning for the people.

The king continued, "Michael, we don't cross into his border and he stays out of ours. This dragon has shown reserve and respect for our kingdom."

"Respect... respect?" Michael countered, "You think living at our border and threatening to kill our people is a sign of respect? And answer me this, why has he suddenly decided to dwell at the edge of the border and blow fire into the surrounding fields?"

The king shook his head, "You are not listening to me. The proper way to go about this is not through a fight with a dragon. How many soldiers would we lose? Are you willing to sacrifice a few men from your band of knights just to kill a rather small dragon that lives, not in our towns, but outside our border?"

Michael couldn't help but smile in sarcasm at the king's use of the word small. Though compared to other dragons he was quite small, this one was no less intimidating. He would still rival the size of an elephant, and his sharp teeth and massive tail would leave anyone cowering before him. "My king, also think about this... if this beast was sent away, the trade routes to the east would be opened. Our neighbors would see it as a sign of goodwill."

The king rubbed his forehead out of frustration. He spoke a little quieter, "Michael... my knight, you are not even thinking rationally now. Those to the east of us are savages. They would have nothing but war from us." His voice was rising at this point, "Please, will you just let me explain my solution before you keep objecting."

Michael took a deep breath and looked back at his knights. They seemed to be waiting patiently while he made his opinion known to the king. Michael had argued his point mightily and, so far, wasn't getting through. He decided to yield to the king. He spoke in a calm voice, "Ok, King, tell me, what do you have in mind for this creature?"

King Sebastian bowed his head gently in a sign of appreciation, "Thank you for seeing the light. I will proceed." He turned now to his advisor, "Hector, please bring in the statue." Hector quickly retreated to a set of large double doors behind the king.

A puzzled look spread across Michael's face as Hector opened the doors. He beheld the statue that two royal servants brought in on a cart. Hector helped guide it into place by the table. Michael couldn't believe what his eyes were seeing. It was a wooden statue of a dragon. It was about five feet in height, beautifully designed, and very well detailed. Hector was a master craftsman, and seemed to have spent hours on this fixture under the king's orders. The teeth and the claws were each uniquely crafted, and even each individual scale looked to be crafted with great detail. Hector spoke up, "We plan to overlay it with gold before setting it on the border of the dragon's territory."

Michael's mouth dropped open as he searched for words. On one hand the structure was a beauty to behold. It was possibly Hector's greatest work. The detail was incredible. But on the other hand, he couldn't believe what the king was proposing. Offering some type of idol to the dragon was not the road Michael wanted to venture down. "No…. no!" he said shaking his head. "This is definitely not the side of the kingdom we want to show the dragon."

"Michael," the king stuck his hand out, trying to calm him, "Hear me out, the dragon will see the time we spent on this and its beauty and he will look on us with favor."

"He will definitely look on us with favor," Michael shouted, "because he will think he is a god to us!"

"Listen, my knight. We just need to leave it at the edge of the territory and let him think what he wants."

"King, you are my king, but in all due respect for you and the kingdom… I will not bring this piece of wickedness before him. This idea is most shameful, and definitely below your dignity."

Hector could not contain his rage any longer. Before anyone could react, he quickly pulled his dagger again and lunged over the round table toward Michael. "How dare you speak to the king in this manner!" he shouted as he passed over the table.

Taking a step back, Michael quickly picked up his shield to intercept the approaching dagger. The dagger hit hard against the shield. The blade snapped in half upon impact. Hector landed on his feet and tried to gather himself quickly. Turning around, he wasn't able to react in time to see Michael's shield being driven into his face. Everyone could hear the crack of Hector's nose breaking.

Hector fell to the floor. Blood was already starting to flow from his nostrils. Michael walked calmly over to where Hector was lying on the ground face up. An expression of terror was clearly visible. Michael slowly unsheathed his sword and held the tip toward Hector's throat. "What were you saying, Snake?" he spoke quietly. Everyone watched in amazement at Michael's poise.

Hector hissed as he spoke, "You're not man enough to drive me through anyway. Go ahead and do it if you choose. I bet you…"

"Men, stop this non-sense," King Sebastian said, rolling his eyes. "Hector, get off the floor and get back over here before you hurt yourself." Pushing Michael's sword aside, Hector quickly got up and ran toward the king's side. The blood from his nose stained his mouth and chin. Michael sheathed his sword as his enemy retreated.

The king continued, "Well, like it or not, we are delivering this statue to the edge of the woods. You can either support me as your king or you can…"

Crash! The king turned to see the statue lying flat on the ground, knocked off the cart. A few of the wooden claws and teeth had broken off during the fall, and there were other large cracks in the body of the structure. A mixture of anger and confusion could be seen on the king's face because beside the fallen statue, he was looking into the face of his only daughter, Belle.

With all the commotion with Michael and Hector, they had failed to see Belle pick up a javelin mounted on the wall and approach the statue. Swinging the javelin as hard as she could, she had knocked the statue off the cart and onto the floor. She now stood beside the broken structure, still in her nightgown, but looking more like a warrior with the javelin in her hand.

"Belle, what do you think you are doing?" her father spoke, a little more confused than angry.

Belle was a little scared as she spoke, "Father, I want to know what is happening. And please," she paused, just for a moment, "I want to know how I can help." Though she tried to look and sound tough, her voice was naturally soft and pleasant. It was always inviting to all who heard it.

The room had gone silent for a moment. Tensions had been rising all morning, and it was as if Belle's presence had brought everything back down to a calm level. All the knights had grand respect for the king's daughter. She was always kind to the townspeople and sought to befriend them when she could. She truly represented the best of the kingdom of Mendolon.

Michael took a deep breath and spoke quietly, "Belle, the dragon has been coming out of his cave the last two days and traveling to the edge of his border, sometimes into our territory."

"You can't prove that," the king countered.

Michael continued, "Regardless, he is burning the fields on the edge of our border, destroying crops and killing a few livestock. I'm sure you've also heard the rumors that he growls at night, giving off a warning to those nearby."

"Belle, we are debating what is the proper procedure to deal with these current developments," her father added.

Everyone stood in silence for a few seconds trying to process everything that had happened and everything they had discussed. The mood had become noticeably less tense. Michael and his knights took seats at the table. Belle quietly sat down before speaking up, "Father, I think we should follow Michael's plan. This dragon has been pestering us for years now, and maybe in the past the people were content to let him live on as long as he left us unbothered… but, Father, now is the time to fight back. He is again bringing fear to the townspeople and threatening us. He is one of the smallest dragons we know of; surely men with half the skill and courage of Michael have slain dragons greater than the one we face. I'd say let's take up arms and confront him at once." Michael couldn't help but smile slightly at Belle's confidence in him.

The king gently sat down at the table. He shook his head in exhaustion. He was angry at Michael. If it weren't for his loyalty and valor in battle, the king would have surely demoted him a long time ago. He rubbed his hands through his thick brown beard as a plan formulated through his mind. He wanted a way to turn this situation around for his own glory and fame… or better yet, for the glory and fame of his lineage.

Standing up, the king grabbed for his crown and placed it on his head. He was ready to issue a decree. "Ok, this is what I propose. Today, we lead a procession through the town with Michael and his knights on the way to fight the dragon. Let the people see we are going to strike."

"I agree, my king," Michael responded.

"But let me say this," the king continued with a smile on his face, "At the front of the procession beside Michael will be my daughter leading the way."

This caught Michael off guard. He did not like the sound of this. "With all due respect, Sire, I do not agree with this decision. Yes, your daughter is skilled with the sword and will be a knight in her time, but I don't think she is quite ready to face a dragon. I know you want..."

"Let me finish," the king responded, "Belle will accompany you on this journey in full battle attire, but she will only go with you so far. Let the people see you ride through town and into the territory, but right before you are to do battle with the dragon in his lair, find a safe haven for Belle. Let her see the battle and claim the victory for it in the end. It will unite the people under my throne, and confirm my lineage against rebellion for a generation."

Michael thought about this proposal from the king. He didn't like the idea of bringing Belle along, but he liked it a lot more than any plan of appeasement the king had offered. Standing up from the table, he cracked his knuckles as he looked sharply at the king. "We will prepare at once, and leave as soon as the townsfolk begin to enter the markets." The king nodded in approval.

Belle stood shocked. She couldn't believe she was about to go on a dragon hunt.

2

$\mathcal{B}$elle led the way on horseback through the center of town, dressed in her own armor. It was a beautiful purple and white pattern. It looked quite fitting for a princess, yet still ready for battle. A small sword was bouncing gently off her side with every step of the horse. She wore no helmet, just a simple crown on her head. Michael and his men were following close behind Belle. Michael chose his eight best men to accompany them on this expedition. He didn't want any trouble from the dragon. The knights were in their traditional battle armor, whereas Michael was dressed in his unique warrior-like armor. It consisted of a grey fabric material with a metal vest covering his chest and traditional metal gloves to cover his hands. He wanted the protection yet valued the ability to be mobile during a battle. Unlike the other knights, he wore a helmet that left his face exposed. The king wanted the people to see the face of the realm's chief knight.

It was prime time for the merchants. The streets were busy with people buying and selling in vast array. Many had stopped their transactions to watch the brigade of soldiers pass through the streets. Some of the young girls ran in excitement to see the king's beautiful daughter pass through their midst. They clapped and cheered at the sight of the princess.

Belle smiled and waved to the crowds as they showed their affection. A part of her felt deceptive leading knights through town like this, knowing that she was not going to engage in battle. In her mind she reassured herself that this was bringing the people hope, giving them something to rejoice about. Her father's presence often brought dissension among the people. She was thankful that she could bring unity.

A young girl ran up toward Belle's horse in a full sprint. She couldn't have been older than nine. She was bouncing with excitement. "Whoa, hold up!" Michael said, holding out his hand to slow the girl. She stopped in her tracks.

"It's all right... let her come," Belle said, motioning with her hand for the girl to come closer. As she approached the horse, Belle could see that the girl held up a flower to her. Belle couldn't help but smile as she gently took it from the girl's hand. It was a daisy. The petals were nearly perfect. Stopping her horse in place, she put the flower in her hair, right by her ear. Giving the girl a small wink, she gave her horse a light kick as they continued on. The young girl waved as she ran back to her mother.

"It seems the townspeople are quite fond of you, Your Highness," Michael said, riding alongside Belle.

"Maybe they're cheering for you, the king's chief knight," Belle said, still waving to the people.

Michael laughed slightly, "I can assure you they're not. The princess of the land is the one they want to see."

"Michael, you know the people love you and appreciate your services to the kingdom."

"Oh, don't get me wrong, I know they see me favorably, but you know as well as I that their true affection rests with you and you alone."

Belle kept smiling and waving to the people. She genuinely loved them. More than anything she wanted them to feel safe and at peace in the kingdom. She was happy that after many years the threat of the dragon that lived at their borders was finally going to be eliminated.

≈⁄∽

It had taken them most of the day to reach the southeastern edge of the kingdom. They were currently on the outskirts to the kingdom's border close to the dragon's territory. A few small villages were located in this region of rolling hills. They were simple farming communities. Occasionally the king would send guards through the area for collecting taxes or for the issuing of new decrees, but for the most part these villages governed themselves.

Michael, Belle, and the knights passed through the center of a small village located in a wooded area. A few houses lined the side of the road. On any other occasion, the people would have only given a slight notice to knights passing through their village, but as of late, the people were anxious to see the kingdom deal with the threats from the dragon. The group of knights was definitely a positive sign for the people, and seeing the king's daughter riding with them was also a joyous sight.

A few times each year, Belle would travel to these outlining towns, usually with a couple of knights by her side. She wanted to see the people's faces. In her heart of hearts she truly loved them and wanted them to experience lives of peace and tranquility within the kingdom of Mendolon. She worked hard at learning names and remembering the occupations of the people she saw more regularly. She knew that one day she was going to be their queen, and they would be her people.

Coming to the end of the line of houses, Michael instructed the men. "This road should take us right into the dragon's territory. We have about another mile to travel and then we will stop for food before proceeding into the territory."

No one responded. The men were loyal and followed his orders without question. They trusted him.

Belle spoke up, "Michael, I'm surprised we are entering on the south side. The dragon has been spotted more by the villages on the northwestern side of the territory."

Michael nodded without making eye contact. "I figure that is where the dragon might be spending most of his time. He may not expect anyone to approach his cave from the southern route."

"I'm surprised that we would need to take such precautions with a group of eight men and this small of a dragon."

Michael smiled as he turned to look at Belle, "Your confidence in me and my men is quite flattering, but I'm trying to eliminate any chance of an incident. This dragon has shown quite a bit of intelligence and I don't want to underestimate him in any way." Michael paused for a moment, "Even though he is small, he is still a fire-breathing dragon."

Most of the women in the kingdom admired Michael for his strength and good looks. He was truly a symbol for the kingdom and King Sebastian would not hesitate to parade him around the villages with a brigade of troops. Belle, on the other hand, admired him for his bravery and humility. She wished more people could see that side of him.

They trotted along in silence for a minute or two. Belle and Michael were about ten feet in front of the others. The sound of the horses' hooves was soothing as they traveled closer to the dragon's territory. None of the men seemed scared. They found their confidence in their leader.

Belle broke the silence, "At times you really surprise me, Michael."

"Oh, how so?"

"You often fall in line with many of my father's wishes and desires. Why are you so loyal to him and give him so much respect?"

Michael spoke calmly, "Belle, I don't know how much you heard this morning, but we were arguing for quite a while about what to do with this dragon."

"Yes, I know, but even still, you are here doing my father's bidding... even bringing me along. You know my father can be a harsh man at times. Why do you have such an allegiance to him?"

Michael waited just a moment before speaking. His mind seemed to be elsewhere. "My allegiance is to freedom, justice, and peace. Yes, your father is harsh at times, but he has provided a stable realm for the people of his kingdom. I will seek to maintain that. I will honor him as our king... for the sake of the people."

Belle was happy for these few minutes alone to talk with Michael. She wanted to speak with him more in depth. All morning she had suspected that something was on his mind. It may have been a simple inflection in his voice, or possibly the way he was not making eye contact, but somehow Belle knew Michael was hiding something. He was truly a man filled with honor and truth, and most of the time he would easily give himself away if he wasn't being completely honest.

"Michael, I know this dragon needs to be dealt with, but he has been here for years and not crossed our borders. Why the urgency? Couldn't this dragon just be making us aware of his presence? Reminding us of his territory."

"Isn't ridding our border of a fire breathing dragon enough motivation?"

Though Belle often came across as sweet and soft spoken, she did have a determined side to her personality that wouldn't give up till she got the answer she was looking for. "Michael, please," she said reaching over and grabbing his arm, "You give yourself away so easily. What is really going on?"

Looking down at Belle's hand holding his arm seemed to soften him. Though at times he tried not to think about it, he knew the rumors among the townspeople that one day they would wed. He looked up at her eyes as they were fixed on his. He knew there was no need in hiding anything, especially since she was accompanying them on this journey. He looked back at his men before speaking, "Belle, something does not add up with this dragon."

"What do you mean?" she said, releasing his arm.

"I mean the whole situation. It's always disturbed me. For one, have you ever heard of a dragon positioning itself directly between two kingdoms, and marking off its boundary? Usually they live far off, hoarding and protecting whatever gold they have accumulated. I have never heard of a dragon dwelling this close to such a populated region, much less two vast kingdoms."

"Michael, that was about twenty years ago when he marked off his territory. You would have been young. Do you even remember that time?"

"I do. I was five at the time. People were filled with fear, wondering what the implications of having a dragon at our borders would mean."

"I can imagine that was a hard time to grow up," Belle said softly.

"For a time it was. I remember as a boy hearing about how the dragon had marked the border of his territory with fire. Among the townspeople they nicknamed the area *Dragon Waste*. Quickly, stories began to grow about the size of the dragon and if this would somehow incite a war with our neighbors to the east. I believe at that time, every boy in the kingdom had visions of growing up to become a dragon hunter."

Belle was anxious to hear more as her father never talked much about it. "What happened, Michael?" she inquired. "Do you remember why the kingdom did nothing about it at the time?"

Michael shrugged his shoulders, "Life moved on. After he marked his territory the people knew to stay out of it. We didn't cross his border and he stayed out of our villages. Other matters then concerned us as a people. King Sebastian, your father, heard rumors of war to the north. We thought we might be headed into it. Our attention was turned there. One day turned to another and the dragon was slowly forgotten."

"You know, when you put it like that, it is strange that we, as a kingdom, have just come to accept a dragon living this close to our border."

"Precisely. The whole situation is odd." Michael paused for a moment as if he was in deep thought, "But at the moment there is something else that has brought even more curiosity to me," he said, brushing his blond hair out of his eyes.

"Oh, and what's that?" Belle said, puzzled.

"The king is right on one thing... for years this dragon has lived at our border in solitude. The only incident was the passing merchant that went into his area. But still, he has never directly threatened us like he is doing now."

Belle thought for a moment about what Michael was implying. She figured she would ask directly, "So what's your point? What do you think is happening?"

"This dragon is being provoked. He would not act like this unless something was making him angry." Michael stared hard into the distance. "And maybe not necessarily some*thing*... but possibly some*one*."

෴

They reached the border of the dragon's territory in the middle of the afternoon. They stopped for a quick meal and to check supplies before heading into the area. A wooden sign stood at the border warning all travelers, "Dragon Waste: KEEP OUT! Enter under no circumstance." Michael gave it only a passing glance as they proceeded forward.

The day grew dreary as they traveled through the territory. Belle wondered if it was going to rain. She figured rain would actually be an advantage in battling a fire breathing dragon. Soon the trail faded away. Plant life had overtaken it. Michael's top soldier, Gideon, directed them according to a map of the area. Gideon was in his late forties, and he had been in the territory a couple of times before the dragon had settled. The dragon's cave was nearly in the center of the territory, and it would be at least an hour before they arrived.

Belle had felt a little anxiety when they first entered the territory, but as the journey dragged on, the anxiety slowly faded. Occasionally glancing at the soldiers, she saw no fear in their eyes. She gleaned much confidence from their demeanor. They followed their captain whom they trusted. He was focused. From their earlier talk, Belle knew that Michael had questions about this dragon. There was a mystery with this dragon, and Michael was ready to explore.

Besides the overgrowth of plant life, the territory did not look much different from the outskirts of Mendolon: a thick forest followed by a small open plain, followed by a cluster of trees. Belle's mind went to the battle that would be fought. She wondered how close she would be. She wondered how much she would be able to see. Or how long would it last? Surely a dragon this small would be a quick victory for Michael, especially with the amount of men that were brought along.

A rustle in the woods startled the company. Everyone stopped and looked to their left. Every man's hand instantly went to the hilt of their sword, except for Michael who went for one of his daggers attached to his belt. For a distant enemy he would not hesitate to throw a small dagger. The men watched closely as a rabbit bounced from a small bush on a hill. The tension eased and the men continued on.

Since they entered the territory, no one had said a word. Gideon and Michael led the way, and Belle was surrounded by knights on both sides. She longed for conversation. She wanted her questions answered. Her mind slowly drifted to her recurring dream. She had a faint hope that something on this journey would jog her memory and help her remember it. Belle felt as if it was on the edge of her mind, just waiting to be grasped. *Oh, how I wish I could remember it*, she thought.

Without warning, Michael stopped the company. They were on the edge of a clearing of trees. A small hill lay just before them. "We're here, men," Michael said in a quiet voice. Belle thought this was odd as she couldn't see the cave from where her horse stood. The men quickly dismounted from their horses and tied them to nearby trees. Belle followed suit.

Michael continued, "Gideon, you take the men around to the front of the cave and wait for me. I will make sure Belle is situated before joining you."

"We will wait," Gideon responded obediently. Michael and Belle watched as the knights walked around the hill, swords drawn, ready to fight. It was obvious the entrance to the cave was on the opposite side of the hill. Belle hoped she would be positioned where she could see the battle transpire.

"Belle, I'm going to position you here at the top of the hill among those two small trees," Michael said, pointing to the top of the small hill. "Common to most dragons, at this time he should be sleeping." Michael began leading her up the hill. She was a little disappointed as a part of her wished that somehow Michael would have allowed her to engage in the fight.

Michael further explained the plan. "Our strategy is simple. We attack the dragon while it is sleeping. If it awakes, it will have nowhere to go. Our numbers should overwhelm him pretty easily."

"What if he decides to breathe fire on you?" Belle said bluntly.

"Highly unlikely. If the dragon is trapped, most of the time they won't breathe fire, knowing that in a confined space the fire might lead to their own demise."

Reaching the trees on the top of the hill, Belle could see there was a steep cliff on the side where the opening of the cave was. Looking over the cliff, she could see she was about twenty feet off the ground. She could also see knights at the base. Michael gave a small wave, indicating he would be ready soon.

"I'd advise you to lay low among the trees. If the dragon seems to somehow get past us, he will probably head for the horses. Up here you will be completely out of the battle."

Michael looked off into the distance when he spoke. He did not face her. Belle could tell his mind was occupied. In the past she had seen Michael before small battles, and this was completely unlike him. "Michael... is everything ok?"

"You can take my shield," Michael said, completely ignoring the question. "You can use it to cover yourself, just in case the dragon is not in the cave. As soon as the battle is done, I will come for you. Remember to stay here."

Michael turned to leave. "Michael," Belle said, reaching out and trying to grab his hand. Failing to grasp his hand, her fingernails tore the cloth around his forearm, just above his gloves. Her grip was tight. Michael stopped. Looking down, Michael could see the torn cloth around his forearm. He looked up at Belle, making direct eye contact.

She continued, "Michael, I'm sorry, but is everything ok? Do you need me in this battle? I can help you guys. I've..."

"Belle," Michael said, placing his hand on her shoulder. "I know you are a capable warrior, and have shown valor, but... I will follow your father's wishes. You will be safe here."

He tried to turn away again, but she held tight. "Tell me, is everything all right? You don't seem yourself. What is it?"

Michael took a deep breath as he looked off into the distance. It seemed as if he was trying to choose his words carefully. "I keep thinking about our earlier conversation about *this* dragon."

"Do you still have questions about this whole situation?"

Michael looked right at her, "I do and the more I think about it... the more questions I have. Something is going on, and I want to get to the bottom of it."

3

*M*ichael came off the hill and walked toward the front of the cave. Forced by habit, he found himself checking the daggers on his belt. He made sure they were all in their proper place and ready to be used if need be. He carried his sword on his back. As opposed to a typical knight's sword, he preferred a shorter one. His current one was about a foot and a half in length. It was light-weight and could easily be pulled in the midst of combat.

He found his knights at the mouth of the cave looking into the entrance. Many of them already had their swords drawn. A couple of them looked worried. Seeing Michael approach, Gideon took a few steps toward him with news. "Sir, we believe the creature is awake," Gideon said quietly.

"Oh, what makes you say that?"

"We can hear his faint growls. He sounds to be about fifty to seven-five yards in." Gideon had always been blessed with a keen sense of hearing. It had proven to be a great asset in battle.

"Well, I guess there is not a moment to lose," Michael said, placing his helmet on his head and drawing his sword. "Follow me, men." With both hands on his sword, Michael proceeded to enter the cave. The knights did the same and followed behind their captain.

The knights were as quiet as they could be as they entered. They had all gone through immense training and knew how to sneak up on an enemy. Every drop of water and every slight kick of a rock seemed to be exaggerated in their minds. With every step, Michael went further into the darkness of the cave and closer to the growling of the creature. Sweat beads formed on his forehead. He was waiting for the right moment to charge the creature. One of his men had the assignment to light the torch just as he sprang into battle.

Michael's mind quickly flashed back to the time of his youth. He remembered as a boy hearing about the dragon coming to their borders. He remembered the fear in the eyes of townspeople. He remembered the desire to one day slay this dragon and bring peace to the realm. The feelings from his youth came back. He was truly ready to put an end to this dragon... to put an end to fear.

Michael quickly looked back at his men, making sure they were still in step with him. He could see them clearly against the light coming from the opening of the cave. Turning toward the back of the cave, he could see nothing, only hear the growling.

The growling became louder with every step. It sounded irregular—in fact, it sounded as if the creature might be hurt. As he stepped closer and closer, he noticed that the growling was a lot less robust than what he had anticipated. In fact, he wouldn't characterize this as growling at all, more like moaning. Something wasn't right, he could sense it... he could almost feel it.

Michael stood for a moment and listened to the growling. It was constant. He studied it carefully. It sounded somewhat familiar. It was a sound he had heard before. He tried to remember where and when. He knew it hadn't been that long ago. Michael closed his eyes to think, to try to remember. Searching his mind, he knew it was from one of his journeys a few years ago. He was traveling abroad on a mission. It was at a time when… he remembered what it was.

Standing at ease, he looked back at his men. "Bernard, light the torch," he said, not bothering to be quiet.

There were a few seconds of silence before Bernard responded timidly. "But Sir, this was not in our plans. I don't think…"

"Bernard, just do it," Michael said unafraid. The torch was quickly lit, piercing the darkness. The men gazed with fear to see a creature by the back of the cave. Two small piles of gold lay around him. The creature was obviously in pain and not at all what they were expecting.

They will never forget the sight they saw. There was no dragon. A lion had been caught and placed at the back of the cave in the midst of the dragon's gold. He was stuck in a large pile of rocks that covered his back hind legs. He was unable to move. His front legs and face were covered in scratches and blood. The lion longed to be released.

Confusion clouded the face of every man. Gideon was the first to speak, "Sir, what is going on? This is definitely unlike a dragon keeping his prey alive. Or is this the trick of some man?"

"Oh, most assuredly this is the work of the dragon. No man could be in here long enough to catch a lion in the midst of the dragon's gold."

Michael and Gideon both took off their helmets in frustration. They desperately wanted answers. Gideon spoke, "Well, why is there a lion caught in the back of his cave? What does all of this mean?"

Michael looked back at Gideon. He wasn't sure what to say. There was a mixture of fear and wonder in his eyes. He remembered something he had said to Belle earlier that morning, *This dragon has shown quite a bit of intelligence and I don't want to underestimate him in any way.*

After a few moments of contemplation, Michael broke the silence with an answer to Gideon's question. "It means it's a trap. We have to get out of here right now! Hurry!"

❦❧

Belle lay on the hill under a bush, wondering how long this dragon hunt would take. She wondered what it would be like to battle a dragon. The castle library had a book with various tales of dragon hunts through the last hundred years. She had read it many times. Some of the tales were extravagant, where full armies were needed to protect cities and keep the creatures at bay. Others were minor where a single brave warrior would institute some sort of plan of trickery, in order to slay the dragon and claim the gold for himself. She wondered if some of those stories were slightly exaggerated as there weren't any eyewitnesses besides the actual dragon slayers.

She heard thunder in the distance. She had hoped that the storms of the day had passed in the early morning. The ground was cold and gave her a slight chill. A butterfly came flying past her eyes and landed right in front of her. It was close, and she could see his pattern clearly. Its wings were a beautiful green and blue pattern. Streaks of black lines ran through the colors, reminding Belle of a church's stained glass windows. She lay perfectly still as she didn't want to disturb this beautiful sight. He was gently flapping his wings, exploring some of the wet leaves on the hill. Belle couldn't help but smile, thankful she could see this simple wonderful sight.

The butterfly suddenly flew away as the thunder grew louder. In fact, it was terribly loud and seemed to be steady. Turning her head slightly to the side and listening closely, she realized this wasn't thunder at all. It was the sound of the air being pushed by the wings of a large flying creature... the wings of a dragon.

Looking up high she could see him. He was a dull red color. And though one would still consider him a small dragon, he was slightly bigger than she had imagined. He looked angry as he flew over her head. His eyes looked intent with evil as he snarled. She could see his razor sharp teeth and the spikes running down his back. She was thankful that Michael had brought as many men as did.

Flying close to Belle, he lowered himself near the front of the cave. Belle crawled from her hiding position and crept quietly to the edge of the small cliff in front of her. Peering over the edge, she could see the dragon was blocking the entryway to the cave. He let out a loud shrieking roar as his mouth opened wide. He was ready to kill.

It was a trap, Belle thought to herself. This dragon had somehow manipulated the men into entering the cave, and now they were trapped inside with no way out except through the dragon. All he would have to do would be to fill the cave with a constant stream of fire until every man was killed. The plan was diabolically ingenious.

Belle began to panic at the thought of the men inside. Fear gripped her.

∾∾

Michael ran toward the front of the cave just in time to see the dragon descend right on the opening. His men were right behind him. They were trapped with no way of escape. The dragon let out a loud roar. "Steady men!" Michael yelled, as he quickly tried to think of a plan.

Before the soldiers could react, the dragon pivoted himself to his side and swiped the front of the cave with his tail, knocking the men against the side wall of the cave. Michael was the only one to escape from the tail's swipe. He had quickly dropped his sword and dived over the sweeping tail as it approached him. Dirt and mud covered his face.

Quickly gathering himself, Michael wiped his face and checked his bearings. His men lay against the side of the cave moaning in pain. They had hit hard against the side wall. Turning to face the dragon, Michael could see the creature standing tall and his neck starting to glow. He knew the fire was coming soon. His men were defenseless and would be killed in an instant.

He spotted a round shield lying right next to him. One of his men had dropped it when he was hit by the dragon. With great speed Michael picked it up and ran toward the dragon. "Dragon!" he yelled as he ran, looking to redirect the creature's attention.

The dragon turned to face Michael, and let out a steady stream of fire. Within twelve feet of the creature, Michael crouched low and held the shield in front of his body. He felt the impact of the fire against the shield. It was extremely hot, and the metal from the shield was heating up quickly. He knew eventually his arm would start to burn. He wondered how long he could hold it. Fire was also coming off the edges of the shield as it was deflected. The cave was also heating up rapidly, turning it into an oven. Michael wondered if this would be his end.

❧❧

Belle watched from the edge of the cliff as the dragon breathed fire into the cave. It was a horrible scene. She knew the men were in there suffering. She wondered what she could do. Trying to think of something, she frantically looked around the hill. A large rock caught her attention. Quickly picking it up with both hands, she lifted it high above her head and threw it down toward the dragon. She watched as the stone grazed the side of his body and fell to the ground. The creature was unfazed by it.

Starting to panic more, she searched for something else to throw: a larger stone, a log... Something caught her eye. It was under the bush where she was lying. Running over to it, she picked it up and gripped it tightly. She had had a fair amount of training with the sword and it was time to put it to use. Running back to the edge of the cliff, she looked over to see the dragon still breathing fire into the cave. She knew this was her moment... and it was now or never.

She gathered all the courage she could find, and with all her strength she jumped off the cliff, her sword pointed downward toward the dragon's body.

∾∾

Just when Michael thought he could hold the shield no longer, the dragon stopped. He let out a loud shrieking groan. Michael quickly threw down the shield that was blazing hot. He grabbed his arm.

Looking up, Michael saw a very curious sight. Belle was on the top of the dragon with her sword planted firmly in him. A dark green substance oozed from the dragon's body. Shaking in pain, the creature threw Belle off of himself. She rolled off the side of him and onto the ground. She hit hard and cried out in pain.

The dragon turned to face the princess lying on the ground. He was angry. He put his foot over her and pressed her gently against the ground. His neck started to glow. Belle's eyes grew big as she knew the fire was coming soon. Her life flashed before her eyes. Curious thoughts filled her mind. She remembered portions of her dream.

Michael, seeing what was transpiring, quickly reached onto his belt and grabbed one of his daggers. As fast as he could, he threw it with all his might toward the face of the dragon. The dagger soared through the air and implanted itself squarely in the right eye of the creature. It went in deep.

The dragon groaned in pain as never before. He reared back and lifted his leg. Belle rolled free to safety. The dark green blood started to flow from the eye of the creature. He took a few steps backward and tried to grasp the dagger with his front legs. His efforts were in vain.

A few of Michael's men had gathered themselves and were now at his side. They now had the upper hand. Assessing his situation, he knew he had to get the dragon out of the entryway of the cave.

"Shields up," he said to the five men at his side. They quickly held up their shields and stood in battle stance. "Get ready, men... charge!" Michael yelled as the men ran toward the dragon with their shields held high covering their chest. As they got close to the dragon, each man lunged forward hitting the dragon with the force of their shield and bodies. The dragon fell back a few feet, catching himself on his left side. The front of the cave was now open.

The dragon was now moving erratically and seemed to be in a lot of panic. He could not see clearly after being blinded in his right eye. He took a swipe toward the men with one of his legs and knocked them all toward the ground. The dragon continued to frantically groan in pain from the sword and dagger planted in him.

Michael was angry. He was angry at this dragon for hurting his men. He was angry at this dragon for threatening Belle's life. He was angry at this dragon for tricking them, luring them into the cave. And he was angry at this dragon for the fear he caused the people of Mendolon over the years. He had had enough.

Slowly rising to his feet, he looked confidently at the dragon... he was unafraid. He was ready to put an end to this dragon. A few moments passed before Michael picked up one of the shields his men dropped and held it in his hand.

Motivated by his anger, he threw the shield with all of his might. It soared through the air and struck hard against Belle's sword implanted in the dragon's side. The sword twisted, opening up the wound even more. A fresh stream of dragon blood flowed from his side. The dragon shuddered in pain as he screamed profusely.

Michael's men regrouped and gathered to his side as they watched the dragon. He scratched against the soil, searching for comfort from his pain. The shrieks grew more irritating to the men. Gideon was the first to speak, "Sir, what is your next move? Should we attack?"

"No," Michael said quietly. "Let him now feel the fear that he implanted in our people all these years."

The dragon had obviously given up. He was no longer worried about killing his intruders. He was in grave pain. His wings began to flap, and before anyone could realize what was happening, the dragon took off and flew into the distance. He was going north, far away from the kingdom. Michael stood watching the dragon until he could see him no more. He was thankful this dragon was gone.

4

$\mathcal{G}$ideon ran to where Belle was lying among the edge of the woods. She was obviously in pain, clutching her side. "Princess, are you ok?"

Her eyes were closed and she was wincing in pain. She spoke quietly, "Yes... I'll be fine. I think I might've broken a rib when I fell."

Gideon crouched beside her on one knee. "Well, it looks like you were ready for a dragon hunt after all."

"Thanks, don't mention it," Belle said, trying to catch her breath. Belle always found Gideon's presence comforting. He had a father-like demeanor, and his thick mustache always brought a smile to Belle.

Michael walked over to join them. "Gideon, how is she?" Michael asked.

Gideon rose to his feet, "Oh, she'll be fine. A little banged up, but in a couple days, she'll be back on her feet."

The other soldiers were attending to a few men who were injured from the swipe of the dragon's tail. Michael spoke up, "Gideon, check on the men. I want a full assessment of our injuries. There is still work that needs to be done."

"Yes sir," Gideon said, nodding his head and walking toward the men.

Michael's attention was now turned to Belle. He was so proud of her, and impressed by her bravery. She had never even seen a dragon before, and to jump on his back from a cliff required a large amount of courage. With a little more training, he knew she was going to be a great warrior.

Dropping to one knee, he put his hand on her head as he spoke, "Belle? Are you okay?"

"Michael... yes, I'm fine," she said, slightly opening her eyes.

Michael spoke softly, "You showed much courage and bravery today. I know I speak for the men in this brigade in saying we are forever in your gratitude."

"Thank you Michael," she said, grabbing his arm. "I guess all those stories about dragon battles weren't exaggerated after all." They had been through a lot and they couldn't help but smile at each other. Never did Belle ever think that she would be in a situation where she would have to save Michael de Bolbec. People in Mendolon were always talking about the strength of the realm's chief knight, and for the king's daughter to save him in a battle was truly ironic.

Gideon and the other soldiers gathered by Michael and Belle. Belle slowly released his arm as Michael rose to his feet. "Gideon, what's your assessment?"

"A couple of broken arms, brushes, cuts, and a few massive headaches, but nothing that should hinder us."

"Good. I want you to escort Belle and the injured men back to the castle. Upon arrival, be sure to alert Hector that we will need nurses to help with the injuries." Gideon nodded his head in approval. Michael continued, "Bernard, I want you to release the lion in the cave."

Bernard's eyes got wide, "The lion? Are you sure that's a good idea? I mean... lions can bite people."

"Thank you, Bernard. I'm well aware of that," Michael responded. "I will remind you that we did just fight a dragon.

Take another man with you, and just get this done. This lion has suffered enough."

Michael took a deep breath as he contemplated what to do next. The men could tell he had something on his mind. He looked out into the woods to the east. He knew that this was the last step in the mission. "Whoever's left, follow me into the eastern woods."

Michael turned and walked toward the east. Two of his men abruptly followed him. One of them spoke up, "Sir, may I ask what are we doing? The mission is accomplished. Why aren't we going back?"

Not breaking stride, Michael responded, "The mission is not done... There is a mystery yet unsolved. We need to find out what provoked this dragon."

✌︎✎

It had been a long day for Michael and his men. Michael had warned them the day before that they might be engaging in a dragon hunt today, so they all had woken up early to prepare. Michael, particularly, had only slept a couple hours as he was anticipating the mission. But even with the lack of sleep, fatigue had not yet set in. His adrenaline was still going strong as they sought to solve this present mystery.

The three men trekked farther into the woods. They were headed east. The terrain was a little different on this side of Dragon Waste. The trees and their branches were thicker, and covered most of the overhead light. Every few feet there seemed to be a large rock that jutted from the ground, oftentimes covered with moss. They all knew that the more one traveled toward the eastern kingdom, the rockier the ground became.

The men traveled slowly with Michael in the lead. No one said a word. They all felt a little strange traveling in this territory unabated. For the past twenty years it was left uninhabited, except for the dragon. And even before the creature took over this region, none of the men had journeyed this far east. They couldn't help but visually explore their surroundings as Michael led them.

The men had not gone far when Michael stopped them. "What is it?" one of the men asked. Michael pointed ahead to an area about thirty yards in front of them. Nothing looked different to the men. There were a few large trees with a couple large rocks lying beside them. It didn't look much different from every other spot in this area of the woods.

"I don't see anything," one of the soldiers stated.

"Look closely," Michael replied, slowly walking forward.

All three men continued closer to the spot where Michael was focused. The two soldiers reached for their weapons. As they got closer to the spot, all three men could clearly see a figure seated comfortably with his back to a tree. He had a small knife in hand and was casually slicing an apple. There was a book by his side. About twenty feet from his spot a tent rested. It was obvious he had been lodging there for a few days.

"Lovely day for a walk in the woods," the individual said, not breaking focus from his task.

All three were stunned by his candor. The knights' eyes were wide, wondering what Michael's next move would be. He was relaxed, not fearing any harm from this trespasser.

The individual continued, "May I interest you fellows in a slice of a Grimdolon apple. You won't find them in your kingdom, and they are a rare delicacy even in mine. I need to be sure…"

"What are you doing here?" Michael said sternly.

"Well, currently I'm taking a break from my book to satisfy my hunger. Reading modern philosophy surely makes one's head spin, and can make one work up quite an appetite."

"No, what are you doing in the dragon's territory?" Michael said, staying focused.

"I think you actually mean former dragon's territory. I assume you boys took care of it." Michael's soldiers just looked at each other. They were obviously confused by everything transpiring.

"We took care of him," Michael replied. "Now tell us what you are doing here?"

"Well, then let me first introduce myself, I am…"

"Yes, I know who you are, or rather what you are… Beast!" Michael replied. He was in fact a beast from the eastern Kingdom of Grimdolon, the land of beasts. Like his kind, he was mostly a mixture of man and lion, with a few scattered characteristics of a wolf. He was dressed properly, in a red jacket and slacks. On his face was an affluent pair of eyeglasses. It appeared that he was either a beast of nobility or worked in an important role for the king of his realm.

"And I know who you are, Michael de Bolbec, chief knight for King Sebastian, and fiercest protector of Mendolon."

"Why are you here? Do you know how dangerous it is for you to be here? Our king has an order of immediate death to anyone who crosses into this territory."

"Yes, I am familiar with all the laws and edicts from your kingdom and they weren't going to stop me."

"But you provoked a dragon!" Michael said angrily. "Do you know what you could have done? He's been burning fields on the edge of our kingdom and killing livestock. You could have cost us the lives of innocent people. And my men today have been badly wounded by that creature."

"Yes, Michael, I know and for that I am very sorry, but I know what I had to do. It was a necessity. Truly, it will all become clear soon," the beast spoke calmly.

Michael ran his fingers through his hair. "Listen, you could have started a war. Our king is going to be furious when he finds out that a beast from Grimdolon provoked this dragon."

The beast took a deep breath and stood to his feet, "I don't know if you are going to believe me, but in the long run I am actually trying to prevent a war from happening."

"What are you talking about?"

"I'm saying that I had to provoke the dragon. I needed to talk to you. I needed to get your attention, and this is the only option I had."

Michael rubbed his chin as he paced to his side. The knights had heard everything but still wondered what was transpiring. The beast did not take his eyes off Michael as he bit into a slice of apple.

A few moments passed before Michael interrupted the silence. "Beast, you are speaking in riddles. Please tell me plainly what you are inferring."

"Michael de Bolbec," he paused for a moment, "I'm trying to tell you that something is coming." He spoke seriously, looking directly at Michael. "And it will strike fear into the hearts of your people and put into motion events that could reshape every kingdom of this world."

Michael was taken off guard by the sudden seriousness of the beast. "How sure are you of all this?"

The beast took off his eyeglasses. "Oh, believe me when I speak. I am risking my life trying to get you this information."

Michael wondered what his next move would be. He knew that he just couldn't let this beast go free. He had broken one of the king's strictest laws. All neighboring kingdoms knew of this law. The king would be swift in his punishment, and this beast would surely face death.

Michael breathed deeply as he looked back at his guards. "Lock him up... be sure the king does not see him. Bring him to my lower chambers and chain him there." The men went to grab the beast, who willingly submitted himself to the knights.

Michael added one last admonition. He spoke softly, "And for now... do not mention this to anyone."

THE BEAUTY OF A BEAST

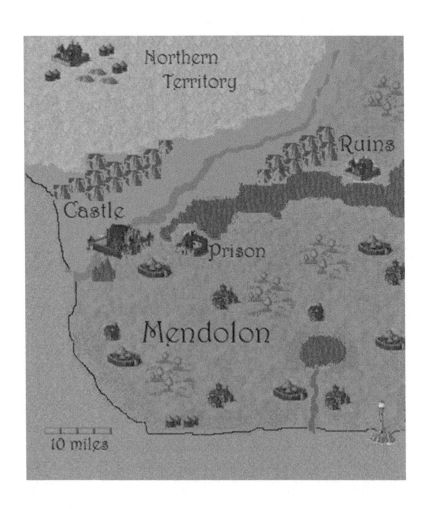

Northern
Territory

Ruins

Castle

prison

Mendolon

10 miles

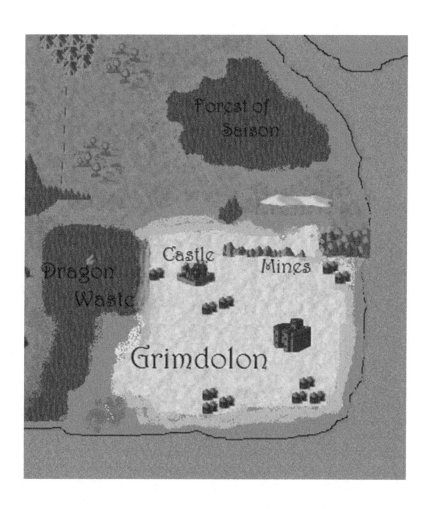

PROLOGUE

$\mathcal{O}$nce upon a time in a distant land there were two kingdoms that dwelt next to one another. They lived in peace but were not fond of each other. They kept their distance and didn't cross into each other's lands for fear of war. This pattern went on for the last hundred and twenty years.

The kingdom to the west was called Mendolon. It was a kingdom of men. It was a rich land full of farming and craftsmen. Foreigners often traveled there to trade for the bountiful supplies of the land. Sometimes their kings were peaceful and sought only the welfare and peace of their own people. Other times, their kings were full of greed, seeking riches and power at the expense of others. Their current king, Sebastian, was a man of ambiguity. He was not hostile to other kings, but did not agree to treaties either. The kingdoms of the world were often confused by his actions. He had one daughter named Belle. She was the pride and joy of the kingdom. The people of Mendolon knew she was the one who truly held the kingdom together.

The kingdom to the east was called Grimdolon. It was a kingdom of beasts. The race of beasts was often described as a mixture of man and lion with subtle characteristics of a wolf. They were known for possessing natural intelligence in regards to philosophy, the arts and the ways of the world. Their land was dry and their soil was rocky. Their only crops grew to the northeast in the kingdom's orchards. They relied mostly on mining and fishing for their livelihood. Others in the world knew very little about the comings and goings of the beasts. It was a small kingdom with a population under eight thousand. The beasts were a passive people that often dwelt in isolation.

For years these kingdoms continued in peace, not disturbing the other. They didn't even allow trade routes to pass between them. Over the years, men had occasionally acquired a beast from a neighboring country as a slave, but this was rare. Men simply did not have any correspondence with beasts. The two kingdoms of Mendolon and Grimdolon dared not cross each other's border. At one point in their recent history a dragon had even taken up residence between the kingdoms and any attempt at becoming allies quickly fell into a distant dream. Stories of the other kingdom became history, and history became legend.

But just when the flow of history seemed to be a steady flowing stream... everything changed. Six months ago random crimes began occurring in the kingdom of Mendolon. There were sightings of a beast. Rumors quickly began to spread that a beast from Grimdolon had entered their villages and begun terrorizing the people of Mendolon. The people called this beast, "The Savage." At first he appeared to be working alone, but as time when on, the people of Mendolon became convinced that he had gained a following and was working with a band of criminals. There was also talk among the people that he possessed some type of magic. The townspeople lived in fear of where the Savage and his followers would strike next.

The people of Mendolon cried out to their king for help. They begged and pleaded with him to find relief. He did all he could to neutralize the threat of the Savage, but nothing seemed to work. The king's most superior warriors, the Knights, worked seamlessly to find their enemy, but it was always in vain. Occasionally they would find some of his followers and prevent an attack from occurring, but most of the time they seemed to be one step behind the Savage's attacks. Through it all the people of Mendolon felt helpless. The questions remained... Who could defeat the Savage? How could order and peace be restored to the kingdom?

๙ ๖

It was late in the evening in Mendolon. The markets outside the castle were filled with people, finishing their buying and selling for the day. There was the usual buying of food and household goods, but mostly the buying of gifts. People felt safe with the castle being close by. Torches lit up the streets. Children laughed as they ran through the markets. It was winter and snow was lightly falling. It was a pleasant scene on the streets of Mendolon.

There were many markets throughout the kingdom. Each village had one, and each was known for its specific specialty. The eastern villages traded tools and farm equipment, while the markets to the south specialized in fruits grown not far from the coast. The western markets, not far from the castle, traded an assortment of everything, but were primarily known for having a large variety of gifts and trinkets. Foreigners would travel many miles and stay in nearby inns just to visit this exquisite market.

Currently, music was being played by musicians carrying various instruments in the streets. One would not travel very far before hearing the sound of a lute close by. Merchants welcomed the music as many thought it relaxed the people of the kingdom. It made them feel at peace while journeying through the streets. With the recent mischievous attacks throughout the kingdom, any semblance of peace was greatly welcomed.

Children laughed, music played, the snow was still falling gently. It was a beautiful scene... until it was all disturbed. A large explosion blasted out from one of the shops. People fell to the ground. The music stopped. Debris flew through the air. The next few moments were chaotic. A thick mist began to disperse on the crowd. People were screaming, running for their lives. The exploding shop was burning, and there were random fires in the streets. Parents ran, frantically dropping their gifts, carrying their children. A few villagers ran through the mist toward the burning shop, wondering how they could help.

The situation seemed like it couldn't get any worse until from out of the crowd, someone yelled, "A beast!" This sent the people into absolute panic. They screamed in fear, knowing that the Savage was attacking. Others in the crowd yelled for help. Still others confirmed the people's fear, shouting, "Run from the beast!" Screaming and chaos engulfed the streets. Many people would later claim they saw a horde of beasts.

It was about ten minutes later that a company of knights came on the scene. The people were beginning to clear out. Their swords were drawn, wondering what they would find. The mist was clearing away, and they saw a few dozen people lying on the ground injured, crying for help.

The leader of the group, Michael de Bolbec, quickly issued orders, "Put out the fires, save everyone. Bring them to the castle's infirmary. It looks like the Savage and his flock has struck again."

"Should we keep our swords drawn?" another knight asked.

"No, it looks like we are too late. The Savage is gone. This was all he wanted."

"What did he want?"

Looking around, Michael assessed the situation further. He took a deep breath before speaking, "He wanted to strike fear in the hearts of our people."

CHAPTER 1

$\mathcal{B}$elle sat under a tree sharpening her sword. Currently, she was taking a break from her training. She was dressed in her warrior attire. It was light gray with a woven purple pattern that clearly distinguished her as the princess. Daily she woke up early to further her training in knighthood. Just having celebrated her twenty-first birthday a month ago, Belle's desire was to be the best in the kingdom. Every morning, under the cover of darkness, she would leave the castle and travel a half mile deep into the nearby woods to train. She went through a strict routine of sword practice, followed by various obstacle course training. She would climb ropes, jump over logs, crawl under brushes, and scale a twelve-foot rock wall. Belle wanted to be ready for anything in battle.

Being the only daughter of the king, she had to wake up early every morning for training. Her beauty and pleasant personality made her the center of popularity and fame in the kingdom. She was always kind and welcoming, even to the poorest peasant. If this location was discovered, word would quickly spread around town and the people would flock to her. In order to have a secluded spot to train, she had to keep this spot quiet. Only a few people knew where she was each morning.

In the past, Belle took time with the townspeople and worked hard at remembering their names. She purposely made trips into the kingdom's towns to visit with the people. Her desire was to ease tension in the kingdom between common folks and royalty. Her father, King Sebastian, wasn't always the most gracious and righteous ruler. He was harsh with people and often handed out stiff penalties for insulting his kingdom. Knowing that one day she would be queen, she hoped to bring peace to the realm.

Belle stood to her feet, holding her sword in her right hand. She rotated her wrist checking the blade. Light gleaned off it as the sun was starting to rise through the trees. She would have to hurry to finish her training this morning. Running off in a sprint, she sheathed her sword on her back. She approached a net that was spread out a foot above the ground. She quickly dove under it and crawled as fast as she could. She could feel the weight of the sword with every inch. Reaching the end, she stood to her feet and ran up a few flights of steps to a rope positioned over a mud pit. She grabbed the rope and swung over the pit. As she reached the end of the pit, she let go of the rope and dove onto the ground, quickly rotating herself into a somersault. She brushed her long brown hair out of her eyes to get a clear view of the twelve-foot-high stone wall in front of her. She began methodically ascending, taking special note as to where to place her footing.

Even though Belle had always been naturally skilled in swordsmanship and agility, this was her routine every morning for the past eight months. Ever since her battle with the Eastern dragon, she had been motivated to accelerate her training as a knight. She wanted to fight for the kingdom's peace and freedom. She wanted to lead her people in these ideals and she wanted the people to trust her and to find their confidence in her.

The events of the last week kept running through her head. The Savage's attack on the markets had been his most terrorizing yet. It was public. Many people claimed they saw a horde of beasts scavenging the shops, wreaking havoc to all in their path. Two people were killed in the attack and many others were injured. The knights that arrived on the scene were able to put out the fires and bring some order to the chaotic scene. But the damage had already been done, and the people were very shaken up. The attack seemed to be a statement by the Savage that he was no longer content to work in the shadows. He wanted to be seen. He wanted to be feared. Belle so badly wanted to catch the hideous beast. She hated that the Savage was terrorizing her people and creating an existential fear over the realm. Her desire was for the people to feel free and to not live in this fear the Savage was bringing.

Reaching the top of the stone wall, Belle quickly caught her breath before jumping to a nearby tree branch. She grabbed the branch with both arms and swung herself to a lower branch a few feet away. She took note of the slight crack the branch made when she grabbed onto it, telling herself to choose a different branch the next time. Swinging her feet back and forth, the princess gained enough momentum to catapult herself forward onto the ground right in front of a scarecrow she had set up. Within a fraction of a second she pulled her sword and quickly cut off the head of the straw structure. Mission completed.

Belle was stumbling less and getting faster each morning. She wanted to show her father that she was truly a knight worthy of all her accolades in swordsmanship and agility. He always doubted her and never truly thought she was as good in battle as everyone said she was. She felt that she still had much to prove to him. This doubt by her father provided an extra motivation to catch the Savage. It would be exactly what she needed to show him that she was worthy of knighthood.

The sound of horse's hooves startled her. She looked up to see Michael, the king's chief knight, coming close. He was one of the few who knew of her training ground. Belle and Michael had been working together a lot more since the battle with the dragon eight months ago. Along with other knights, they had been responding to the Savage's attacks and rescuing any townspeople that might be in danger.

On this day, Michael was dressed like a commoner, which was a rare scene these days, as he was most always wearing his armor. He had been working constantly to find the Savage. Michael came within a few feet of Belle before stopping his horse and dismounting.

"I hope no one saw you come this way," Belle said, wiping the sweat from her forehead, and sheathing her sword.

Michael smiled as he spoke, "Belle, you can assure yourself that a true knight of the realm knows when he's being watched or followed."

Belle nodded, knowing this to be true. Michael was the best and she knew he would always be careful to never give her spot away. "Sorry, I just want to stay focused. This area has provided a great solace for me to complete my training. I'd hate for it to be found out."

Seeing that she had been training hard, he held out a small water skin for her to drink. "Thank you," she responded, taking a drink.

Michael casually walked around her training area, admiring the obstacle course and challenges she had set up. "You've made some improvements since the last time I've been here. You've done well."

"Thanks," she said, putting down the water skin. "I don't want there to be any doubt about my knighthood. I want the people to know that I'm ready to protect them."

Michael brushed his blond hair out of his eyes. "Belle, you know the people of Mendolon are aware of your abilities. Your heroics with the dragon are becoming a legend in neighboring kingdoms. People are starting to ask about the 'Princess Dragon Slayer.'"

Belle couldn't help but smile at Michael's flattery. Though there were tensions in the kingdom, it was obvious to all that Belle and Michael had grown closer. The rumors began to pick up again about an eventual wedding. Both tried to suppress any thought of a relationship at this time as the most pending duty ahead was catching the Savage.

"So Michael, what is the meaning of this visit?" she said, hoping to quickly change the subject.

Michael turned and walked close to where she was standing. Even though he knew that they were alone, he wanted to be sure there was no chance someone could hear what he was about to say. "I think we might have found the Savage's main hideout."

"What? Where?"

"Shh... No too loud... The old ruins north of the kingdom."

"That is many miles away from the western markets," Belle responded, a little puzzled by his suggestion. "I don't even know if that's under my father's control anymore. I thought one of the northern kingdoms inhabited that area."

"It would make sense as to why we can't find him. Also, it would explain why his attacks are sporadic."

Belle was shocked. The fight against the Savage was becoming hopeless, but now to receive news like this was incredible. It was the biggest lead they had received in a long time. So many questions raced through her mind, "Who knows about this?"

"Just myself, Gideon, and Hector."

"What? You told Hector. Are you sure that's a good idea?"

"Yes, He's been designing new armor for me that will make it easier to maneuver in a battle. I need it to be ready for tonight."

"What about my father? Does he know?"

"Not yet. I'm trying to keep this as quiet as possible. Take no offense, but your father has been quick tempered as of late and I don't want him ordering an all-out assault. The nations around us and the empire to the far north are primed for war; any careless action could be interpreted wrongly."

"But you know he's going to find out soon."

"Certainly," Michael responded, not in the least bit concerned. "I want to break the news to him later in the day after Gideon has come up with a comprehensive strategy. I want the king to see that we can infiltrate the ruins with a small company of knights."

Belle stood staring at Michael. She couldn't believe what she was hearing. The past six months had been some of the worst days for the kingdom. So much time and effort had been placed in trying to find the Savage, and to now know his location and to hear of a plan to take him down was overwhelming.

"Michael, make no mistake that I'm coming with you," she said, taking a step closer to him.

"Of course, that's why I came to find you, so you can be preparing."

"When do we leave?"

"At nightfall. We will meet early after midday to discuss our plan of attack. We will need to be as coordinated as possible. I believe the Savage's followers will most likely be gathered at the ruins as well. We cannot take any chances."

Belle knew that her training was done for the day. All of her energy needed to be preserved for the attack later that night. She knew Michael would need her ready in this confrontation. "I'll be ready," she replied confidently.

Michael mounted his horse and grabbed the reins. "I'll see you in the king's war room after the noon meal. Everyone should be well informed by then."

Michael was about to turn and leave the area when Belle stopped him, "Wait! one more thing." There was one question still on her mind that she couldn't shake. "How did you find out about the ruins? How do you know the Savage is hiding out there?"

Belle did not take her eyes off of him. Michael de Bolbec was the most honest man she knew, and she could easily tell when he was hiding something, or not being completely honest with her. He ran his fingers through his hair, wondering how much information he should disclose. After a few moments of silence, Belle spoke up, "Do not hold back from me. We've been through a lot so far."

The young knight looked off into the distance as he wondered how to respond. "Belle... I have a source that is helping us decipher the actions of the Savage."

Belle was quite surprised, "Michael, you never told me this. Who is this 'source' that you have?"

Michael searched for words. He had given so much information so far, and any more would truly be an extra burden for this morning. "All in time... Everything will be clear soon enough."

Belle was even more confused. She wondered at exactly what was going on, "But... Michael... are you sure this information is correct? How do you know you can trust this source of yours?"

Michael took a deep breath as he looked toward the ground, searching for words. He shrugged his shoulders before looking at Belle and speaking, "In honesty... I'm not sure if I do trust him... but at this point he's our only option. And he may be the best chance we have of securing peace in our realm."

"But what if this is a trap tonight? What if this source of yours is leading us to our doom?" Belle said, speaking with obvious concern in her voice.

Michael looked squarely at Belle, knowing there was a lot of truth to what she was saying. Much like her, he was eager to catch the Savage and was willing to take risks in order to secure his imprisonment. He knew that eventually drastic measures would have to be taken in order to catch this villain. Michael responded in the only way he knew how, "Well… for the sake of peace among the people of Mendolon, that is a risk I'm willing to take." Michael quickly kicked his horse as he rode to the south.

Belle watched him as he left. She couldn't help but admire him for his bravery.

కుడిం

"What?" King Sebastian stated. It was the middle of the afternoon and he couldn't believe what he was hearing. "You think you found the hideout of the Savage?"

"That's correct, Your Majesty," Michael confidently stated, "And we are prepared to strike tonight."

The king stood from his seat and put his hands on his head. He gently pulled on his long brown hair, excited about the news. Finding the Savage had consumed his thoughts these last months. He couldn't believe that Michael had located his hideout. "Well, what are we waiting for? Let's get all our soldiers mounted at once. Let's attack him before he can strike."

"King, let's slow down, just a little," Michael said, holding up his hand to quiet him. "The Savage has been one step ahead of us in every way. If we start mounting up soldiers, he will somehow get word and prevent our attack. He might even use it to his advantage."

"Michael, are you crazy? We can't wait," Sebastian said, frustrated. "We have to strike now."

"Yes, my King, I understand, but using an army is not the way to attack. He's crafty and somehow he has eyes on the kingdom. Most definitely he will see us coming."

Sebastian sat down, trying to calm himself. He closed his eyes and gently stroked his beard. He spoke softly, "Well, what do you suggest we do?"

Michael nodded his head in approval. He wanted to show the king patience, and that a well thought out strategy had been devised. "We attack the Northern Ruins tonight under the cloak of darkness. Hector and Gideon are planning a strategic attack from the northwest. The Savage will not see us coming. We will penetrate any defenses he might have, and overthrow his hideout before he realizes what is happening."

"How many knights are thinking about taking?"

"About a dozen."

King Sebastian nodded his head in approval. He realized the wisdom in the plan, and he was excited to finally take down this menace to the kingdom of Mendolon. It had given him far too many sleepless nights, and the fear that the Savage was bringing to the people of the kingdom was starting to reach him as well. He was happy to have a plan in place to take down this beast. Still, one question plagued his mind, "Michael, may I ask, how did you come to find the hideout of the Savage?"

Michael stood, wondering what to say. He knew he couldn't reveal his source to the king for fear of possible treason. He decided to dodge the question, "King, you just authorize the attack, and let me worry about where I get my information."

The king smiled with contempt at his chief knight. If anyone else in the kingdom had spoken to him like that, he or she would have been locked away immediately. Any other time the king would have at least reprimanded him, but for right now he had other things on his mind. "Very well then, get your men ready. I look forward to hearing of a successful campaign."

CHAPTER 2

The Knights of Mendolon approached the Northern Ruins. Snow was lightly falling through the air. They were about a mile from their destination, regrouping at the edge of a wooded area. The ruins consisted of a small decaying castle with a wall around the perimeter. Though the castle had much wear and tear, the wall itself had held strong. Over a hundred years ago, these ruins had served as the castle of Mendolon, but since then the kingdoms of the north debated about whose land it was. King Sebastian didn't care about the area, and he let the kingdoms of the world do with it as they wish.

Michael and Belle were with a dozen other knights. Gideon, Michael's second in command, was among those in the troop. The king's assistant, Hector, was with them as he had devised the plan of penetrating the walls and entering the ruins. The plan was for Michael and Belle to scale the back perimeter of the wall and clear away any guards on the top. Next, Belle would find the front gate, and open the doors for the brigade of knights to enter. By the time the Savage and his followers figured out what was happening, it would be too late.

"Knights, try to stay hidden for as long as you can when approaching the gate," Hector said, giving out orders. The hissing of his voice sounded even more frightful at night. His dark green apparel along with his black hair gave him a very sinister look. "Most likely the Savage will have a few guards stationed on top of the wall with arrows. Keep close to cover if possible." Gideon nodded his head in approval.

Hector then turned to face Michael and Belle. Strands of his long black hair covered his face. He continued, hissing as he talked, "The two of you need to be quick. I don't know how many men the Savage has working with him and it is best if we keep the element of surprise in our favor for as long as possible." He paused a moment to clear his throat. "When you reach the top of the wall, do whatever you can to keep the men from calling for reinforcements."

"I understand," Michael responded. "Belle and I will clear the wall. She'll look for a quick way to open the front gate. I'll try to find and capture the Savage." Michael turned to the others, "Gideon, after you and the knights are inside the wall, try to detain any of the Savage's followers. Belle, once the courtyard's secure, enter the castle and rescue any hostages the Savage might be holding in the dungeon."

"Yes, Captain," they all responded in agreement. Everyone understood the severity of this mission. The Savage had been terrorizing the people for months, and this was the best shot they had at putting a stop to it. Hector had even made Michael and Belle special armor for this mission. Michael's was a dark grey suit made of a flexible thin metal that form fitted to his upper body. He had a small sword on his back and a belt full of daggers around his waist. A simple hood was over his head to conceal his hair. Belle's armor was a warrior's outfit that was her usual grey with a few dark purple patterns. It was durable and flexible for battle, yet still gave the distinction of royalty. Being that she was the king's daughter, Hector always thought Belle's armor should be worthy of a princess.

Everyone was ready to disperse. Michael and Belle would be taking a more northern route for a mile to the back wall, while the knights would travel south to the front gates.

Michael turned to walk away when Hector stopped him, "Michael, be careful in that armor. The material is flexible, but nowhere near as strong as a traditional suit. It will not hold up against a direct stab from a sword. Your speed and the element of surprise will be the best advantage you have in that armor."

Michael couldn't help but smile at Hector's warning. "Hector, I appreciate the concern. I'm beginning to think we've become friends."

Hector snarled, and gritted his teeth. "Just take care of the princess, and come back alive." Michael nodded in agreement as he turned to walk away.

❧

Belle scaled the back wall of the ruins. It was an easy climb as it was made of thick stones that jutted out, making for easy hand holds. There were also cracks in the wall that were large enough to fit one's hands. Michael was just in front of her and about at the top. They were trying to be as quiet as possible as they didn't know who they would meet at the top of the twenty-foot wall.

Belle felt sweat beads rolling off her forehead with every climb. It was getting close to midnight, and she hadn't taken her evening medicine. She wondered if it would calm her nerves at this point. Once they made it to the top, she knew that her job would be to cover Michael with her bow, while he directly engaged the guards. For the past few months they had worked with each other enough to know each other's fighting styles and when the other would need a helping hand. They truly were great partners.

Reaching the top of the wall, Michael flung himself over, and then quickly reached back and helped Belle ascend the last few feet. "Watch closely," he said, looking directly into her eyes. "I'm going to try to make this quick." Belle nodded in approval.

Michael ran off with a sprint toward the first guard who was watching an area to the back left of the castle. He was dressed in dark clothing but was without armor. Under the darkness of night, he had failed to see Michael and Belle reach the top. When Michael came within fifteen feet of him, the guard realized that an intruder was approaching. Before he could react, Michael pulled a dagger from his belt, and threw it at his right shoulder. It easily penetrated where his shoulder met his arm. The guard screamed in pain. With his left fist, Michael quickly punched him in the stomach, buckling the man over, and then with his right hand he rammed the guard's head into his knee knocking him out cold. The body fell to the ground.

About twenty feet away, another guard was getting an arrow ready. Michael sprang toward him and rolled into a somersault. Belle quickly fired an arrow that penetrated the guard's arm. The bow dropped out of his hand. Quickly arising from his somersault, Michael jumped and spun into a fierce spinning kick. His boot connected with the side of the guard's head, knocking the guard off the wall outside the ruins. The guard fell to the ground not far from where Gideon and the other knights were stationed. Gideon motioned to the men. That was their cue to start approaching the gate.

Michael barely had time to react when he saw the blade of another guard swiping downward toward him. He quickly jumped out of the way, and punched the guard right in the face. He heard a cracking sound. The guard stumbled a few feet back, and before he could gather his wits, Michael drew a dagger and threw it at the guard's wrist. It pierced his skin, and the man gave a loud shriek, dropping his sword. In order to quickly quiet the man, Michael lunged forward and kicked him in the stomach with his knee, knocking the guard backward off the wall and into the courtyard of the ruins.

Michael watched in disappointment as his body hit the ground. He knew it would only be a matter of seconds before he was found. Belle quickly ran over to where Michael was standing. He turned to face her, "Well, I guess the plan is now accelerated. Let's go."

Michael and Belle ran off with a sprint toward a staircase that would bring them to the front gate. Michael bounded down the steps as quickly as he could, often skipping three or four steps. Belle was right behind him. Reaching the bottom of the steps, he didn't even stop to check and see how many guards were stationed close to the gate. At this point he figured speed would be his best advantage.

Running into the courtyard, he saw three guards that looked as passive as any guard could possibly look. Swiftly Michael drew a dagger and flung it at the tallest one, puncturing his bicep. He yelled out in pain. The other two guards were confused to see a dagger suddenly in their comrade's arm. Michael sprang forward and kicked one of the unharmed guards out of the way. Pivoting, he threw his right elbow into the head of the guard with the dagger in his arm. He fell backward.

The last guard still standing threw a punch at Michael. It was easily blocked, and Michael kicked him in the stomach. Turning around, Michael threw a dagger toward one of the guards lying on the ground. It penetrated his side, and he was not to be worried about any more. Turning to the guard who tried to punch him, Michael grabbed him by the head and flipped him over his back. He quickly got down on one knee and delivered a punch directly to his forehead, knocking him out.

Michael turned around to see the guard with the dagger in his bicep, swiping toward him with a sword. He promptly jumped backwards and reached for a dagger. Michael was ready to throw it when he saw Belle block the guard's sword with hers. She pulled back and took a swipe at him. He blocked, and then pulled back to take a swing at her. She jumped out of the way and spun herself around, sweeping his legs. The guard fell onto his back. His head hit hard. Dazed, the guard tried to arise. Belle then struck him as hard as she could with her forearm. She would have a large bruise, but the guard was no longer a threat.

Michael put the dagger back on his belt. From what they could see, there were no more guards in sight. The coast was clear. "Nice work," he said, relaxed.

"Not bad yourself," Belle returned, sheathing her sword. "I can tell you've been training with the daggers. Your accuracy was flawless."

He nodded slightly in approval, "All for the service of the kingdom." He removed his hood, and brushed his blond hair out of his eyes. His mind quickly went back to the task at hand. "Belle, get the gate open for the men, and search the castle for hostages. Have our men arrest all the guards and have them placed outside the gates after the castle is cleared. I'm going after the Savage," he said, running toward the castle.

"Be careful," Belle yelled to him. There was obvious concern in her voice.

❧

Gideon and the knights were about thirty feet away when the doors began to open. Belle had removed all the barriers and pushed with all her might to open the doors. The men could tell she was struggling and quickly ran to assist her in prying them open. The knights grabbed both doors and pulled. It was just a few moments later before the doors were completely open.

"What took you so long?" Gideon said sarcastically. His thick mustache curled as he smiled.

"Oh, you know Michael, he's always taking his time," she responded. She felt a lot more relaxed now that she had the knights inside the castle walls. "Gideon, you and your men search the courtyard. Make sure all threats are neutralized."

She turned to the knight Bernard, who was responsible for the torches. He carried them in a bag on his back. "Bernard, come with me. I'm going into the castle, looking for prisoners."

"But... the Savage is a monster... and it's really dark in there," he said, worried. Bernard was very skilled with the sword, but often struggled with uncertain fears.

"Yes, Bernard, that's why you're coming with me. You have the torches."

Gideon broke in, "We will do as you command, your Highness. We await your return."

"Thank you, Gideon," Belle said, running off toward the castle. Bernard followed close behind.

꧁꧂

Michael crept through the hallways of the castle ruins. He was as quiet as possible. It was dark, but thankfully there were a few cracks in the walls that let in light. He wondered where the Savage might be hiding. Before the mission, he had looked at a map of this abandoned castle and memorized a few key locations where one might find the beast. Currently, Michael was heading for the throne room.

Turning a corner, he saw a small torch on the wall giving off a faint glow of light. He hid in the shadows, wondering how many people were inside. He heard no one and saw no one. He quickly moved through the light and close to the double doors of the throne room. Reaching the throne room doors, Michael crouched down in the shadows. He checked the daggers around his belt to make sure everything was in the proper place for a quick attack.

He pulled on the right door and found that it opened easily. He slid into the room quickly and hid in the shadows.

Scanning the area, he found that it was empty. A large crack in the wall let in the moonlight. He could see two large dilapidated thrones at the end of room, and to the left of them a single door which led to the king's personal living quarters. Quietly he moved through the long throne room toward it. He decided to pull his sword just in case he had to engage in close range combat.

Reaching the door, Michael found that it stood slightly open. He peeked into the room but saw no one. He opened the door a little more to let in some of the light. The chief knight slowly looked into the room and could clearly see that it was empty. He opened the door more to let in as much light as possible.

It was obvious that someone had been living in this room. There was an unmade bed on the far wall, along with scraps of food by its side. Along the side wall he saw a desk with about a dozen books stacked in order. Papers were scattered on the desk and the floor. He made his way over to them to see what he could find. Some of the books seemed to be on the history and customs of the people of Grimdolon. Others were on the tales of dragons and one was on the legend of the Undying Land across the Sea. He recognized many of the writers as being scholars from northern providences. He found them curious. Looking through the scattered papers, he couldn't find anything that looked valuable. It was mostly just notes that someone had taken from studying these books.

He was about to turn and leave when he noticed another book on the floor behind the desk. It was open and looked to be shredded. Some of its pages were scattered around. Michael bent down to get a closer look. Picking it up, he could see that it was a history book on ancient kings and kingdoms of distant lands. He wondered why the Savage needed it. Many of its pages were torn and missing and others were ruined. He laid it back on the desk. Being a lover of books, he closed it reverently. In a strange way he felt sorry for it, hoping no more harm would come to the book.

❧❧

Belle and Bernard were on the east side of the castle descending a flight of steps. They were headed to the castle's dungeon. Belle had her sword drawn and was in front. She stayed close against the wall and meticulously moved from step to step. Fear gripped her. She wondered what they would find at the bottom of these steps. Bernard was behind her with a small lit torch. He was constantly checking in front and behind to see if he could see anyone.

Reaching the bottom, Belle peered through the doorway into the dungeon. There were five prisoners sleeping on straw, locked away behind steel bars. Three were middle aged men, one looked to be a teenage girl, and the other was an elderly woman. They were all dressed in rags and looked greatly unkempt. There was one guard in a chair, sleeping against the wall. The keys to the prison were hanging on his belt. *Looks to be an easy task*, Belle thought to herself.

Belle slowly took a step into the room, her sword in her hand. She was trying to be as quiet as possible as not to wake the man. Looking over at the prisoners she could see one of the men stirring. She turned her focus toward the guard and slowly approached him. Each step was meticulously taken.

She was about ten feet from the guard and ready to engage when she heard a loud crashing sound coming from the doorway. The guard was completely surprised and fell backwards out of his seat. Belle glanced behind her to see that Bernard had tripped on the bottom step and had fallen through the doorway. All of the prisoners were also startled and wondered what was transpiring.

The guard looked up and saw Belle standing in front of him. He tried to gather his wits. He quickly stood and drew his sword. Belle stepped closer to confront him. He swung his sword at her. Belle blocked easily, and kicked his knee. The guard stumbled and took a step back. Belle swung at the guard, and likewise he held his sword up in order to block. Belle pulled back, and swung again; this time to his right side. He blocked again. Belle quickly pulled her left arm back and punched him square in the cheek bone. The guard fell back against the wall and before he could react, Belle hit him again, except this time with the hard handle of her sword. The guard lost consciousness and fell to the floor.

Belle took a deep breath and sheathed her sword. She noticed her hair had come undone during the fight. Since the guard was no longer a threat, she took a moment to tie her hair back in a ponytail. She took her time as she was quite out of breath at the moment.

She turned around to see Bernard gathering himself and brushing the dirt off his armor. Disappointed with himself, he looked at Belle with great embarrassment on his face. "Your Highness, I'm so sorry. I was just entering to see how I could help, when I took notice of the prisoners, and my feet got caught and I..."

Belle didn't know what to say. She could tell Bernard was very sincere. She patted him on the shoulder like a child, "Bernard, what's done is done. Let's get these prisoners freed and to safety." She crouched down beside the unconscious guard and grabbed his keys.

"Oh, one more thing," Bernard said, timidly. "You won't tell Michael about this... will you?"

Belle looked up at the twenty-year-old knight, feeling compassion for him. She couldn't help but smile slightly, "No... I don't see any reason why we need to tell Michael. This can be our little secret."

"Oh, thank you so much."

"No problem, let's get these prisoners freed."

Taking the keys, Belle fumbled through them, trying to figure out which one would unlock the door. The prisoners saw what was transpiring and began gathering what little possessions they had. Two of the middle-aged men were helping the elderly woman stand to her feet. The teenage girl began to tear up seeing Mendolon's princess standing at the prison doors trying to get them open.

After a few minutes of trying a number of the keys, she finally heard the clicking of the lock, and the prison door swung open. Bernard quickly entered the cell and picked up the elderly woman in his arms. "Thank you, thank you," the teenage girl said, giving Belle a quick squeeze.

Belle addressed the group, "How is everyone? Are you able to move?"

One of the men stepped forward. "Yes, none of us are injured physically, just malnourished." He pointed at Bernard, "If he can carry the old woman, I think we are all good to run out of here as fast as possible."

"That won't be necessary," Belle spoke softly, trying to reassure them. "Our men have mostly secured the castle. We should have nothing to worry about. Most of the guards have been detained… everything's going to be all right."

The men stood silent, looking at each other. One spoke up, "You have the Savage and his beasts detained?"

Belle was a little confused, "No, but shortly, the Savage should be detained. All the guards we found were human. We believe we got most of them."

The man across from Belle stood wide-eyed, shaking his head. "Your Highness, you are wrong. The Savage has been torturing us with his own legion of beasts. He also runs experiments on us, trying to see what we are most afraid of. If you haven't captured the Savage or his army yet… I suggest everyone evacuate right away. He has a weapon I don't think anyone is ready to face."

"A weapon?" Belle said, troubled. "What is it... What does he have?"

The man took a deep breath. "He has... fear, and he seems to wield it like a sword."

Belle now knew they had underestimated this enemy.

CHAPTER 3

$\mathcal{M}$ichael continued his quest through the castle. Cracks in the wall gave him just enough light to guide his way. He stayed in the shadows as much as possible. His dark grey warrior suit helped conceal him. He was now journeying through a long hallway. An old rug lined the floor. So far in his exploration of the castle, he hadn't seen anyone.

Reaching the end of the hall, he found a stairwell to an upper floor. He briefly looked inside and checked the corners, scanning for a surprise attack. He saw no one and heard no one. Quietly he entered the stairwell and proceeded up the stairs. The area felt cool. It was dark. He drew his sword from his back. He didn't want to get caught unprepared. The chief knight wanted to be ready for anything.

It was times like this that he thought of his late father, Albert de Bolbec. He was the bravest knight in all the realm. There was no equal to him in character or in swordplay. He was truly a legend. When Michael was young, he lost his father in a battle in the northeast. Michael then determined in himself, that even as a young man, he would take his father's place and become the best knight in the entire realm. As he grew up, it was obvious that he had the same genes as his father, and that being a knight was part of his destiny. He knew that if his father could see him now, he would be proud of his son.

Ascending the steps, he could see the faint glow of a light at the top of the steps. With each step the light became stronger. He could see the top of the steps. He relaxed his breathing and continued to climb as quietly as possibly.

Reaching the top step, Michael could see that the light was coming from a large candle in this room. He slowly removed his hood and peeked in the room to get a better view. It was some sort of study. There were a couple of bookcases against the wall, along with a large table in the center of the room. Books and papers were scattered on the table, along with a few miscellaneous objects that looked to be used for experimentation. Michael could also see a skull, and beside it a cage with a few mice inside. There were many other fascinating items in this room, but none of them caught his attention. For in the middle of the room... he saw a figure.

The figure was dressed in an all-black coat that stretched down to his boots. A hood covered his head and face. Michael could not make out any of his features. His arms were also covered. He was frantically moving about the room gathering any papers and scrolls and stuffing them into a leather bag. Michael caught a glimpse of his torso and could see he was heavily armored. He watched closely and could also see the long nails and fur on his fingers as he gathered objects. Michael knew right away that this was the Savage.

Michael wanted to watch his movements for just a moment, seeing if he could glean any information concerning what he was doing. He couldn't believe he was face-to-face with the creature that had eluded him and his men the last six months. He could feel his anger rising inside of him. This creature had brought so much pain and suffering to the kingdom. He was ready for peace to be restored.

It was without warning that the beast stuffed the last scroll into his bag and turned to the doorway, heading straight toward Michael. Michael knew he would be seen instantly. Without giving it much thought as to how to engage this creature, instinctively Michael jumped from the shadows and kicked him directly in the middle of the stomach. The beast fell backwards into the room, bumping the table. He dropped his bag, and his papers were scattered along the floor. His hood was still covering his head and face. Michael lunged forward and took a swipe with his sword. The beast moved to the side, barely dodging the sword. Quickly, the beast turned and jumped on the table, reaching for the candle. Michael was just about to pull one of his daggers, when the beast grabbed the fire of the candle and the room went completely dark.

The darkness paralyzed Michael. He couldn't see a thing. Without warning Michael felt a boot from the beast kick him squarely in the jaw. He yelled in pain as he fell to his side. Quickly gathering himself, he planted his back against a nearby wall and tried to quiet his breathing. He could hear the initial sounds of movement by the Savage, but then everything went silent. A dagger was still in Michael's hand, and he was ready to attack... but in the darkness, he wasn't sure where.

❧❧

Gideon and his men checked the courtyard. The guards had been gathered together and tied up. Many of them were in pain. Everything was now quiet. Gideon twirled the ends of his mustache in nervousness. Things seemed to be a little too quiet, and there was no sign of any other guards. The knights were now regrouping at the front gate.

"Did you find anything?" Gideon asked his men.

"No... no sign of anyone," one of the knights responded. "It looks like if there was anyone else, they had already cleared out."

Gideon rubbed the top of his head, running his fingers through what little hair he had left. He was in his late forties and had been on many expeditions through the years, but still he had never seen anything quite like this. He was a little confused by this whole ordeal. He spoke quietly, "Then I wonder why the Savage had guards only watching over the walls. Something doesn't add up."

He was looking back and forth around the courtyard. Nothing seemed out of place. He then explored the front gate. Gideon was just about to walk away when something caught his eye. Just outside the doors of the gate, he saw an odd looking set of footprints in the snow coming from outside the walls. They were running through the gate. He went out to get a closer look. Kneeling down, he could see the prints were obviously of someone stumbling. He looked to the left of the gates and could easily trace them to their original spot.

The footprints came from the spot where the guard fell from the wall after he was kicked off it by Michael. Upon close examination, he could see the guard had landed in a spot where snow had piled from the wind. *He survived the fall*, Gideon thought to himself. *If he was able to stumble through the gate, he might've warned others. I have to let our men know right away.*

Running back to the gates, Gideon cried, "Men, we have to brace ourselves, there was..." It was too late. As Gideon was approaching the gate, the large wooden doors slammed shut. He feared for his men.

Inside the walls, the knights were confused by the sudden shutting of the doors. They drew their swords and quickly stood in a circle with their backs to one another. They all looked around frantically for where their enemy might appear.

A mist began to descend on the courtyard. The knights wondered where it came from. The guards who were still tied up cried out in terror. "Please, no, you can't do this to us. After all we've done. No, stop!" The mist grew, creating a fog in the air. The guards squirmed, trying to get free from the ropes that bound them.

The mist became so thick that the knights couldn't see a thing. "Steady, men," one yelled out. All the men held their swords out, wondering what they would face.

At first it was just the faint sound of a growl. It sounded like a vicious lion, except with a higher pitch. Fear gripped the men as panic started to settle in them. The growls became louder and more dreadful. It was the cry of a wild beast that was hungry for blood. "A beast!" one of the knights shouted. Soon they were all crying out in fear.

"A beast!" one would yell.

"Get away," another screamed.

The scene was chaotic. Through the mist they all saw nothing but terrorizing beasts, gritting their teeth. All of them were over six and a half feet tall. Their eyes were blood red, and their claws were untamed. What little clothes they were wearing were rags. They pounced on the men, stripping them of their swords. The men tried to fight off the ravaging beasts in any way they could. The ones who were still on their feet ran frantically.

It was at this time that Belle and Bernard arrived in the courtyard with the prisoners. They heard the screams of the knights within the misty area. They were all stunned for just a moment. "We've got to help them," Belle said, drawing her sword.

One of the male prisoners quickly grabbed her arm and held her back. "Princess... I'm sorry," he spoke softly. "There's nothing we can do at the moment but wait, and hope they survive." Belle felt utterly helpless.

Listening outside the doors, Gideon heard everything. It truly frightened him. He wished more than anything that he could be inside those walls helping his fellow knights in whatever way possible. He began beating on the doors. "Open up... open up!" he shouted, hoping someone on the other side would hear him. He took a step back and drew his sword, hoping someone would respond. The screaming continued on the inside. It was driving him crazy. He began kicking the doors, hoping for some response. Maybe, just maybe, he could lure the attackers outside the walls.

A moment later the doors began to slowly creak open. Gideon could see nothing but the mist. It started to slowly move out of courtyard through the doors. He wasn't sure how to react. If the attackers came out the doors he wouldn't be able to see them coming. He moved out of the center of the doors and to the side. His plan was to hide behind the opening doors for just a moment while the heavy mist cleared out. If an enemy stepped out of the walls and spotted him, he would be ready with his sword.

The attack went on for just a few more seconds. The mist was starting to become less dense as it was dispersing through the gate and out into the open. One by one the beasts got up and ran through doors, leaving all the men alive but injured. One knight remained lying on his back, trying to fight off a beast. Loud screaming came from the man, while the beast growled. Seeing that the others were running through the gate, the last beast stopped his fight with the man and held the knight's head down against the ground. The beast lowered his face as close as he could to the knight. With a hideous growling voice, the beast spoke, "Warn your king that the Savage is coming for his kingdom, and he cannot be tamed." The knight could feel the beast's breath against his face. He continued, "Nothing can stop him. Fear will overcome!" The beast roared loudly in the knight's face once more before letting go and running off.

Gideon was hiding behind the doors when he saw the horde of cloaked figures run though the entryway. He presumed they were beasts. The mist seemed to leave when the last one left. Gideon thought it best not to engage them in battle since a whole horde had basically run through at once. His mind was now completely focused on his fellow knights. After waiting another minute, he sprang from the shadows and ran through the doors. His men were on the ground in pain, and many were in shock from what had just occurred. Belle and Bernard were already ministering to a few of the men who had severe wounds. Gideon looked around to see if he could find answers to what occurred. He turned to Belle, "Belle, what happened?

"I'm not sure. We arrived as the mist was falling on the men. They weren't able to see their enemies and were attacked. They were helpless," Belle said as she put pressure on a neck wound of one of the knights. There was great urgency in her voice. "What were you doing outside the walls?" she asked.

"I was exploring a pair of footprints in the snow when the doors shut." He had many questions about the attack, "Was that really a group of beasts that attacked our men?"

Belle was troubled, burdened by everything that was happening. "I'm not sure. They didn't seem like typical beasts from Grimdolon. They were vicious and terribly fierce."

The freed prisoners began to help Belle and Bernard in whatever way they could. Belle shouted out orders and told one of the men to search for medical supplies. Gideon saw she was beginning to panic. "Belle, tell me what can I do to help?"

"Take care of these men. I'm going to find Michael!" she shouted.

❧

Michael sat against the wall with his sword in hand. He sat in near complete darkness. There was just a little light coming from the doorway that helped him get his bearings. He wondered if the Savage was still in the room. A few minutes had passed, and he hadn't heard a sound. He wondered what his next move should be.

Feeling the area around him with his hand, he began to move ever so slightly through the room toward the doorway.

The room was completely silent, and Michael was careful, as he didn't want to disturb anything and give away his position. He was thankful for this new armor Hector had designed. It proved to be immeasurably valuable at this time.

Reaching the doorway, Michael quickly moved out of the room into the top of the stairwell. He looked around frantically for any signs of the Savage. Even in the cold winter air, sweat beads rolled off his forehead. He waited a few moments before moving. Occasionally he heard a sound, but quickly realized he was hearing noises coming from outside the castle. He wondered how his men were fairing.

It was at that moment that Michael heard footsteps coming up the stairwell. Looking down the steps, he could see Belle ascending. She was holding a torch and checking her bearings as she climbed the steps. She looked worried. As she got close, Michael called out to her, "Belle, hold your position!" Belle quickly put her back to the wall, and pulled her sword.

She answered back, "Michael, are you all right?"

"Yes, I'm fine. I confronted the Savage in this room a few minutes ago. He may have escaped, but I need to know for sure."

Belle waited a few seconds before answering. "What would you like me to do?"

"Use caution, but come, meet me here. I'll explore the room with the torch." Belle began to slowly ascend the rest of the steps, watching for any enemy that might come her way.

Upon reaching him, Michael whispered to her, "Hold the torch into the room. I want to make sure this beast is gone." Belle nodded in approval. She did as he asked and Michael ducked low and scanned the room. It appeared empty, confirming his suspicion that the beast had left earlier.

Pulling back, he looked up at Belle, "Hand me the torch. I'm going to enter the room and light the candle I saw earlier. Watch the room for me." Belle had many questions, but she knew they would have to wait. She handed over the torch and Michael entered the room. Belle grabbed her bow and pointed an arrow into the room. She would easily let it fly if she had to. Michael quickly found the matches beside the candle and lit it. The room brightened as the wick caught fire.

Michael turned, checking the room one more time. "I believe it's safe to enter, Belle. It looks like the Savage fled the room when I confronted him earlier."

"Michael, I hate to say it, but that might not even be our biggest problem. It appears that rumors are true. The Savage has a horde of beasts assisting him. They attacked us earlier."

"What! What happened?" Michael asked, desperate for information.

"In the courtyard a thick mist fell on our men. They couldn't see a thing. A band of beasts descended on them, brutally attacking them."

"Is everyone ok?"

"I don't know. Gideon and Bernard were attending to them when I left to find you."

Michael couldn't believe what he was hearing. This mission was supposed to be the end of the Savage's reign of terror, but it seemed like things were only getting worse. He ran his fingers through his blond hair and took a deep breath, "Where are the beasts now?"

"They left. It appears one of the guards we knocked from the wall tipped them off. I would assume he opened the doors for them to escape."

"Well then... we must hurry," Michael said sternly. He turned to the table in the center of the room and began searching through many of the scrolls and books.

Belle could tell he was looking for something, "What are you doing? Shouldn't we be leaving?"

Michael didn't take his eyes off the task at hand, "The Savage was working on something before he left. I think he got word we were coming and began packing up some of his work."

Belle was puzzled, "What? Are you sure? How do you know this?"

"I watched him before I attacked. He was moving quickly and was recklessly throwing a lot of papers and scrolls into a bag that he was..." Michael stopped mid-sentence. Looking onto the floor he saw the shoulder bag the Savage had dropped during their fight. There were a few papers that had fallen out when Michael kicked him. He cleared a spot on the large table and spread out the contents of the bag.

Belle looked inquisitively at the contents. She saw maps of the villages of Mendolon, along with notes along the margins. There was also a map of the castle, along with detailed accounts of who worked and resided there on a daily basis. There were notes concerning where to attack, if a siege on the castle was planned. Michael grabbed one of the scrolls and slowly unrolled it. They were surprised by what they saw. On the scroll were names of the knights and what some of their routines were, along with the names of some of their relatives and family. Belle even saw a list recorded of her daily activities, including her morning training routine. "What is all this?" Belle said quietly.

Michael stood silent for a few moments before answering, "It looks like the Savage's plans are deeper than we anticipated." Michael rubbed his chin, deep in thought, wondering what to do next. He took a few more minutes to read some of the materials before issuing an order, "Belle, we need to get our men out of here, and back to the castle."

Belle was still puzzled by everything, "But... Michael, what does this all mean? What are the Savage's plans? What does he want?"

Michael took a deep breath. "I'm... I'm not entirely sure... but whatever it is, it can't be good."

CHAPTER 4

A few days had passed since the raid on the Northern Ruins. The knights were still recovering from the attacks from the beasts. Most of the men were not seriously injured, but they were dealing with the psychological scars of being attacked by the horde of beasts. Many of them felt incapable of further confronting the Savage and his followers.

After the raid on the castle, Michael, Belle, and Gideon led the evacuation of the castle. Leaving the ruins, they took a southern route back toward Mendolon. Hector had arranged for a caravan of wagons to pick up the knights and any hostages. He met them a few miles from the abandoned castle. It was a difficult journey as many of them were paranoid of another attack from the Savage.

At present, Michael and Gideon were sharing with King Sebastian the information they had gleaned from the Savage's notes found in the upstairs study of the ruins. It was early morning and tensions were high as Michael pleaded his case, "King, the Savage is not what we thought. He is much more calculated and cunning than we have anticipated. We must use all our resources and take every precaution."

The king rested in his chair while he listened to the men. His eyes were closed and his left hand was over his face, hoping this would all go away, "Michael, I hear what you are saying, but this will throw the whole kingdom into a panic."

"King, did you hear me? The Savage is watching us. He's not working alone. Somehow he has spies watching us."

"Please, King, hear what Michael is saying," Gideon added. "He truly knows what is best for the kingdom."

The king slammed his fist against the table and stood up in a fury. His long curly brown hair bounced as he stood. "You think he knows best?" the King said angrily. "Last I checked, I was still king!"

Michael held his hands up, trying to calm the situation. "Listen, Your Majesty, try to hear what I'm saying. The Savage is not going to continue to *just* plan acts of terror and mischief. He is planning a coordinated attack against the kingdom and your reign."

"You don't think I see that?!" the king shot back. He ran his fingers through his beard as he paced back and forth. He was trying hard to calm himself. The Savage had been a nuisance for the past six months, and the king hoped that this enemy would have been disposed of by now. It was frightening news to hear that the Savage had notes concerning a layout of the castle as well as the daily schedule of all the knights.

After a few moments, Michael decided to break the silence. "Please, King, will you grant me to speak my mind? Let me say what I think, and then you may do as you wish."

The king took a deep breath and sat down comfortably in his chair. He nodded and held out his hand toward Michael, as if to say "proceed."

"Very well," Michael said. "I suggest we call to arms all the soldiers and able- bodied men of the land and make them aware of what is transpiring. Set watches throughout the villages. As my men start to recover, I will spread them throughout the land. They can give instruction to the townspeople as well as provide a presence of comfort among the people. Any information or leads concerning the Savage will be brought directly to Belle or myself. And then…"

"Oh Michael…" the king stood up again. He was frustrated.

"What's the matter, my king?"

King Sebastian cursed under his breath, "It's so close to the time of our Winter Ball… In the past this has been our time to show our confidence and strength to the kingdoms of the world."

Gideon shouted out, "But that's not the purpose of the Winter Ball. It is…"

Michael quickly cut him off. "Gideon," he spoke softly, putting a hand on his shoulder. "Let me handle this one."

Michael turned to King Sebastian and continued. "Listen. I'm not saying to cancel the Winter Ball or any of the other celebrations. I think they will actually give the people hope." The annual Winter Ball was the most festive event of the kingdom. All the nobles and most of the knights of Mendolon would be in attendance along with their families. Many of the kingdom's wealthy citizens would also be present, along with a few dignitaries from Mendolon's few allied nations.

"Well, is there anything else you would suggest, O Great and Wise Knight?" the King said sarcastically.

Michael took a deep breath, "Yes, there is actually one more thing." He paused just a moment to absorb the weight of what he was about to say. "King, I think you should seek refuge in one of our allied nations over the sea."

"What? Are you crazy?" the king shot back.

"Listen, Your Majesty. The Savage has detailed plans concerning the castle and the people in it. It seems like you will be the eventual target."

The king pulled his hair in frustration. "But… I can't…. I just can't… not right now."

Michael continued, "Don't worry about the kingdom, my king. I will be advising my men concerning the security of the castle, and I can rely on Hector for running the castle itself. Your daughter, as always, will serve as a symbol of hope in your absence." The king closed his eyes and shook his head. He did not like what Michael was saying, but in his heart of hearts he knew that what he was suggesting was the best plan of action. Any objection he tried to conjure in his mind seemed pointless.

Michael continued. "It won't be long. I know I can catch this beast. Trust me, King. This is the correct plan of action."

There seemed to be a strong tension in the air as Michael and Gideon waited for King Sebastian to respond. At times he could be unreasonable, so they wondered what he would say. He seemed to be thinking intently about the suggestions made. The king rubbed his forehead in deep contemplation. It was a full minute before Sebastian broke the silence, "Very well, I will leave at once. I will be accompanied by a small troop of soldiers. I will travel north."

"What? Where are you going in the north?" Michael responded. "I would think traveling over the sea would be the safest route."

The king turned to walk away, "You heard me. I will go to the north to the Lost Mountains. I will stay in seclusion until the Savage is captured."

❧❧

It was getting late in the afternoon and Belle was still training on her obstacle course. After discovering the Savage's plans, she knew she had to change her routine. She no longer came out in the early morning to the course but rather waited until the afternoon. She also took a handful of soldiers with her to help stand watch as she trained. They proved themselves valuable in that a couple times she had called on them to assist her in her training.

She had heard of her father's plans to travel north, and this motivated her even more to defeat the Savage. The winter season and particularly the Royal Winter Ball was a majestic time of celebration for the kingdom of Mendolon. For Sebastian to miss it was quite a big deal. It was the one time all year that the people truly saw their king as a benevolent ruler as opposed to a wealth-obsessed tax collector.

Currently she was practicing sword fighting with Bernard as the other soldiers looked on. They used long blunt swords to practice dueling. Bernard was very skilled in technique, but Belle's speed often got the better of him. At this moment, Bernard had her backing up in a defensive position. She never wanted anyone to go easy on her just because she was the princess. She always told them to give her their best. She was thankful that Bernard never held back.

Belle jumped back as Bernard took a furious side swipe with his sword. Belle crouched and spun into a side kick, sweeping his legs out from under him. Bernard fell hard to the ground on a small patch of snow, dropping his sword. Quickly standing up, Belle held the dull tip of the sword to Bernard's chest as he lay on the ground. Bernard let out a deep breath… he was exhausted.

Belle pulled back her sword, "C'mon Bernard, let's go another round."

"Your Majesty, I think I might need a break. We've been at this for over an hour," Bernard said through heavy breathing.

"But don't you want to beat me? I'm starting to get tired, and you really are doing better," Belle said, trying to encourage him.

"Ok," Bernard's eyes were closed as he lay on the ground, "Just let me take five minutes… and then I'll continue to help you train."

She sheathed her sword, "Very good. Take all the time you need, Bernard."

Belle walked to a nearby tree where she kept a water skin. Lifting it high, she took a large sip of water. *Maybe taking five minutes was a good idea after all*, she thought. She was thankful for these last few days to get away and train. Since the night of the raid on the northern ruins, she had not slept well. Her recurring dream had returned, and it consumed a lot of her thinking. In some regards it was becoming an obsession with her.

Her dream was a pleasant dream in many regards. She was entering the Royal Winter Ball, and there were crowds of people welcoming her as she entered. She was dressed beautifully. Her dress was full and eloquent. It was a deep purple color. She wore white gloves and her brown hair was curled and pinned up. As she walked by the guests, they welcomed her and commented on how beautiful her dress was. She found her herself smiling and quietly saying "thank you" as she passed by individuals. Music played gently in the background.

In her dream she would make her way to the dance floor. She could hear the sound of violins. When the guests cleared the floor... the dream started to turn. Something was not right. She felt that she was not supposed to be there, and it wasn't unfolding properly. In the dream she was pulled between desires of wanting to stay and wanting to leave simultaneously. She would scream out on the dance floor, "Please, let me go. I don't want to be here. This is not right. I must go now!" It was at this point that she would always wake up and remind herself that it was only a dream. This had been her normal routine off and on for the past nine months. But for the last few nights since the raid, it had occurred every night.

Bernard was just now getting onto his feet and stumbling over to where Belle stood. He collapsed on the ground right by her, resting his arms under his head like he was ready to take a nap. "Belle, I'm ready to start again, whenever you are," he said through muffled speech.

Belle took another sip of water, "Oh… it's ok, Bernard. I might take a few more minutes to rest if that's ok with you."

Bernard took a deep breath. "If you insist," he said, drifting off to sleep.

The soldiers who were watching the southern perimeter reached for the hilts of their swords as they heard a horse approaching. They quickly relaxed their grip when they saw Michael come into view on the road. He was dressed in his warrior gear, as he wanted to be ready at any moment for an encounter with the Savage. He didn't seem to be in a hurry, but Belle had worked with him enough to know that he had something on his mind. Entering the area, he dismounted his horse and approached Belle.

"What brings you out here today, Michael?" Belle said, greeting him.

"I guess you've heard about your father's plans to hide in the north," he spoke quietly.

"I have," Belle said, brushing a strand of brown hair out of her face. "I think it's a good plan."

"Yes, and then I'm going to…" Michael stopped mid-sentence. "What's with him?" Michael said, pointing at Bernard lying on the ground.

Belle looked over at Bernard sleeping on the ground. He was snoring at this point. "Oh… him. Yeah, he's just waiting for me to rest up, so we can continue with my training."

"I see… that's very gracious of you, Your Highness," Michael said, smiling slightly. He continued, "Anyway, the king is hoping to depart as soon as he can. He should be fine as he's taking a band of soldiers with him, and he's traveling roads that belong to our allies. He's left you and me in charge until he gets back."

"Well… he does think we make a great team," Belle said jovially. Michael tried to stay focused but couldn't help but blush just a little at Belle's comment. They had been working so fervently for the past few days that Michael hadn't given much thought to the king's eventual plans to see them wed.

He continued, "The castle's dungeon will be cleared out for the most part, but I'm going to move a special prisoner down there."

Belle was confused, "What? What are you talking about?"

Michael looked off into the distance, contemplating the magnitude of what he was about to say to Belle. He took a deep breath before speaking quietly, "It's my source. The one I was telling you about."

Her eyes grew wide, "The one who led us to the Northern Ruins?"

"Yes, that's the one. He's been imprisoned in the barracks of my house."

Many questions flooded Belle's mind, "Who is he? Where did you find him?"

Michael looked around again to make sure no one was overhearing them talk. He got close to Belle's face, and talked softly, "Eight months ago after the dragon hunt we found him living in the woods. He is the one who provoked the dragon."

Belle was utterly shocked, "What! You have him in your barracks? Why didn't you turn him over to my father?"

Michael anticipated all these questions, "Listen Belle, you know how hasty your father can be. I knew he would order an immediate execution of him. I didn't want that to happen. He said that he had information concerning the Savage that was helpful, and so far he has been accurate." Belle paced just a little as Michael's information sank in. What Michael did in hiding his prisoner was a case for treason against the king. She knew Michael would not do such a thing unless there was validity to what he was saying. She was stunned. She greatly wondered where all this would lead.

"Tell me more about him," she said, hungry for information.

"He's a young noble from another kingdom. I would guess he's a little younger than me. He is very intelligent and very knowledgeable of this world."

"How..." Belle stumbled over her words. "How was he able to pin down the location of the Northern Ruins?"

"After every attack from the Savage, I brought him back clues and evidence and he was able to piece everything together and come up with a location of where the Savage was hiding."

Belle paced slightly, turning to face the sun that was beginning to set. She comfortably crossed her arms as the information sank in. She felt the information Michael was sharing with her was invaluable. It motivated her even more to find the Savage and capture him. She wanted to accelerate the plans. "Well, I'd say that settles it. Especially with the notes we got from the ruins. Let's have your source look at them. If you're confident in him, let's get all the information we can from him and catch the Savage."

Michael ran his fingers through his blond hair as he looked off into the distance. Belle could tell he had something on his mind. "What is it, Michael?" she said, grabbing his arm.

"Listen, Belle. This is where it gets interesting. He's now refusing to talk to me."

"What? Why?"

Michael shook his head, "I'm not entirely sure. But ever since we got back from the ruins, he says he wants to talk with someone else."

"Who?"

Michael looked directly into Belle's eyes, "You, Belle... he wants to talk to you."

"Me? Are you joking?... Why?"

"I'm not sure. I've tried to bargain with him, but he refuses. His one request is to talk to the princess of the land."

Belle continued to pace as she thought about what Michael had just said. She thought everything sounded quite curious. Intuitively she had a lot of precaution, but the desire to catch the Savage outweighed everything. Turning to Michael, she shrugged her shoulders and smiled slightly. "Ok, I don't see what the problem is. Let me meet with him and get the information we need."

Michael took a deep breath, seemingly reluctant to let this plan go through. He spoke quietly, "Very well... let's meet at the castle after sunset and I will brief you on everything he's told me so far."

Michael turned to walk away, but Belle quickly reached out and grabbed his arm. She wasn't finished yet. Belle knew him well enough to know that he was hiding something, and, more specifically, he hadn't answered one of her questions. "Michael, before you leave... I need to know something. Please tell me, *who* is he?... and what's his name?"

Michael nodded his head slightly and looked off into the distance. He knew this question would come, "His name is Jean-Luc Pascal, and he's a beast."

CHAPTER 5

$\mathcal{M}$ichael led Belle through the back halls of the castle toward the dungeon. The area of the castle was dark with only a few small torches lighting the hallway. Belle couldn't believe how everything was unfolding. The thought of her father going to the north was still fresh on everyone's mind, and now she learned that Michael secretly had a beast imprisoned for the last eight months. She wondered if everything would ever truly return to normalcy.

Belle tied her hair back into a ponytail as she walked, trying to get herself mentally ready for this task at hand. "I still can't believe you had a beast living in the small prison in your house," she said to Michael.

"Yeah, sometimes it's strange even for me to think about," Michael said quietly. "But truly, I felt as if I had no other choice."

They came to a stairwell at the end of the hallway. Michael turned to face her, "Belle, this is where I leave you. Try to relax, but don't give him too much information about yourself, as I don't fully trust him yet."

Belle nodded her head in approval. She felt a mixture of both anxiety and wonder as she thought of meeting this beast. "Michael, is there something that makes you doubt him? Has he been untrustworthy in some regard?"

Michael shook his head as he looked back down the hallway from where they came. She could see the apprehension on his face. "No, nothing like that... I just feel like," he paused a moment. "I feel like he's hiding something... like he's leading us on. I think he wants something from me, and I'm not sure yet what it is."

They stood in silence for a few moments wondering what to say next. Michael scratched his head as if he was in deep thought. Belle wondered if he was starting to have second guesses about letting her talk to the beast. She spoke up, grabbing his arm, "Listen, Michael, I'll be careful. Please, don't worry about me. I'll remember the mission and try to get as much info as I can from him."

Michael felt reassured by Belle's confidence. "Ok. Gideon is coming here soon. I told him to wait here just in case you need anything. Things are moving quickly, and I'm going to head home. I'm going to be leading the knights into the towns tomorrow trying to set up small local troops of soldiers to watch for the Savage. Take as much time as you need with the beast. Try to glean as much information as you can from him. I'll check in with you in the early morning in case he led on to any valuable information."

"Thanks, I'll do my best." Belle said, turning to descend the steps.

"Oh, one more thing, Belle," Michael said, stopping her in her tracks.

She turned to face him. "Yes?" she replied.

"Do listen carefully to every word that he says... he tends to subtly speak in riddles," Michael said, trying to prepare her as much as he could.

Belle nodded her head, slightly confused. She wasn't sure how to respond to this last comment. She simply turned and descended the steps.

The steps spiraled down to the lower dungeons of the castle. The stairwell was dark; the only lights came from the main floor and the dungeon. Belle walked down carefully, making sure not to stumble. She wished she would have taken her medicine a little earlier on this particular night. She felt anxious. Just for a moment she instinctively reached for the hilt of her sword before remembering that she was in her own castle. It had been a couple of years since she had been in the dungeon. All prisoners that were kept in this prison were either captured in close proximity to the castle or needed to be interrogated concerning the larger workings of Mendolon. All others were taken to the large prison chambers a few miles east of the castle. Currently in this dungeon besides the beast, Jean-Luc Pascal, there were only three lower level criminals. They had been caught trying to rob the castle's markets in the last few days.

Reaching the bottom steps, she could hear the playing of a violin coming from the farthest prison cell. The other three prisoners were located close to the steps. They stopped chatting at the sight of the princess emerging from the stairwell. The dungeon was dark. Belle could barely make out the faces of the men. "Good evening, M'lady," one of the prisoners said, greeting her.

Belle smiled slightly as she proceeded down the hallway toward the sound of the violin. She brushed a strand of hair out of her face as she walked. There were about five cells on each side separating the beast's cell from the other prisoners. Michael said that he wanted to keep him isolated as well as comfortable in his conditions.

The beast's cell came into view as it was more lit up than the rest of the dungeon. As Belle walked closer, she could see that it was not a typical prison cell. It looked comfortable. There was a well-made bed, along with an end table with a lantern sitting on it. There were also a couple of wooden chairs along with a beautiful rug and a large bookshelf that seemed to contain fifty books or more. As she stepped right in front of the cell, she could see a figure in the middle of the room playing a slow-methodical piece on the violin. It was Jean Luc Pascal, the beast.

He looked to be just under six feet in height. He had long curls of brownish-blond hair rolling down his back. He was very thin for a beast, looking no larger than a man with broad shoulders. Like most beasts, he was a mixture of lion and man, with a few faint characteristics of a wolf. Besides the other night at the ruins, Belle had only once seen a beast traveling a northern road. Jean-Luc looked much more like a man than the one she had seen in the past. He was dressed properly in a red jacket with a white shirt underneath, dark slacks, and a worn pair of shoes. He wore eyeglasses, which gave him even more of the look of a man.

Seeing Belle in the corner of his eye, he finished playing his piece and turned to face her. He peacefully put down his violin on a nearby chair. "Good evening, Your Highness," he said as properly as could. Belle stood silent, not sure what to say. She had never spoken to a beast before. This was not what she expected.

Jean-Luc comfortably took a seat in one of his chairs, adjusting his glasses. He broke the silence, "I'm really glad Michael allowed my request and let you come see me."

"Yeah," she said, still a little stunned by the whole situation. This was truly like nothing else she'd ever experienced. She spoke quietly, "You're... you're a lot smaller than I anticipated."

Jean-Luc couldn't help but laugh slightly, "Well... it's a pleasure to meet you too, Your Highness."

"Oh, no... I'm sorry," Belle said, stuttering over her words. "I've just never met a beast before, and ... this is not what I expected."

"What did you expect?"

"I'm not sure. To be honest, this whole situation is very different for me. I just learned that you were helping us catch the Savage, and that Michael has had you imprisoned for the past eight months," Belle said with poise.

"Well, as in everything that Michael does, I would say he has treated me very fairly. For being imprisoned, he has actually made my stay as comfortable as it can be - even helping me to feel at home in my new cell," Jean-Luc said, looking around at all the amenities in his cell. He seemed completely comfortable as he spoke. He shrugged his shoulders, "And to be honest with you... I did provoke the dragon which has to be worth some form of punishment."

"Why were you in the dragon's territory on that day?" Belle said, amazed at how relaxed she had become so soon.

He nodded his head in approval at the question, anticipating it would come. "I needed to get Michael's attention. I needed to warn him about the Savage."

"Do you know the Savage, personally?"

"I would not say he is a friend, rather someone I'm just familiar with." He stopped to point at something behind Belle, "Bernard came down earlier and left a chair for you."

Belle turned to see the chair sitting against the wall. "Thank you," she said, retrieving the chair and taking a seat.

"Now, where was I... Oh yes, the Savage. His real name is Dominique Delano. Supposedly he was doing some mining in the northern parts of Grimdolon. I heard about him from some of our townsfolk."

"What did they say about him?" Belle asked inquisitively.

The beast took a breath, "To be honest, those working around the area described him as being mad. He can't be reasoned with or controlled. They say he had a lust for power and clearly knows what he wants. It drove him to madness."

"What was he doing in Grimdolon's mines?"

"Not sure, exactly. There are many mysterious materials to be found in those mines. I'm sure you've heard the rumors about our mines." Belle nodded in agreement. From childhood schooling, everyone knew that Grimdolon was known for its mining and that it was the kingdom's main source of wealth. Their land was rich in minerals and other various resources that could be used for anything from medicines to synthetic materials. The beasts of Grimdolon also found gems and other rubies in certain areas of the mines.

Belle was hungry for more information. She wanted to figure out what the Savage was currently planning. She continued, "Michael and I found his plans in the Northern Ruins. We know that he is planning some sort of attack on the castle, and particularly, my father."

Jean-Luc nodded his head in approval, "Correct. He thinks that he will be able to overthrow the kingdom of Mendolon with a small band of followers. He will stop at nothing until he accomplishes that goal."

Belle was on the edge of her seat at this point. She didn't want to miss anything Jean-Luc was saying. "The notes we found at the Northern Ruins had a list of every knight in the castle along with a thorough map of the castle. I must admit, it was quite frightening to see," Belle said honestly. "Do you know what specifically he is planning?"

Jean-Luc stood up, rubbing his chin in deep contemplation. "I'm not sure yet... I need a little more information before I can come to a conclusion." He paced his cell, trying to put pieces together. The beast stopped for a moment before looking directly at Belle, "Can you think of anything else you've seen in the ruins that might help us with this mystery?"

Belle rubbed her forehead, trying to think of anything she saw or heard, "No, nothing comes to mind."

Jean-Luc paced near the front of the cell. He was sure there was something that could help him piece all this information together. He was wondering if he had missed something in all the conversations he had had with Michael.

Belle tried to think of something to say that would help the situation. She broke the silence, "Some of the townspeople say he has magic."

This stopped Jean-Luc right in his tracks. He looked at Belle with a slight smile on his face. "Magic?" he said inquisitively.

"Yes, that's what I've heard, and I guess I saw a little bit of it the other night while we were at the ruins. He created this smoke screen as his fellow beasts attacked our men. The Knights couldn't see what was coming."

Jean-Luc stepped as close as he could to Belle and spoke through the bars, "Belle... may I call you, Belle?"

She became a little nervous with how close he was to her. "Sure, that should be fine. Michael said we are close to the same age."

"Very well... Belle, I will encourage you with this thought, and if I were you, I would greatly take it to heart." He looked directly at Belle, "Perception is not always reality... Just because Sir Delano is spreading rumors that he has magic, doesn't mean he actually possesses it."

Belle stood up, stepping a little closer to the prison bars. "Wait... you're saying that the Savage spread those rumors himself about having magic?"

"Precisely. He does not operate in reality. He just manipulates everyone into thinking that he has more power than he really does."

A strand of brown hair fell in front of Belle's eyes, and she brushed it to the side. "Jean-Luc, how is he doing this? How is he eluding all our knights and successfully striking different parts of the kingdom?"

Jean-Luc stood silent for a moment, seemingly caught off guard by something Belle said. Belle wondered why the silence all of a sudden, "Jean-Luc, are you ok?"

He closed his eyes for a quick moment and shook his head, "Sorry... As I was saying, he manipulates you. Fear is his main weapon. The Savage wants you living in fear and constantly wondering what he's going to do. He is not operating in reality... only perception."

Belle was confused by this whole exchange with the beast. She feared he was talking in riddles like Michael had warned her. Worse yet, like Michael, she could tell that this beast was hiding something from her. She felt like he was starting to play games with her. She became frustrated. "I feel you are hiding something from me. Please, tell me plainly what you mean by all this, Beast."

Jean-Luc nodded in approval and calmly walked over and picked up his violin. He took a seat close to the bars where Belle was seated. It looked as if he was trying to carefully choose the words he was about to say. Belle could tell he was calculating the depth of everything he was saying. This worried her greatly. The beast took a deep breath before speaking to her, "Well... you are actually correct, Your Highness." He took off his glasses and was now looking straight at Belle. "I do have secrets, but I'm not ready to disclose them yet. If I gave everything to you at once, you would be finished with me."

"Secrets... what are you talking about?" Belle was starting to get a little angry at this point.

"Belle... you must open your eyes." Jean-Luc's eyes were still fixed on Belle as he spoke very intently in a hushed voice, "Look around you, Your Highness. You know this kingdom has secrets. They surround your life. Widen your gaze. Open... your... eyes."

Belle stood silently, looking at the beast. She didn't know how to respond. She started to become somewhat frightened of Jean-Luc and what he may be implying. The princess was ready to leave. She turned to walk away. "That'll be all today... Beast."

She was a few steps down the hall when Jean-Luc quickly stood up and stopped her. "One more thing, Your Highness."

Belle turned to face him as he spoke. "You said that in the Northern Ruins, you and Michael found a list of all the knights along with their daily schedules."

"That's correct," she said softly.

"Did you find anything concerning Michael de Bolbec in the Savage's notes?"

Belle thought for a second as she tried to remember everything she'd seen that night. "Actually... no we didn't. Nothing about Michael."

"Let me draw one conclusion," Jean-Luc said with wide eyes, grabbing the prison bars in front of him. He spoke in a rushed voice, "The notes on Michael weren't there in the upper room of the ruins because the Savage and his followers had taken them out. They probably had been referring to them frequently as of late. I would easily venture to say that Michael is their first target, and they are going to strike against him as soon as they can. I would make sure he is safe."

Belle put her hands over her mouth as she remembered Michael's last words about heading home to get some sleep. She knew he was in danger. She quickly ran out of the dungeon.

CHAPTER 6

$\mathcal{M}$ichael stirred the fire in his fireplace. It was a cold December evening and he wanted to be sure it burned strong through the evening. He hadn't been sleeping much as of late. Between his discussions with Jean-Luc and his constant research on the Savage, sleep had become a forgotten luxury. He had another busy day tomorrow so he wanted to be sure to get a good night's rest before venturing out into the towns.

His home was located east of the castle about three miles. The house was considered quite large for someone who wasn't royalty. It consisted of five bedrooms, a study, a kitchen and small dining area, along with a library. It was made of stone, and contained both a second story and a basement. His great-grandfather had built it many years ago, and through the decades many of his family members had lived there.

Michael took off his boots and set them by the fire, hoping they would dry during the night. Working late nights and early mornings as of late, he appreciated the opportunity to relax. Earlier he had made himself a cup of tea. He reached for it and took a sip. *Steeped perfectly*, he thought to himself. He rested his head against the back of the rocking chair.

He closed his eyes and thought of the townspeople he would face tomorrow. How he wished that he was traveling to the towns tomorrow bringing good news. For the past six months, he felt like his only interaction with the people of Mendolon had been warnings and precautionary visits to their towns. Earlier this year he had hoped that ridding the eastern border of the dragon would be a momentous occasion, but it actually opened the greater mystery of the Savage. In his heart of hearts, Michael longed to ride through the towns telling people that peace and justice had been secured for years to come. He wanted this for the people of Mendolon more than anything.

He took another sip of tea as he felt the temperature in the air drop. Putting down his tea, he went to retrieve a blanket from his bedroom. Walking the hallway, he grabbed his bicep and flexed. His muscles were still a little sore from the raid on the ruins a few days ago. It was only at down time moments like this that he realized how sore they were. It reminded him that as strong as he was, the ultimate victory could not come from him alone. Even as the realm's bravest knight, he was finite.

Reaching his bedroom, he grabbed a blanket off his bed. He was about to exit the room when he realized the temperature in the room was much cooler than the rest of the house. It stopped him in his tracks. He looked to the south side of the room and there he saw a window was open. Michael quickly got down on the ground and pulled a small blade he hid under his bed. There was no reason for that window to be open. The obvious conclusion was that someone was inside his home.

He stood against the wall and looked down the hallway back toward the living room area. The house was silent; he heard nothing. He slowly made his way down the hallway, checking each room he passed by. His mind wondered if this was a common burglar ... or something more sinister.

As he got close to the fireplace room, Michael could see that it was starting to fill with smoke. He wondered if the intruder was spreading his fire and if he was going to be a victim of arson. He began to move a little faster. His weapons were kept in a small armory closet off the main living area. At a time like this he really wished he had his daggers handy.

৵৶

Belle quickly ran up the steps from the dungeon. She found Gideon at the top, on the verge of sleeping. She startled him with her urgency, "Gideon, we've got to head to Michael's house, and we must leave at once."

He quickly shook himself awake and stood up. "Why, what's going on?"

"Jean-Luc, the beast, thinks the Savage is going to target him first," she said moving quickly down the hallway.

Gideon followed her. "What makes you think that? We didn't find anything in the Savage's notes concerning Michael, and besides, his private residence has been a secret for years."

"I don't know how, but Jean-Luc says that the Savage knows more about us than we think. He ultimately wants to overthrow the kingdom, and he plans to do it by first taking down the kingdom's chief knight."

"What do you suggest, Your Highness? Most of the knights are still recovering from their injuries."

"Gideon, call a few dozen of the castle's soldiers into service. I'm afraid of what we might face at Michael's dwelling."

৵৶

Reaching the main living area, Michael quickly realized that the room was not filled with smoke at all. It was a thick fog-like mist in the air. He knew instantly that this was an attack from the Savage. He gripped his sword tightly, not able to see much of anything. The fog continued to spread rapidly.

He was almost at his armory when he heard a figure spring from behind him. He quickly turned and met the figure with his sword. It was a ravenous beast, who looked to be hungry for blood. Michael met him with his eyes and looked into the monstrous face. The creature growled at him as their swords pressed against each other. Michael jumped back, and felt the hands of another creature behind him. He quickly turned and slashed the beast. The creature groaned, as Michael figured he might have taken off one of his fingers in the swipe. Being aware of his surroundings, he turned around, and blocked another swipe of the sword from the first beast. He couldn't see much in the mist, and it took him completely off guard when he felt another creature land a punch to his left side.

Michael stumbled to his right, and then felt another beast's bicep around his throat squeezing. Pushing back with his feet, he slammed the beast against a nearby a wall. This helped him get his bearing to where he was in the house. The beast squeezed tighter. He felt his mind begin to fade. He knew it was now or never.

With his sword still in hand, he stabbed the beast's forearm that was squeezing his neck. The beast loosened his grip as he screamed in pain. With his right elbow, Michael turned and hit the beast in the head. He spun around completely and took a swipe with his sword. He was not sure of the damage he had done.

Another beast grabbed him from behind. Startled, he dropped his sword. He took no time in flipping the beast over his back. He picked up his sword and took off running to where he thought his front door was, hitting his toe on a chair on the way out. For a moment he had forgotten that he had taken off his boots earlier in the evening.

Michael was almost at the front door when he saw it open, and two more large, angry beasts entered the doorway. They both had swords, and there were others still in the house. He knew he wouldn't survive a battle with all of them. Quickly, he looked for an escape. Turning to his right, he could see the faint light from a window. He threw his sword down and sprinted toward it. He dove head first with his arms out in front. The glass shattered as he hit it and passed through to the outside. His body naturally went into a somersault as he hit the ground. His hands began to bleed heavily from the shattered glass.

Getting to his feet, Michael was stopped directly in his tracks. There in front of him was a brigade of rough-looking men standing around the spot where he landed. There were about a dozen of them standing in a semicircle around him. Michael was pinned between the men and his house. The men had somber looks on their faces and their clothes were disheveled. What Michael noticed most of all was that each man had a bow and arrow in hand, and they were all pointing them directly at him. He knew this was his point of surrender. He put his hands up showing that he was not prepared to fight back.

A few minutes passed and no one said a word. The men just stood staring at Michael with their arrows raised. Finally, two of the men moved out of position and a dark figure passed into the circle. Michael knew who it was. He had seen him before, just a few nights earlier. It was the Savage.

He was dressed in all black with a hood over his head. Even though it was dark, Michael could see portions of his face this time. His eyes particularly seemed to glow from under the hood. They were a deep red color. Michael could also see a little bit of the dark brown fur from his face. He saw the same hands as he had a few days ago. His claws looked a little longer this time. They reached out toward Michael and threw his face into the ground.

"That's for striking my men at the ruins," he said with a deep, vicious voice.

Michael wondered if he should try to fight back and somehow gain the upper hand. He thought otherwise as he would probably be met with a dozen arrows if he tried.

The Savage then delivered a swift kick to Michael's ribs as he lay on the ground. He groaned in pain, grabbing his ribs. "And that's for striking my beasts tonight," the Savage said with an even angrier tone.

Michael brushed his blond hair out of his face. "Well…" he moaned as he spoke, "at least you could've made it a fair fight. Five or six against one doesn't seem very fair."

The Savage laughed quietly as he spoke, "It would seem that the 'Great Knight of Mendolon' is not as strong as the people think."

Michael rose to one knee, and spoke with vengeance. "And blinding a guy's vision during a fight doesn't seem very honorable. But I have to remember that a beast that targets women and children at markets doesn't have any honor."

This seemed to infuriate the Savage. He quickly walked back over to Michael and drove his face back into the ground. He pushed as hard as he could as he spoke through gritted teeth, "Listen, you Mendolon filth. You will not speak to me like that." He stopped to growl in his ear, "I know your comings and goings. I know you have Jean-Luc tucked away in your silly little castle that I will soon rule from."

Michael tried to raise his face out of the snow on the ground, but one of the troops holding an arrow quickly came and drove his foot into his back, putting further weight on him. The Savage got down close to Michael's ear as he spoke, "I imagine Jean-Luc has told you how I operate." He growled again in his ear. "I take away your vision, your perception. The only thing you are able to see are my beasts striking you…. Your sight is gone and it leaves me to move in … with fear."

Michael had had enough. He decided he wouldn't go down without a fight. With all his strength he quickly rolled himself over. In one swift moment he sat up and punched the man with the arrow in the stomach with his left fist, and then took a swipe at his face with his right. The man fell backwards dropping his bow and arrow. He turned to attack the Savage, but it was too late. An arrow was sent flying through the air from one of the men and it penetrated Michael's flesh next to one of his shoulder blades.

Thankfully, the arrow did not go deep. He stopped briefly to wince in pain. The Savage quickly hit Michael with his fist on the side of his head. He fell to the ground. "That's enough, men. Tie him up, and let's take him to our lair."

A few of the men approached Michael and tied his hands behind his back. Another threw a black cloth bag over his head. All he could see was complete darkness.

∾∾

It was just over a half an hour later that Belle, Gideon, and a troop of soldiers arrived on the scene. Michael's house had been damaged profusely in the attack. The Savage and his followers had broken through windows, doors, and even a section of the roof. Debris was scattered everywhere and it looked as if a number of things had been stolen from the house. Belle had only been to Michael's house once years ago with her father. She remembered the trip fondly and hated seeing his house like this.

"The Savage really came at him with full force," Gideon said, looking through some of the debris scattered around. Belle didn't respond. She felt on the verge of tears. She was scared for her friend.

Gideon opened the armory closet beside the fireplace. "It looks like the Savage didn't find Michael's personal armory."

Belle took a quick glance at it. "Take all the weapons and bring them back to the castle," she requested. "Gideon, have the men search the house and gather anything that looks to be of personal value. Word will begin to spread of this attack to some of the nearby residents. I want to be sure all of Michael's belongings are well-secured."

"It will be done," Gideon said, nodding his head. He began the task at once.

Belle took one more look at the house before heading outside. She had seen enough. Stepping outside, Belle took a deep breath of fresh air. She put her hands in front of her eyes trying to hold back the tears. Horrible thoughts gathered in her mind as to what may have happened to Michael. She worried that he may not even be alive. The thought sickened her. She sat down on the steps outside his front door. "You have to be strong," she whispered to herself. Belle had never met her mother, as she had lost her shortly after she was born, but it was especially at times like this that she wished her mother was around to help her glean strength.

She started to sing a song she'd learned from one of the castle gardeners, "Daffodils, lilies… the beauties of the fields. The crops are growing high and strong… what will they yield? The season comes and then they're gone, through all the changes of the year, help me be strong."

The princess felt a tear roll down her cheek. She wiped it away and stood to her feet and then let her hair down to help her relax. She knew the time called for her to be strong and to start thinking of a plan. Where was the Savage now hiding? How would they find him? Every angle would need to be explored. She would spare no expense. Looking back into the house, she beheld its ruined state. Was there a clue she was missing? How would she open her eyes, widen her gaze? What would Michael advise her to do at a time like this?

Belle was about to enter the house again when something on the doorframe caught her attention. She examined it closely. It was a clump of dark grey fur stuck to the doorway. It looked to be from a beast, possibly the Savage. Even though it seemed insignificant, she wondered if she should have this examined further. *Who could help with something like this?* She thought to herself, *I wonder if anyone could make any sense out of …*

A passing thought came to mind… she knew of another possibility to explore.

CHAPTER 7

"You can't be serious!" Hector hissed as he followed Belle through the castle's back hallway toward the dungeon.

She didn't break stride as she spoke, "We have to trust him. He is the only one we know who has inside information on the Savage."

Hector grabbed Belle's arm, stopping her in her tracks. "I didn't like the fact that Michael brought a beast into our dungeon but now *you* want to release him and let him explore Michael's house. You don't even know if he's telling us the truth, and you want to trust him?"

Belle pulled her arm away from Hector and turned to face him. More than an hour had passed since examining Michael's house. Gideon and his men had found nothing significant at Michael's home that would lead them to the Savage. Belle's idea was now to bring Jean-Luc to the house and see if he could find anything among the debris that would be helpful. She knew it was a very risky move, but she thought it was truly their best option. "We have to do this. Michael is captured, and we've got to save him before it's too late. I don't see what other options we have at this point."

Hector pulled his black hair in frustration, "But the king will never have this. Letting a beast out of prison to capture another beast is insanity."

"Hector, he led us to the Northern Ruins, where we almost caught the Savage. It was the first lead we've had to catching this villain. Let's bring him to Michael's house, and perhaps he can see something that we can't." Belle pleaded with him, "Maybe there's a clue, or some sort of detail that we haven't uncovered. We must do whatever we can to catch him... Will you not at least consider it for my father, so he may return?"

Hector shook his head, thinking hard about Belle's proposal. He did not like her idea, but he knew it was possibly the best option they had to catch the Savage. Hector feared that with every passing day, the Savage was gaining more followers. Especially with Michael captured and the king not even in Mendolon, he greatly feared that the Savage was gaining the upper hand on the whole kingdom.

Hector spoke quietly, "What if he tries to bargain with you?"

Belle nodded her head and brushed her hair out of her eyes. She was prepared for this question, "I'm not sure what he wants, but I know my limits."

Hector breathed deeply. He knew this truly was the best path forward to catching the Savage. He gritted his teeth as he spoke, "Just be sure this results in the demise of the Savage." With that, he turned and walked back down the hallway.

Belle watched as he walked away and eventually left her sight. She knew the mission that now lay before her. She wondered to what extent Jean-Luc could help. She began to slowly descend the steps toward the dungeon. It was dark, and there were no sounds coming from the dungeon this time. It was after midnight and Belle figured the other prisoners were probably asleep at this point.

Reaching the bottom of the steps, she saw that her assumption was correct. The other prisoners were resting peacefully. A torch lit her way to Jean Luc's cell. She found him sitting in one of his chairs, relaxed. His arms were folded and it looked as if he had been falling in and out of sleep. His glasses were still on and he was still wearing his red coat. With Michael captured, she felt a great urgency to get answers from him, but she also remembered Michael's admonition that Jean-Luc seemed to speak in riddles. The princess knew she would still have to proceed cautiously with him.

"Jean-Luc," Belle said quietly.

He raised his head and looked up at Belle. He stood to his feet. "Your Highness, welcome back. I wasn't expecting you this soon." He was calm, but there was obvious curiosity in his voice. "What has become of Michael?"

"We were too late. You were right. The Savage came for him and took him. His house was in shambles."

"Hmm... this is unfortunate," Jean-Luc said, shaking his head. "I did not anticipate this move by Sir Delano. I figured he would strike the castle first, but it appears that his moves are more calculated. It looks like he is biding his time before an all-out strike on your father's dynasty."

Belle sat down on the chair that had been placed there earlier in the evening. She remained focused. "I wished we would have seen it sooner. Michael was our leader. We can't afford to lose him. If the Savage is manipulating us with fear, Michael was our best option against him. He knows no fear."

Jean-Luc took off his glasses and cleaned one of the lens with the end of his coat. He smiled slightly as he spoke, "Well, in actuality, that's where you are wrong, Your Highness. Michael does know fear."

"I know you've spent a lot of time with Michael lately, but I've fought with him in battle and I can tell you he's not afraid of anything."

Jean-Luc put his glasses back on his face. He was relaxed as he spoke, "Michael does, in fact, know fear, and that's what makes him so strong. Men like Michael seem unafraid at times because they know that their lives are ultimately fragile. They do not trust in themselves but know that they must trust in things greater than themselves. That's how he deals with his fear."

Even though Belle did not want to be too hasty with him, she knew that time was limited and she wanted to keep the conversation focused on how to save Michael. She quickly changed the subject, "Jean-Luc, we searched his house but didn't find anything that would direct us to the Savage's location."

Jean-Luc remained calm. "Yes, Belle, you have to remember that the Savage, Sir Delano, is like a calculated mad man. He does the best he can to keep his locations secret."

Belle took a deep breath before going further. She knew that what she was about to say would change the whole conversation. "Jean-Luc, we need your help. We want you to come with us and explore the house. See if you can find anything that will help us determine where they took Michael."

Jean-Luc couldn't believe what he was hearing. He sat quietly for a few moments before responding, "You want to release me?"

"No… well, yes, sort of, we just want you to explore the house with us and see if there is anything we've missed."

Jean-Luc nodded his head as he listened. Things were accelerating faster than he anticipated. "Well, that's very good, Princess. Aren't you a little worried I might run off during this excursion?" Jean-Luc said confidently.

Belle nodded her head in agreement. She was at a slight loss for words, and truly wondered if this was a good plan. She looked down at her boots as she spoke, "Jean-Luc… it appears that we have to trust each other."

Jean-Luc gave her a half smile before speaking, "Very good, Belle, I'm glad to hear you will not be keeping me in chains."

"Of course," she said quietly, "Talking it over with Gideon, we knew you would never agree to it if you were chained, and we want you to trust us, like we are trusting you."

"You are learning well, Your Highness. Please, tell me, what else is there for me? Surely you discussed the conditions of bargaining before coming down."

Belle was speechless. "I... I'm not sure. We were in a hurry to get Michael freed. What... what is it you want?"

Jean-Luc reached over and grabbed a cup that was on a nearby table. He casually took a sip, never taking his eyes off Belle. He gently placed it back on the table before speaking, "Well, it seems that things have changed quite a bit. Belle, it seems like you have inadvertently handed me all the power in this negotiation."

Hearing Jean-Luc say this brought lots of anxiety. Ironically, she greatly wished Michael was by her side during this dialogue. She wondered what exactly Jean-Luc was talking about. Even more, she wondered if she could really trust him. "Please, Jean-Luc, we must act fast. What is it you want?"

He stood from his chair and paced with his hands behind his back. Belle could tell he was in deep thought. He rubbed his chin as he thought about how to accurately relay his request. Moments seemed to drag on as Belle tried to guess what he would say. The dark prison was completely quiet aside from an occasional dripping of water a few feet from Belle. The silence added to her worries as she sat waiting for Jean-Luc's request.

After a minute or two, he turned to face Belle and spoke quietly, "Your Highness, I desire what most beasts desire." He paused briefly, "To be treated kindly in the world of men."

Belle was puzzled at the request, "Of course... please go on."

"I want to go to the Winter Ball. I want to meet the nobles of your kingdom. I want to freely mingle among the guests, and I would like the pleasure of escorting you to the ball, Princess."

Belle stood to her feet. She was shocked by the request. Many ideas circulated in her mind. The first thing she thought of was her dream. She wondered if there was any connection with Jean-Luc's request. Second of all, she wondered how Jean-Luc's request would be taken by the rest of the kingdom. The kingdoms of Mendolon and Grimdolon were not allies and people may not be accepting of a beast at their ball, especially since one of his very kind had been terrorizing the people for the past six months. She didn't think this was a good plan. She tried to counter, "What if I petition my father to open up trade routes with Grimdolon? Surely that would be a great benefit to your kingdom. The people would…"

"Your Majesty, surely my accompaniment wouldn't be that bad." Jean-Luc spoke with a smile, "And honestly, I can be a gentleman."

Belle shook her head as she brushed the hair out of her eyes. "Jean-Luc, this situation is serious. Michael is captured by the Savage. We have to make haste to save him. There's no time to lose."

He took off his glasses and spoke sincerely, "I know, and I'm very sorry about that, but I feel my request is simple and more than fair. Please, Princess… will you accept my proposal?"

Belle took a deep breath. She knew in her heart of hearts that Jean-Luc's request was rather small if it would result in the rescue of Michael de Bolbec. His request also gave her a small amount of reassurance that he would not run off while exploring Michael's house. At the moment, the best option seemed to be to agree to the plan. "Ok, I accept your offer. I'll make sure Gideon and the others are ready to leave at once."

"Wait!" Jean-Luc said, stepping forward and grabbing the bars to his cell. "First of all, thank you for accepting my offer,

Belle. I look forward to it." Belle nodded in approval, trying to stay focused.

He continued, "I want to propose that we wait till the morning to leave. We can start at first light."

Belle quickly objected, "But we can't wait another minute. Who knows what the Savage is doing to Michael. We can't waste any more time. There are…"

"Belle," he said quietly, interrupting her. "We will be in a much better situation if we wait till morning. I don't want to miss anything in the darkness. I want to be able to see everything."

"But what about Michael?"

"I imagine that the Savage has bigger plans for him, and he will be kept alive. Sir Delano is calculated, and it seems that he will try to use his hostage to his advantage." This brought Belle a lot of fear. She wondered how the Savage might try to manipulate Michael. She remembered the hostages in the ruins talking about the experiments the Savage ran on them, testing to see of what they were most afraid. In the end Belle knew she would have to agree with Jean-Luc's demands. He now seemed to hold all the power.

She spoke sternly, "We will leave at first light. Be prepared."

"Thank you, Princess," he said quietly.

&

Michael awoke with his arms stretched out, chained to the wall. Trying to move his hands, he realized that one of his little fingers was broken. He had trouble breathing and guessed one of his ribs was also broken. It felt as if every muscle in his body was sore. He could see that a considerable amount of blood had come from a wound in his head. The last thing he remembered was having a black bag thrown over his face and then being beaten by the Savage's followers. He wondered how much time had passed since the invasion of his home.

Looking around, Michael found himself in a very dark, damp place. There was a torch on the wall about ten feet in front of him. Its light was faint and made it difficult for him to find his bearing. At first he wondered if he was in some type of cave, but he quickly noticed the brick structure of the wall. He realized it was manmade. He wondered if he was underground, possibly in a dungeon. He looked feverishly for a clue to his whereabouts.

It wasn't long before he heard voices approaching him. He held his head up, trying to see who was coming. Just a few moments passed before he saw a creature dressed in a black cape and hood step into the torchlight. He threw open his cape, and Michael was able to catch a glimpse of his ferocious hands covered in fur with long nails protruding from the fingers. He spoke harshly, "Welcome, Michael de Bolbec." The Savage quickly drew his arm back and struck Michael squarely on the side of his head. He let out a groan as the sting of pain rushed through his jaw.

He continued, "Your kingdom is going to crumble, Michael, and there's nothing you can do to stop it."

Michael looked to the side and spit a considerable amount of blood out of his mouth. "What do you want?" he said, mustering what little voice he had.

The Savage laughed under his breath. Michael could not see his face, but he could see the piercing red eyes emerging from under his hood. The Savage grabbed Michael's face and turned it to look directly into his eyes. "I have big plans for you, Michael de Bolbec." He growled slightly before continuing, "You are seen as a symbol for this kingdom and I plan on using that. You will become a symbol of fear for Mendolon."

Michael looked back straight into the Savage's eyes. He didn't back down. The expression of his face turned to anger at the mention of terrorizing the people of Mendolon. His mind went back into thinking like a knight instead of a prisoner. What could he learn about this beast? How would he escape these chains?

❧ ❧

Belle entered her bedroom tower. It was late. She had much anxiety and didn't know how she would be able to sleep. From her conversation with Jean-Luc, many reservations passed through her mind. A part of her worried if she had let him have too much power over her, and promising him an invitation to the Winter Ball would be too much. Another chief concern was the fact that Michael would spend the night in the custody of the Savage. She greatly hoped Jean-Luc knew what he was talking about in reassuring her that Michael would be kept alive. It all felt like more than she could handle.

She quickly put away her armor and dressed into her nightgown. Belle figured she would at least try to get some sleep before the morning. She wanted to be at her sharpest when examining Michael's house with Jean-Luc. Crawling into bed, she rested her head on her pillow and readjusted her blankets. It was a peaceful night. She could hear a light breeze blowing outside against her window. With her father gone, along with some of the servants, there were no faint traces of voices heard from downstairs. It was truly peaceful.

The princess began drifting off to sleep when, all of a sudden, she thought of something. Sitting up in her bed, she looked over at her nightstand and saw her medicine sitting by her lantern. Realizing she had forgotten to take it earlier, she quickly reached for it and drank it down. Hopefully, it would help her sleep.

111

CHAPTER 8

$\mathcal{B}$elle and Hector waited at Michael's house along with a company of soldiers. Soon enough a carriage would arrive bringing Jean-Luc Pascal to inspect the area. Gideon and Bernard were attending to him. The sun was just starting to rise over the trees to the east. The temperature was a little warmer than usual for this time of year.

Currently Hector was complaining that the carriage hadn't arrived. "Your Highness, this plan of yours seems to be falling apart already. I thought you said they were to arrive early this morning. What's taking them so long?"

"Hector, please, calm down. I'm sure Gideon is just taking his time to make sure everything is well-secured before they transport Jean-Luc."

Hector paced back and forth pulling at his disheveled black hair. His long green robe collected snow as he walked back and forth. "First, you want to involve a beast in this manhunt, and then you waste our time not having him here at the right time. You are showing yourself unfit for the knighthood you desire."

"Listen, I'm doing the best I can," Belle said, trying to hold back her anger. "My father's gone and Michael is captured. More than anyone, I want the Savage captured and everything back to normal."

"Well, then you need to start listening to me. I am your father's top advisor. If he were here, I wouldn't be ignored like I am now."

"Hector, all of us are needed to catch the Savage. We just don't have any other option at this point. This might not come to anything, but I think it is best to at least try and see if Jean-Luc spots anything."

Hector growled under his breath and looked off into the distance as he tried to think of what to say next. He hated that the king's daughter was giving the orders at this point. He felt confident that the king would have left him in charge if he knew that Michael was captured. He gritted his teeth as he spoke, "If anything goes wrong with this beast, I will hold you personally responsible."

Belle nodded in approval, "I understand. Like I said, I believe he will truly help us…"

Belle wasn't able to say anything else. At that point a two-horse carriage came down the path leading to Michael's house. She could see Bernard riding up front with the driver. It was obvious that Jean-Luc was inside. Belle turned and stopped to walk down the path to meet the carriage. A few soldiers followed suit. Belle was anxious for answers to Michael's whereabouts.

The carriage stopped as Belle met them on the path, not far from the house. "Good day, Your Highness," Bernard greeted her.

"Same to you, Bernard."

The door to the carriage opened and Gideon climbed out. He stroked his mustache as he climbed down the steps.

"Did everything go well in bringing him?" Belle said, questioning Gideon.

"Yes, everything went fine. He was very compliant and didn't say a word in the carriage. I chained his hands as a precaution."

Belle could tell Gideon looked a little worried about bringing him to Michael's house. "Is there anything else, Gideon?"

Gideon looked directly at Belle as he spoke quietly, "I'm not sure. But like Michael said before, I don't think he's being completely honest with us. I feel like there is some game he is playing with us. Like we are pawns, falling into his trap. Something is going on that we don't know about."

Belle knew what Gideon was saying was correct. They all had felt it at one time or another. Jean-Luc was hiding something. It made everyone nervous. She felt as if she was standing on the edge of a cliff, wondering if this was the right route to take. She hoped this plan would truly turn out for good and not for harm. Belle looked back at Michael's house before speaking up, "I don't know what other choice we have. I think this is a risk we have to take."

Gideon scratched his short hair, thinking hard about this whole unfolding of events. He shrugged his shoulders. "I think you're right; we don't have any other option at this point."

"Very well... let's bring him out."

"Bernard," Gideon said loudly, "Bring the beast out." Without hesitation Bernard stuck his head in the carriage and ordered Jean-Luc out. Hector and the rest of the soldiers joined the rest of the group by the carriage. It was just a few moments later that Jean-Luc emerged from the carriage's door. He had on his signature eye-glasses along with his red coat and a white shirt underneath. His long brown hair was tied back. Unlike many beasts, he was wearing boots, which to many, signify that he possessed a large amount of wealth or was some type of nobility back in Grimdolon. He stood tall on the steps of the carriage and took a deep breath of fresh air with his eyes closed.

Belle was the first to speak, "Thanks for coming, Jean-Luc."

He calmly walked down the steps and examined the group. He smiled politely before speaking up, "You're welcome, Princess. Happy to help."

Everyone was silent, not sure what to say. There were many in the company of soldiers that had never seen a beast speak before. They were stunned. Jean-Luc continued, "Well, I must admit that I haven't been able to get outside much these days... but lovely weather you're having. Your kingdom is quite nice with a fresh dusting of snow."

"Thank you," Belle responded.

"You're welcome. Now... what do you say we get these chains off and start exploring the house? Time is wasting."

Gideon approached Jean-Luc with a key. He started the meticulous work of unlatching some of the locks and unwrapping the chains. Hector objected loudly, "What are you doing? You can't unchain this beast. What if he escapes?"

Belle turned to face him, and spoke quietly, hoping Jean-Luc wouldn't hear, "Hector, this is what we agreed to do. We want to show our confidence in him. Hopefully he will give us information we need."

Hector shook his head in anger. He spoke very loudly so Jean-Luc would hear. "This is crazy. This beast doesn't need to be walking freely. He should be in chains."

Jean-Luc looked up and faced Hector. He quickly countered, "Well, I'm sorry, my good fellow... but most of us aren't where we should be these days. I imagine the museum would be a most appropriate place for you. I would think people could learn a lot about abnormalities in personalities by studying you."

"Watch your tongue, Beast," Hector said as he walked away.

The chains fell to the ground. Jean-Luc rubbed his wrists, grateful for the freedom. "Thank you," he said very quietly. He adjusted his coat, and began walking toward the house. His pace was slow and he seemed to be looking all around, observing his surroundings. He did not seem to be in much of a hurry.

"Jean-Luc, is there anything you would like to see of first priority?" Belle asked.

"I would like to see the house first," he said, still walking slowly.

"Of course you want to see the house." Belle was a little frustrated by the answer. "Any specific room you would like to see in the house?"

Jean-Luc looked over at Belle and smiled slightly, realizing his answer was a little too obvious. "Belle, how about you take me to the house and show me anything you think is significant."

"Right this way."

Belle led him inside the disheveled home. It was still in disarray. Hector was inside, speaking with a couple of soldiers. "Good day, gentlemen," Jean-Luc said as he walked past them. Hector snarled in return.

Belle led him to Michael's bedroom where the window was still open. "We believe the Savage entered through this window."

Jean-Luc closely examined the window for anything strange. "I don't believe the Savage entered at all," he spoke without breaking his concentration. "Sir Delano seems to hide in the shadows these days. He has enough followers to do his dirty work."

Jean-Luc looked down at the floor where he saw a small knife. He picked it up and examined it. He seemed intrigued by it. It was dirty and had a few chips in the blade. Instantly, Belle became nervous. What if she had underestimated Jean-Luc? What if he was biding his time till he was able to escape from prison and find a weapon? What if he attacked her? Many thoughts passed through her mind as her hand instinctively went toward her sword at her side.

Jean-Luc looked up her and spoke, "Obviously this was dropped by one of the Savage's followers. Were any other weapons found in the house?"

"Yes, we found Michael's armory by the fireplace room. It seems as if he wasn't able to retrieve any weapons during the ambush. A fight happened by the fireplace room. We found Michael's sword close by."

"Well... shall we have a look?"

Belle and Jean-Luc entered the main living area of the house only to find that the whole brigade of soldiers and knights had joined them inside. To Jean-Luc's disappointment, it was crowded. He wanted room to explore. Hector quickly approached Belle and pulled her aside. He was angry. "Your Highness, I must say, you're wasting our time. The Savage is probably ready to strike again, and all you want to do to watch this manipulative beast try to find a way to escape."

"Hector, give him time. We haven't been here long."

"Princess, this beast doesn't know what he is doing. For all we know he could be working with the Savage."

Belle put her hand up, trying to calm Hector. "Listen, please, for the sake of the kingdom, let's give him a few minutes and watch and see if he finds anything." Hector and Belle turned to watch Jean-Luc for a moment as he examined the room. He was observing a spot on the wall. He was looking at it closely, squinting his eyes just a little as he focused on it. He then touched the spot with his fingers and examined them. Without warning, the beast then put his fingers to his lips and tasted the substance he found.

Hector couldn't bear to watch anymore. He turned to Belle and spoke loudly, "That's it, Your Highness, I will not sit around while this beast walks around freely and makes a fool of the kingdom! I'm heading back to the castle to see if there's anything that will lead us to Michael." Hector turned and shouted an instruction to the men, "Soldiers of Mendolon, we're heading back to the castle. Follow me."

The men started to exit the house when Belle grabbed his arm. "Hector, listen to me. Give him a chance. I'm almost certain he won't try to escape. Let's trust him just a little."

An angry look formed on Hector's face. Belle could see his yellowing teeth through the strands of dark black hair over his face. He spoke through gritted teeth, "You stay here and follow this dim-witted beast. I don't care if he runs or stays here. I'm going to save Michael, and one day you will thank me for saving this pathetic husband of yours."

Belle took a step back. She was incredibly angry at Hector. She didn't know how someone could be so cold, especially at a time like this, when Michael's life was on the line. She was worried about him and truly feared for his life. Hector's words cut deep. Michael was a person of great honor, and the thought of him being tortured was unbearable. She pulled her sword and held it to her side. She couldn't remember a time she was so furious. "You need to watch your words, Snake."

"You couldn't do it if you wanted, Princess." He laughed slightly. "You better be glad your father is the king. If not, I would have put you in your place a long time ago... little girl."

They stared at each other for just a few moments before Hector turned and left with the soldiers. Belle wanted to stop the men and plead with them to stay. A part of her was very frustrated at everything transpiring, but another part of her was truly scared. She wanted their help. She wanted guidance. Even though she now had this reputation of being a princess dragon-slayer, there were times when she just wanted to be a simple princess in her land. She wanted to be vulnerable- to cry with others if need be.

The room cleared, leaving only her and the beast, Jean-Luc, who seemed unfazed by everything happening around him. Looking outside, Belle could see Gideon and Bernard out front as the soldiers walked past them. She was thankful they were sticking with her on this mission.

She took a seat on a nearby chair. "Jean-Luc, it looks like the kingdom is losing faith in me."

Jean-Luc was crouched down on the floor looking at something. He smiled as he spoke, "Belle, this will work out nicely. The area is now uncluttered. Plenty of room to explore." Belle couldn't help but smile a little at the irony of Jean-Luc's positive attitude. She was thankful he was as calm as he was.

He held up something small in his hand. "Your Majesty, I'm finding little bits of hair all over this room, obviously from the fight that ensued. This might sound strange, but did anyone find a cluster of hair by any chance?"

Belle was shocked by his question. It was like he could almost read her mind. "Yes… as a matter of fact, here by the door." She led him over to the front entryway and showed him the cluster of hair she found the night before.

"Interesting," Jean-Luc said, studying it closely. He adjusted his glasses to get a good look at it. He then reached out and grabbed the clump of hair with his thumb and index finger on his right hand. He felt the texture of it, and then held it up to the light. "Well, well, well… it looks like the Savage didn't completely cover his tracks this time."

Belle looked over her shoulder to see Gideon and Bernard watching them from a few feet away. They waited patiently for any command Belle might give. "I'll be right back," she told Jean-Luc. He nodded in approval, not taking his eyes off the clump of hair.

Approaching the two knights, Belle spoke quietly, "Thank you so much for staying. It means a lot."

"Anything for you… Your Highness," Gideon said, smiling through his thick mustache.

"We explored the house. Jean-Luc seems to have found something of interest with the bits of fur around the house."

"Do you think he will be able to lead us to Michael?" Bernard asked anxiously.

Belle shrugged her shoulders, "I don't know. He hasn't said much yet about his findings. All I do know is that Michael trusted him with the information we found at the Savage's ruins. I think, for Michael's sake, we should let him take his time."

Gideon rubbed his chin as he listened. "Yeah, I agree with you, Your Majesty. I think he's our best chance at finding Michael."

"Could he tell if Michael was injured during the fight with the Savage's followers?" Bernard asked.

"No, but yesterday we think we found some of his blood by one of the windows. Not much though."

Bernard took a deep breath and shook his head. He admired Michael and was thankful Michael had given him a chance at being a knight, even with his long list of gaffes. Bernard felt a tear roll down his cheek as he thought about his leader and friend under the clutches of the enemy.

Belle rubbed his arm and smiled, "Don't worry, Bernard. We will get him back. We'll do whatever it takes."

"Thanks," Bernard said, wiping his nose.

Belle knew it was time to get back to work. "Well, I'm going to go see if there is anything else that…"

Gideon interrupted her, "Wait… where is Jean-Luc?"

Belle turned to see that he was gone.

❧

Northeast of Mendolon, not far from the mines of Grimdolon, King Sebastian stood in a dark room of an old cabin located in the dense woods. It was lit only by a single candle. There were a handful of soldiers with him. Tensions were high. In the middle of the room sat a beast from Grimdolon. He was beaten and tied up. Blood covered the fur around his head. He was a large, older beast, and he had put up quite a fight with Sebastian's men before eventually giving up.

The beast was a miner from the northern area of Grimdolon. He was one who was working closely with the Savage before he started his escapades in Mendolon. Sebastian wanted him captured and interrogated. He wanted to see if this beast could help in any way with the capture of the Savage.

"Tell me, Beast," Sebastian asked, "What do you know of Dominique Delano, the one they call the Savage?"

"I know nothing. He worked in the mines east of me. My crew was looking for diamonds and gems."

Sebastian turned to the soldier beside him. "Hit him," he said casually. A soldier, dressed in full armor approached the beast and hit him squarely in the face. He groaned in pain.

Sebastian bent down and got right in the beast's face. "Do you want to tell me the truth now, Beast? We know you're in charge of a division of the mines. Tell us everything you know about him."

The beast took a deep breath and tried to regain his composure. He was a stubborn beast who had spent many years in prison before working the mines. He didn't like being bossed around. He spoke with his eyes closed, "Look, he was anxious for a job. I knew it was a little unorthodox, but we tried to keep his hiring quiet, and I figured we'd give him a chance. We needed workers."

"Go on!" Sebastian demanded.

"Even though the workers quickly realized he was a little strange, we decided to keep him… that is until we discovered he was stealing portions of our gleanings."

Sebastian nodded in approval. "Yes, I know all of this. Tell me more about *who* he is. Why is he attacking Mendolon? What does he want?"

The beast looked to the side toward the ground and spit some of the blood that filled his mouth. He looked at the king in front of him demanding answers. King Sebastian of Mendolon was the last person he wanted to help in any way. He had heard the stories about him and wasn't about to give him what he wanted. He stared directly at him as he spoke, "O wise king, by the questions you are asking I take it you've never met him."

Sebastian could feel his blood pressure start to rise. The beast continued, "I find all of this quite astounding... since you did try to hire him."

"What?"

The old beast smiled back at the king, "Don't think I don't know. He was stealing from our mines for you."

The king couldn't take anymore. "I've heard enough!" he said angrily, leaving the dark room.

"Wait," the beast shouted. Sebastian turned to face him. The beast continued, "May this terror that's happening in Mendolon be a lesson to you, King, of what happens when you try to employ a madman." The large beast leaned forward in his chair, "And now you've lost control."

The king briskly left the cabin. He slammed the door shut behind him. Even though it was morning, the density of the woods along with the trees overhead made the morning seem very dark. Sebastian found it most appropriate as it was how he felt at the moment. Life was spinning out of control, and he longed for stability.

Turning to his left, his eyes met with the character in the shadows who was leaning against the side of the cabin. Sebastian had called for him. He was an assassin from the north. Sebastian had called on him for protection while he was away from the kingdom. He was dressed in full armor with a mask covering his face. Sebastian walked over to where he was standing. The figure stood upright waiting for the king's command. Sebastian looked to his right and to his left before whispering to the character, "Kill the beast inside. I have no use for him."

❦

Belle raced into Michael's house. "Jean-Luc!" she shouted, wondering if he'd gone back inside to investigate. She looked all around the fireplace room. No trace of him. She turned and went down the hallway. She continued to call out, "Jean-Luc... Jean-Luc." She heard nothing. *Where could he have gone?* she thought to herself.

She started to panic, running back outside. Gideon was checking the woods at the edge of Michael's property. Bernard was nowhere to be seen. A myriad of thoughts passed through Belle's mind. Fear was starting to creep in. She wondered why she ever trusted this beast. Michael specifically told her not to fully trust him. He warned her about Jean-Luc having ulterior motives. She feared what would happen if Jean-Luc was never caught.

She turned to her left and sprinted to the side of the house looking for any sign of the prisoner. The wind started to blow gently against her face. The snow was drifting slightly. She didn't know if she should reach for her sword or not. Jean-Luc didn't seem as if he wanted to hurt her. In fact, just the opposite. In the short time together, it was as if they had become friends.

Reaching the back of the house, she could see Bernard with his back turned to her examining something. She ran toward him, wondering what was transpiring. "Bernard," she yelled out. He turned to see Belle running toward him. He said nothing.

Upon reaching the knight, she could see all her fears were in vain. In front of Bernard was Jean-Luc crouched down, examining a spot on the ground. It looked to be a boot print on the ground. Belle felt silly for her sudden surge of panic. Jean-Luc looked as if he was in deep thought, studying the spot.

Belle breathed heavily trying to catch her breath. "Jean-Luc, what are you doing? Did you find anything?"

"Interesting," he said under his breath.

"What is it?"

He slowly rose to his feet. He adjusted his glasses before speaking. "It is faint, but I detect a trace of freshly molded clay mixed with a hint of sewage."

Belle was confused, "I don't understand, Jean-Luc. What are you implying?"

"I'm trying to say, there is only one place in Mendolon that has an underground sewage system, and some of its caverns are newly molded."

Belle couldn't believe what Jean-Luc was implying. "Are you saying the Savage and followers are in the sewage caverns just south of the castle?"

"Exactly," Jean-Luc said with confidence. "I would say, let's go immediately."

CHAPTER 9

$\mathcal{B}$elle, Jean-Luc, Gideon, and Bernard traveled to the south of the castle. The sun was high in the sky as it was just after noon. There was an entrance to the castle's sewage caverns on this side of the castle. Jean-Luc requested they leave immediately for the tunnels. He felt as if the element of surprise was their best virtue. Bernard had a slight phobia about underground tunnels, but Belle and Gideon did not stop to question their excursion. Michael needed saving and if this was where he really was, then they dare not hesitate.

Their entrance to the caverns was built around a small freshwater stream that led to the western sea. These caverns had been constructed less than a year ago, and the sewage system of the castle was still not fully functional. Bernard particularly was thankful for this fact. They advanced slowly into the opening by the stream. The opening was an arch that was about fifteen feet high and twelve feet across. It resembled a cave with a stream running through it. Belle couldn't help but think of the Dragon's cave she had been in earlier in the year.

"Try not to make too much noise as we enter the caverns," Jean-Luc said nonchalantly. "I believe there will be an echo."

"Do we have a plan once we get in there?" Belle asked, readjusting her hair into a ponytail.

"Let's stick together as best as we can," Gideon said. "If anyone sees Michael or thinks they know where he is, don't hesitate to direct me to him."

"What if it's a trap?" Bernard asked.

"Hopefully Jean-Luc is right, in that this attack will catch them completely off-guard," Gideon added.

Belle led the way quietly through the caverns as she was anxious to save Michael. There was a small dry walkway on the side of the tunnel beside the stream. She was out in front with Jean-Luc behind her and the other two knights in back. She had never been in these caverns; she had only seen them as they were constructed into a sewage system for the castle. They were built by redirecting a waterway close to the castle. A small portion of these caverns were built years ago and were meant to be a large dungeon for prisoners. Sebastian's family did not like the idea of a massive dungeon on the castle's premises. He decided to move Mendolon's main prison off site. It was now located east of the castle.

She wondered what they would face in these tunnels. Would there be a horde of beasts that they would confront? Or possibly the Savage himself? Looking around at her companions, she wondered if they were enough to combat whatever foe they would face.

Moving through the caverns, the four traveled further into the darkness. Belle suppressed her fear as much as she could. She was determined to save Michael. Turning around, she could see Jean-Luc as a small amount of light was coming from the opening of the tunnel. He was confident, seemingly unmoved by everything around him. She was amazed by his wisdom and demeanor. It was hard for her to grasp that they were approximately the same age.

After walking in the darkness for what seemed to be fifteen minutes or more, they came to an intersection in the tunnels. Three paths lay in front of them. Belle peeked around the corner down the tunnel on her left. It was a dry tunnel with no water flowing. She could see a torch burning along with about half a dozen men under the light. Some were sleeping, one was eating, and the others looked to be gambling with a game of dice. There were a few weapons sitting by the men's sides, but not enough to be of any concern.

Belle turned back to speak to Jean-Luc. She whispered to him, "Six or seven men around this corner. We can easily surprise them. It should be quick."

Jean-Luc nodded in agreement. He leaned in to whisper in her ear. She could feel his mane against her cheek. "I would guess they are guarding Michael. If you engage the guards, I'll take Gideon in closer with me and see if we can find Michael or maybe even the Savage."

"Agreed," she said. She waited just a moment for Jean-Luc to relay the plans to Gideon and Bernard. Belle grabbed her bow from her back and quietly pulled an arrow from her pouch. Michael had done so much for her and the kingdom of Mendolon. It was time for her to repay the favor.

"Let's do it," Jean-Luc whispered to her.

The next few minutes were quite chaotic. Belle quickly turned the corner and aimed at one of the men. She released the arrow, and the man cried out in pain. Gideon and Bernard sprang into action as the other men tried to get their bearings. They did not know what was transpiring. Some tried to grab their swords, while others were trying to see what had happened to their comrade.

Belle grabbed another arrow and shot it at another one of the men. He screamed out in pain. Bernard and Gideon engaged a couple of the men in a sword fight. The weary men were no match for the knights of Mendolon. Jean-Luc looked on as the swords were clanging. Bernard fought vigorously and was able to knock his opponent's sword out of his hands. As Gideon's sword was locked with another man's, the aged knight was able to use his strength to push his opponent against the wall before knocking him out with the hilt of his sword.

Belle was about to pull another arrow when she felt the slash of a sword against her upper arm near her shoulder. She dropped her bow. Jean-Luc ran forward and tackled the man, sending his sword flying. Bernard quickly came over to help. The man surrendered in fear, seeing a beast on top of him. Jean-Luc reared back and hit him with his fist as hard as he could, knocking out the man.

He ran to Belle to see the damage done. She was on her back grasping her right arm with her left hand. "Let me see it," Jean-Luc urged. Pulling back her hand and tearing away the fabric on her sleeve, he could see that it wasn't deep. "It will most likely leave a scar, but I think you'll be fine."

Belle sat up as she spoke, "Don't worry about me. Bernard and I can handle these men. Take Gideon and find Michael!"

"We'll find him, Your Highness," Jean-Luc said, running past the fallen men and further down the tunnel. Gideon quickly joined him, following close behind.

The Savage looked on as his men were defeated. He stood in the darkness in the tunnel across from where the fight was raging. He was disappointed, angry that this hideout was found so soon. The caverns had provided great access to spy on the castle, and a refuge of escape when he knew the knights of Mendolon were pursuing him. He knew that he now had to change his plans. The Savage looked down at the knife in his hand. A plan formulated in his mind. This was not what he had planned, but he knew that drastic plans had to be taken. Nothing could stop him from his plan of conquering Mendolon and infecting the whole kingdom with fear.

❧

Hector called out orders among the soldiers. They had arrived back at the castle earlier in the day and were now regrouping at the castle's war room. There were maps spread out on a round table and about a dozen men stood about dressed in full armor. They were tired and losing hope in the king's advisor. He hit the table as spoke.

"You men are not looking hard enough. The Savage has to be located close to the castle. He's watching us."

A young soldier from the group stepped forward, removing his helmet, "Please, Sire, we've checked every dwelling in these parts. These are simple townspeople who are terrified of that beast."

"He must have allies," Hector shouted, his black hair falling in front of his face.

"Please, under your orders we've been on high alert for the past three days. We've not seen our families. They are scared."

"I don't care!" Hector shouted, hitting the table hard. "If you haven't noticed I'm trying to protect everyone in this whole blasted kingdom, your families included!"

The men thought he sounded even more like a snake when he was angry. Another soldier stepped forward, "Listen, Sire, maybe if we see what this other beast has to say, maybe…"

"I don't care what any other beast has to say. We are going to find the Savage before he destroys us."

Everyone in the room was then caught off guard when they heard footsteps on the far stairwell. The room fell silent and all eyes turned to see who it was. They were surprised to see one of the castle servants descending the steps accompanied by a teenage boy. This seemed to infuriate Hector even more.

"What is the meaning of this?" he said, excoriating the servant. "You know better than to interrupt us."

"Much apologies, Your Grace, but this boy arrived at the castle a few minutes ago with an urgent message I think you'd like to hear."

The boy stepped forward. He was shy and intimidated by all the eyes watching him. Hector spoke up impatiently, "Well... let us hear it. We don't have all day."

The boy took off his hat and looked down at the floor. By the look of his clothes he was obviously a peasant and had never been inside the castle, much less spoken before the king's chief advisor. "I was down on the western shore playing near the castle's waterway."

"You know peasants aren't supposed be close to that area!" Hector shouted.

"I know... I ... I know I'm not supposed to, but I saw something down there, and I thought I had to come at once."

"Yes... what is it?"

"I saw the Princess Belle, along with two knights. I could tell by their different armor. They looked like they were on a mission, and the strange thing was they had a beast with them. I hid myself and tried not to watch, but I've never seen a beast before and I think..."

"Stop!" Hector said, holding out his hand. "Where did you say they were going?"

The boy was nervous. "I'm not sure, but they seemed to be approaching the castle's water system, but I don't know what happened, and..."

"That is enough," Hector said, interrupting him. "Thank you, Peasant." He looked toward the servant, "Be sure he is rewarded for his help."

"It will be done, Your Grace."

Hector turned to address the soldiers, "Men, take up your arms. We leave immediately for the western shore by the castle's sewage outlet."

❧❧

It wasn't much longer that Gideon and Jean-Luc arrived back at the site of the fight. Bernard had defeated the last of the men, and was now helping Belle wrap her wound. They were surprised to see them back so soon. "Did you find anything?" Belle asked inquisitively.

"No," Gideon responded, "There is nothing further down this tunnel. I think these men were supposed to be looking out for intruders."

"I guess our next option is to try these other tunnels," Belle said, standing to her feet. She rotated her arm to make sure the bandage would stay on. She was thankful that the cut on her arm wasn't deep. She felt a little embarrassed for letting her guard down during the fight.

She continued, "Let's try the tunnel across the way." Gideon and Bernard nodded in agreement as they crossed the waterway to the tunnel opposite them. The water was about knee deep. At this point Bernard was very thankful the sewage system was only partially functional.

Belle was about to enter the water when she slipped on a wet stone close to the water. Jean-Luc reached out his hand and caught her before she was able to fall in completely. Their eyes met as Jean-Luc spoke, "Careful, Your Highness. The stonework is a little slippery."

"Thank you," Belle said, gathering her footing. They quickly made it across the waterway to where Gideon and Bernard were waiting. They then proceeded slowly, with Gideon and Belle in front. Bernard tried to quiet his breathing, but found it difficult to calm himself. He was terrified of what he may face. He was terrified of the Savage. The traumatizing battle at the Northern Ruins had left a deep imprint on his mind. Seeing his comrades in utter terror was not an image he could erase. Some of them still hadn't fully recovered from being ambushed by a horde of angry beasts.

Belle and Gideon also wondered if this was going to be the moment they would meet the Savage face-to-face. They didn't know what to expect. Rumors had spread among the townspeople of his power and his magic. They wondered if they would encounter him alone or would he have others with him? Belle wondered if it was actually a good plan to come just the four of them, or should they have waited for reinforcements? She held her sword in her hand, ready to strike at the first thing she saw.

"I think I see a light up ahead," Gideon said, interrupting her thoughts. There was a turn coming in the tunnel, and there was a faint flicker of torchlight coming from it. They progressed toward it, ever so slowly. No one said a word for the next minute as the light became stronger with every step. A part of Belle, hoping to find Michael, wanted to run right around the turn.

Everyone was in complete focus when a figure passed in front of the light into their tunnel. He was moving at full speed toward them. They could hear him growling ravenously as he progressed toward them. "Stop," Gideon yelled out, holding up his sword. The figure did not stop. As he came closer they could tell it was a large beast. Belle quickly sheathed her sword and grabbed her bow. The beast was only a few feet away when she let the arrow fly into the leg of the creature. He stumbled, falling to one knee. Gideon jumped toward the beast and knocked him on his side. He held his sword to the beast and the creature knocked it out of his hand. Belle and Bernard ran to help restrain the beast. Jean-Luc, seeing the other three locked in a fight with the creature, saw this as an opportunity to search for Michael.

Even though it was dark, the three knights could see they were fighting against a large beast, one dressed in rags. They could tell the beast was bleeding badly and obviously in pain from a wound around his mouth. The arrow in his leg was also causing him a large amount of pain. He growled ravenously as the three held him down. With one of his hands free Bernard pulled his sword and was ready to strike when Belle called out, "Wait!"

Bernard stopped instantly. Belle noticed that the beast was starting to slow down in his struggle. "I think he's giving up," Belle said confidently. Belle and Gideon continued to hold down his arms and his growling faded into a low murmur.

The three watched the beast, slightly mesmerized by him. Bernard was the first to break the silence, "What... what should we do?"

"Bernard," Gideon said, "Grab the rope. Let's tie him up and take him out of the tunnel." Bernard swiftly opened his pouch, searching in his bag for the rope.

As the beast stopped resisting, Belle turned to Gideon, "Do you think we caught the Savage?"

A puzzled look came across his face, "Possibly... I'm not sure."

≪≫

Jean-Luc ran further down the tunnel toward the torch. He turned the corner to his right. The torch was burning bright and beside it was Michael de Bolbec, the great knight of Mendolon. He had cuffs around his wrists that stretched his arms out, chaining them to the walls of the tunnel. Jean-Luc could tell that Michael was injured. He quickly made sure everything was clear, and then approached Michael. His head was slumped forward and he was passed out.

Assessing the chains, Jean-Luc found the locks on the cuffs were weak. Usually he kept his claws fairly short for a beast, but he was thankful that were just long enough to pick the locks. He worked meticulously at it while listening for any sounds of an enemy. The first lock didn't take him long to open. The first cuff fell to the ground and Michael's body dropped to his right. Jean-Luc caught him before his body could hit the ground. Michael woke up, a bit startled.

"What... what's happening?" his faint voice said.

"Michael, my friend, it looks like irony has struck. You've been in chains, and now I am the one rescuing you."

Michael tried to gather himself as quickly as possible. At first he thought his mind was playing tricks on him when saw a beast working to release his wrist, but after a few seconds he realized that Jean-Luc was the one freeing him. "How... did you ... you get out?"

Jean-Luc laughed slightly. He didn't answer Michael's questions, but kept focused on the chains.

Michael wiped his eyes as he tried to speak, "You're supposed... you're supposed to be locked up."

"Well... sorry to disappoint you," Jean-Luc said as the other cuff fell to the ground. Michael was still weak, so Jean-Luc picked him up and carried him back toward his companions.

"They... they shouldn't have let you out," Michael said, falling back asleep in Jean-Luc's arms.

Jean-Luc took a deep breath as he turned the corner, carrying Michael's body. He spoke softly, "Dearest Michael... I fear you might be catching on to my plans."

CHAPTER 10

hree days passed since the rescue of Michael de Bolbec from the Savage. Jean-Luc had carried Michael out of the sewer tunnels while the three knights made sure the injured beast was securely restrained and taken from the caverns. Hector, along with a company of soldiers, arrived at the tunnels shortly after the knights exited. Michael was swiftly taken to the castle's infirmary along with the injured beast. Hector's men were then able to enter the tunnels and capture all of the Savage's men. They were brought to the castle's dungeon where they were kept for interrogation.

Things seemed to calm around the kingdom of Mendolon. Rumors spread among the people that the Savage had been captured by the princess. Tensions relaxed and the townspeople began to travel more freely among the villages. The markets were open again. Belle didn't issue an official statement from the kingdom of Mendolon for a couple of reasons: One, because her father had still not returned and she didn't want to issue anything official without his guidance. Two, she was uncertain if the beast they caught in the tunnels was truly the Savage. They all thought it was strange that he had given up so easily when they found him there.

Currently, Belle, Gideon, and Hector were in the castle's war room discussing what they all thought in regard to the nature of the injured beast. They had all tried to interrogate the beast earlier the last few days but found that he was not cooperating. Gideon was frustrated and rubbed his forehead as he spoke, "I don't know what to make of this beast."

Belle chimed in, "It is very curious the way he gave up the fight immediately. As I said before, it makes me wonder if he was a prisoner of the Savage, released to throw us off course."

Gideon rubbed the ends of his mustache in deep contemplation. Michael was still recovering from his imprisonment and wouldn't be in full strength for another several weeks. Gideon wished he was present at this discussion. He would have been a great help in deciphering this riddle. Gideon looked at the far wall as he spoke, "Or maybe this is another deep rooted trick by the Savage. Maybe his capture was on purpose so he can actually get into the castle. Maybe he's right where he wants to be."

Belle walked over to a nearby window and looked out, trying to ease her mind. She was dressed elegantly in a white and gold flower dress since she planned on venturing into the markets today. It was a dress truly worthy of a princess. Currently two things consumed her mind: Michael's recovery and the new demeanor of peace among the people of Mendolon. The people greatly rejoiced in the rumors that the princess of the land had caught a rogue beast in the castle's tunnels. She hated to think that this newfound joy might be in vain.

Hector, still seated, interrupted the silence, "I say we press the other prisoners harder. Do whatever it takes to make them talk."

Gideon shook his head. "No… they're not talking. They fear the Savage more than any of us."

"Who are they?" Belle spoke up, brushing a strand of hair out of her eyes.

"It looks like they are just a bunch of thieves and criminals that the Savage hired from distance lands. I wonder how much of his plans they actually know," Gideon responded.

The room went back to silence as the three of them pondered what their next step would be. The kingdom's Winter Ball was just a week away and they wanted to be certain they could reassure the townspeople the kingdom was safe. Belle turned from the window and walked quietly toward the table in the center of the room. She took a seat before speaking, "What of the beast? I know he has been silent thus far, but maybe there is some way to get him to talk to us."

"Possibly," Gideon said, nodding as he spoke. "His injuries seem to be quite extensive. I think we should give him a few days before we try to interrogate him."

Hector hit the table as he stood to his feet, "You imbecile! Don't you realize my men have already tried that option?"

"Your men?" Gideon said, startled. "You think you're in charge now?"

"Yes, my men." Hector quickly shot back, "I am the king's chief advisor! Who else would be in charge of the royal soldiers when the king is gone and his chief knight is..."

"Stop it," Belle interrupted. "This won't help anything." She stood to her feet. "Hector, you say you've already tried to interrogate this beast... correct?"

"Yes... Your Highness," he answered with a slight bit of sarcasm in his voice.

"What did he say? Were you able to get anything out of him?"

Hector looked down at the table and began to laugh. His stringy black hair hung down as he laughed. Belle and Gideon looked at each other puzzled. "What is it, Hector?" Gideon said quietly.

"You fools... this beast is not talking to us."

"Why not?"

Hector ran his fingers through his hair, giving them a clear view of the sinister expression on his face. "This beast will never talk to us because someone has permanently thwarted that."

"What do you mean?"

Hector laughed again. "I mean that someone has cut out his tongue." Belle and Gideon looked each other confused. This situation continued to baffle them.

∽∾

Belle rode on horseback through the markets east of the castle. Bernard was walking by her side in full armor. He was acting as her bodyguard as there were many people in the street. Belle had had enough of discussing the Savage with Hector. She wanted to be out among the people, and even though there were still unanswered questions, she was thankful to see the people at peace, carrying on simple commerce. Families were joyously shopping with children running back and forth between their parents and the shops. At any other time, most of the townspeople would have stopped and taken notice of the princess riding through the markets, but at this particular time, most were thankful of the rumors of the Savage's apprehension and were excited to be shopping in the markets.

Belle rode through the center of the streets. A few young girls stopped to smile at the princess. She could tell they were admiring the silver tiara she wore. Belle simply smiled and waved as she passed by. Bernard couldn't help but smile himself at the sight of how much children loved the princess of the land.

"The people seem so happy, Bernard," Belle said. "It's great to see the market completely open again."

"I agree, Your Highness," Bernard said, shaking his head. "I actually think this is the most people I've ever seen here."

The newfound joy of the people seemed to relax Belle and Bernard. Normally, when Bernard was in full armor, he habitually kept one hand on his sword, just so he would be ready to strike in an instant. On this occasion, a townsperson would walk up close to Belle and give their greetings, but even still, Bernard felt no threat anywhere around them.

Bernard broke the silence, "Any item you to wish to purchase today, Your Highness?"

Belle smiled and looked down at Bernard, who was leading her horse, "No, I'm just enjoying seeing the people shop. It makes me thankful for the simple gifts of peace and tranquility that we so often take for granted."

"I agree, Your Highness."

"How about you, Bernard? Is there anyone special that you need to purchase a gift for?" Belle had a mischievous look on her face. Most of the knights knew that Bernard had a particular interest in one of the castle's servant girls who was close to his age.

He blushed slightly as he looked up at Belle. "Maybe a simple gift would be appropriate," he said with a smile.

Belle and Bernard rode through the market for another hour or two. Clouds started to form overhead as it got later in the day. Belle wondered if it would rain before too long. Thinking of Bernard and how much he had walked, Belle thought they ought to start bringing this trip to a close. As they started to head back toward the castle, Bernard spoke up, "Do you think Michael would mind visitors at this time?"

Belle thought for a moment. "I think it should be fine. His mother's been with him most of the day. If you want to go as soon as we get back, I will hold off my visit till later in the evening."

"Are you sure, Your Highness?"

Belle knew that Bernard greatly admired Michael and would want to visit him as soon as possible, "Yes, Bernard, you go ahead. I'll stop in and see him when you're done. I'd hate to burden him with too many visitors at one time."

"Thank you, Your Majesty. I promise I won't be too long. I'll notify you as soon as I'm done. Is there somewhere you will be waiting?"

Belle looked off into the distance as she answered Bernard, "No, there is actually someone else I need to visit first."

≪✦≫

Belle headed down the steps to the castle's dungeon. No matter what the time of day, it was dark. A few of the castle servants would make sure the torches on the walls were kept burning. The last couple days had been busy in the dungeon as the Savage's men were kept down there. Gideon, Hector and others had been down frequently to interrogate them and search for answers. Their efforts had come up short as the Savage's men weren't talking. Hector had them moved to the large prison east of the castle. The dungeon was now quiet again. Only two prisoners remained: the injured beast and Jean-Luc Pascal.

Belle had wanted to talk with Jean-Luc since they got back. Many various duties had come up and this was the first opportunity she had to speak with him. Above anything, Belle wanted to thank him for his efforts and for not betraying their trust. He had done very well in the tunnels, fighting the Savage's men and rescuing Michael. Any questions or doubts she had about Jean-Luc were quickly vanishing.

Reaching the bottom of the steps, Belle looked into the injured beast's cell. He was lying on his side curled up in a fetal position. She figured he was sleeping. A passing thought came to her mind to wake him and see if there was any way she could get anything more out of him. Even if he was missing his tongue, maybe there was some way this beast could answer some of her questions. Quickly thinking otherwise, she decided to leave him alone. She knew any attempt to question him at this point would be in vain, and besides, if he wasn't the Savage, then she figured he deserved some of her pity.

Belle moved further down the hallway toward Jean-Luc's cell. She walked slowly as she didn't want to startle him. Standing in front of his cell, she peeked in to see him reading a book. He was relaxed, sitting comfortably in his chair with his glasses on. The light brown hair of his mane was tied back, and he was dressed comfortably as if he was going to bed soon.

Belle stood staring at him for a few seconds before breaking the silence, "What are you reading?"

"Grimdolon poetry," Jean-Luc said, not taking his eyes off of his book. "Bernard found this book in the depths of your library. He is quite a nice fellow if I must say so myself."

"I'm glad he's taking good care of you."

Jean-Luc smiled slightly as he put down his book and turned to face Belle. "It's nice to see you again, Belle."

"And you too," Belle said politely.

Jean-Luc grabbed a cup from a nearby table and took a drink before speaking, "Is there anything I can do for you on this fine evening?"

Belle looked down at her feet. She blushed ever so slightly. She felt a large amount of gratitude for Jean-Luc's help with the rescue efforts in the tunnels. Looking up at Jean-Luc, she brushed a strand of hair out of her eyes before speaking, "Jean-Luc, I want to thank you for your help in the tunnels. I truly don't think we could have done it without you. The kingdom owes you a large amount of gratitude for your service."

Jean-Luc smiled back at Belle. "The pleasure is mine, Your Majesty," he said, giving a small nod.

"And Jean-Luc..." Belle paused, briefly. She looked directly at Jean-Luc. "Thank you for coming to my aid during the fight." Jean-Luc's smile grew larger. He could tell Belle was very sincere in her gratitude. He closed his eyes, not wanting to say too much. The beast realized he was starting to win her trust. He didn't want that to change.

They were silent for a few seconds as Jean-Luc pondered what to say next. He decided to simply change the direction of the conversation. "Belle, I heard you stop for a moment at the bottom of the stairwell. Were you considering trying to interrogate the injured beast?"

Belle shrugged her shoulders, impressed by Jean Luc's observations. "I don't know... Hector feels like it is in vain trying to get any information from him."

Jean-Luc nodded his head, "Well... Your Majesty, in this instance Hector is correct. I imagine he told you the beast has a debilitating injury. He won't be speaking with you anytime soon." Jean-Luc paused just a moment before continuing, "And even if he could, he wouldn't. He fears the Savage much more any of us."

Belle stepped toward the prison bars. "Jean-Luc, are you saying you know for sure that this injured beast is not the Savage?"

"Oh, I am quite certain of it, Princess."

A look of confusion came on Belle's face, "How... How do you know this?"

Jean-Luc chuckled slightly, "There are many things about this predicament that I'm quite confused about, but one thing I know for sure is that this injured beast is not the Savage."

"Jean-Luc, tell me how you know this."

"Patience, Belle... Patience." Jean-Luc paused briefly before continuing, "For one, this would be highly uncharacteristic of how the Savage has worked in the past. He is always sheltered by a number of criminals. He doesn't seem to act alone." Jean-Luc rose to his feet, "Also, this beast doesn't seem to match the evidence found at Michael's house. I can tell this beast was not at Michael's house."

Belle paced slightly as she began to process what Jean-Luc was saying. In the back of her mind she kept reminding herself of Michael's admonition that Jean-Luc tended to speak in riddles. "Well, who is this beast and why would the Savage cut out his tongue and have him captured?"

"I believe his name is Remy, and I would guess that he was one of the mine workers that helped the Savage, Sir Delano, steal some of the mining resources."

Belle was confused, "Why would he turn himself in like this?"

Jean-Luc adjusted his glasses, "Isn't it obvious?... Remy was just a pawn. Sir Delano turned on him and had him caught by us as a simple diversion. But first he cut out Remy's tongue to make sure he didn't give away any of his plans."

Belle was starting to get a little upset, grabbing the prison bars in front of her, "Jean-Luc, please speak to me plainly. A diversion for what? What is the Savage doing by all of this?"

Jean-Luc took a deep breath and sat down again. He took another drink from his cup and looked straight at Belle. He spoke quietly, "Princess... you must remember what I said before... the Savage only operates in perception, not reality."

"How so?"

"He wants all the people of Mendolon thinking he is caught. He wants the kingdom and the townspeople to let their guard down before he attacks again. Somehow he will find a way to plant rumors among the people that he is caught."

Belle felt frustrated, hearing Jean-Luc's information. She didn't know what their next move should be. A sense of hopelessness came over her. She wondered how long this villain would wreak havoc in the kingdom. The princess had had many sleepless nights, and just when she thought the end was near, it was snatched away from her. Looking behind her, she walked over and grabbed the chair Bernard had originally placed by the wall.

Jean-Luc could tell she was frustrated. "Well, don't be upset, Belle. We are making progress. Hopefully soon we can get a step ahead of him."

Belle took a deep breath and shook her head. She rubbed the back of her head as she tried to think of something to say. She was at a complete loss. "Ok... Jean-Luc, what's next? What should we do?"

Jean-Luc was silent for a few moments. Belle could tell he had something on his mind. A big smile came on his face as he leaned forward, "Belle... what we need to do more than anything is get ready for the Winter Ball. I've never been to one, of course, and I'm quite excited."

Looking down at her feet, Belle smiled at the irony of the situation. Jean-Luc continued, "Surely you don't mean to cancel the ball?"

"No... I guess the ball has just been the furthest thing from my mind these last few days."

Jean-Luc continued to smile, "Belle, we have so much to do. I need to know what you're wearing so we can coordinate colors, and of course, I will need to find out what type of flowers you like, and..."

Belle couldn't help but laugh at this point. "Jean-Luc, you're in a dungeon. How do you think you will be able to buy flowers?"

"Well, I was hoping I could grow some for you, though we don't tend to get much sunlight in these parts."

Belle blushed as she stood to her feet and looked toward the stairs. "Jean-Luc, I really should be going. I'll come back tomorrow, and we can talk about the Winter Ball more in depth."

Jean-Luc calmly stood to his feet and took a bow. "I look forward to it, Your Highness."

"Goodbye, Jean-Luc," Belle said, bowing in return. As she made her way toward the steps she turned and look over her shoulder one last time... toward Jean-Luc's cell. She couldn't help but smile.

CHAPTER 11

*B*elle peeked into Michael's room in the infirmary. She could see his mother by his side placing a cold cloth on his forehead. Michael was lying in bed with bandages covering his arms. Belle thought he looked a bit thinner. She knocked on the door as she pushed it open.

"Come in," Michael's mother said as she turned to see who was entering.

"It's me," Belle said with a smile, entering the room.

"Oh, welcome, child," she said, standing and giving Belle a hug.

"It's great to see you," Belle said, returning the hug. Michael's mother, Helen, had always enjoyed seeing Belle. She loved her greatly as both a princess and as a possible future daughter-in-law. Helen was a kind-natured woman who never seemed to worry. She always wore a big smile and always considered others above herself. She lived in the southern part of the kingdom by the ports. In the last twelve years she had remarried after Michael's father was lost in battle. They had a daughter nine years ago who adored Michael.

Releasing Belle, she looked back at Michael. "He's having a very good day. He was even out of bed this morning. Doctors say he should be back to his normal self in a couple of weeks."

"Oh, mother," Michael spoke up. "You ought to be heading home. Your family needs you. The castle has good doctors. I should be fine."

She smiled back at her son, "Michael, it's like they say... once a mother, always a mother." Belle couldn't help but smile at their interaction. She continued, "And besides, you still have a fever."

Belle laughed slightly. "Michael, I think we need to start bringing your mother with us in battle. Her resiliency would be a valuable asset."

"Belle, don't get her started... she might actually consider it." The three of them had a good laugh together. They were thankful that Michael was safe and seemed to be on the road to recovery.

Michael's mother, realizing that it was starting to get late, thought she ought to be heading home. "Well, my son, I do think this time you are correct. I probably should be going. Belle, it sure was good to see you."

"It truly was great to see you too," Belle said with an affectionate smile.

"Mother, will you be ok traveling home by yourself this late? It looks like it is going to rain, and..."

Helen shook her head, "Michael, you worry too much. I'll be fine. You rest up. I'll come and see you again in a couple of days."

"Thanks, Mother... love you."

"Love you too," Helen said, walking over and giving her son a hug. She then looked toward Belle, "Take care of him."

"I will," Belle said, reassuring her.

Michael's mother said goodbye one last time before leaving the room. Belle quietly walked over to Michael and took a seat beside his bed. "How are you really doing, Michael?"

He shrugged his shoulders, "A few broken ribs, sore arms, along with some deep cuts on my back, and like Mother said, a terrible fever, but... other than that I feel great."

Belle laughed a little and rubbed his forearm, trying to comfort him. "Knowing you, Michael, I'm sure you will be back to your old self in a few days."

He smiled back at Belle and reached over and grabbed her hand, squeezing it tight. He was grateful for her visit. Michael was thankful to have her in his life. It was great to call her both partner and friend. "How are *you* doing?" he asked her.

Belle looked away from Michael as tears started to form in her eyes. She brushed her hair out of her face as she tried to gather herself. She took a deep breath before speaking, "I'm thankful to have you back." The tears started to roll down her cheeks. "When we learned you'd been captured, I thought we'd lost you forever. I felt lost, helpless... afraid."

Michael nodded in agreement, trying to empathize with the princess. In his heart of hearts, he truly wished the whole kingdom could see this moment. Her affection and care for people was truly something to admire and surpassed anything he'd ever seen in any other person of royalty.

They sat in silence for a few moments before Michael spoke up. "How were you able to find me?"

"Jean-Luc was able to figure out your location by examining clues at your house," Belle said calmly.

"What has been your impression of him?"

Belle shook her head, trying to find the right words to say. There were many things about Jean-Luc she was still unsure of. "I don't know, Michael... I think you're right. It does seem like he's speaking in riddles. I can't figure out his plans."

"Do you trust him?"

Belle smiled as she looked down at her feet. "I don't know. He has done everything we've asked him, and he's been true to his word. At this point I think I have to, as I have no reason not to." Michael took a deep breath as fatigue started to set in.

He closed his eyes. "Michael, I can come back another time if you're feeling tired," Belle said softly.

"No… it's fine," Michael said with his eyes still closed. "Were you able to get any information from the beast you captured?"

"No, we weren't able to. He's unable to talk. We're wondering if this beast is the Savage. Jean-Luc is sure he's not, but Gideon and I…"

"Jean-Luc is right," Michael said, interrupting. "The Savage is using this beast to buy himself some time. He wasn't expecting to be found in the tunnels, so he used this beast to briefly throw us off course and to manipulate the perception of the townspeople."

"Yeah… that's what Jean-Luc says."

"What else does he say?"

Belle sat quietly for a few moments trying to gather her thoughts before she spoke. "He says that we need to open our eyes and see clearly what is going on. He says that our perception of everything is wrong and is not reality. There are secrets, he says, that have not yet been uncovered."

Michael opened his eyes and looked straight at Belle. "This is what worries me about him. Like you, I want to trust him, but a part of me is afraid to."

"I agree, Michael… but I don't know what else to do. I think he's the best option we have to find the Savage."

Michael closed his eyes again. The medicine he took earlier was starting to have its effect. He felt himself starting to drift away.

Belle wasn't sure what to say. She actually wondered if she should say anything at all. Michael seemed to be getting more tired, and she figured it would be best to leave and let him get some rest. "Michael, all this can wait for the morning. You need your rest."

Belle rose to her feet and she started to leave. Michael grabbed her arm and opened his eyes. "Belle, if I may make one request."

"Yes... anything."

"Would you mind singing a short melody as I fall asleep?" Michael said through his weariness.

Belle smiled as she sat down beside Michael. She loved to sing and was happy to do it for her friend. She briefly thought about what song to sing before she began. The princess chose a song her nursemaid used to sing to her when she was a little girl.

She sang softly, "Through clouds and stars, and skies of blue... drift off to a land that's meant for you... from there you'll find your peace and rest... there're beaches and waves and beautiful sunsets... now I will go if I may... so sleep peacefully and dream away."

Michael quickly fell asleep. He looked to be in near perfect peace. "Sweet dreams, Michael," she said as she stood to leave.

❧

Jean-Luc sat in his dungeon cell, fiddling with the strings on his violin. He was unable to sleep. He had been imprisoned for a long time and he was ready to leave. The events of the rescue kept playing through his mind. He had greatly enjoyed getting out of his cell and doing something profitable. The brief taste of freedom reminded him what he was missing in the outside world. "Patience, patience," Jean-Luc kept telling himself. He did not want to get ahead of himself.

He had broken a violin string earlier in the evening while trying to tinker with the tune of the instrument. The violin was his escape on these long nights in the cell. It occupied his mind and was helpful in getting his mind off his current state in the prison cell. Currently, he was trying to see if he could salvage the string he had broken. He had broken many strings during his time in prison and he dreaded requesting another one, as he felt he had already exhausted his allowance.

Jean-Luc heard footsteps coming and stopped to listen carefully. It had to be the middle of the night. He wondered who could be coming. Putting down his violin, he tried to analyze the footsteps. The individual was just a few feet away when Jean-Luc realized who was coming, "Hector, you are staying up late these days. I think there are some mice running around here if you are dealing with late night hunger."

"Shut up, Beast," Hector said as he came in front of Jean-Luc's cell. His green clothing could be recognized anywhere.

"Well, I'm just trying to be hospitable, since it is late and you..."

"Quit your fooling. Do you think you can fool me?"

Jean-Luc adjusted his glasses and thought for a moment before answering. "Is that a trick question?" he said calmly.

"You listen here, Jean-Luc Pascal. I've heard about your plans to attend our ball and I'm on to you. Unlike others in this castle, I've spent time in Grimdolon. I have been with your kind."

"Hector... what is your point?"

Hector stepped right up to the bars and nearly put his face through them. "The point is that I know what your plan is. You can't fool me. I'm going to do whatever it takes to stop you."

Jean-Luc rested his hands in his lap and looked directly at Hector, "No... no you won't. You need me, Hector. You know you can't stop the Savage without me."

Hector pulled on his hair in frustration, and gave a faint hiss. He was getting angrier by the moment. "Don't begin to think you have the upper hand. I'm the king's advisor. I'm in control here. I'm..."

Hector stopped midsentence as Jean-Luc abruptly stood to his feet. He looked deeply at Hector. "Do you feel... in control?"

The two men stood in silence, looking at one another. Hector didn't know what to say. Jean-Luc stepped close to the prison bars and continued, "Because ever since I stepped into the dragon's territory eight months ago, I've had two main objectives, and currently I seem to be on the path to completing both."

Hector clinched his teeth in anger. He knew Jean-Luc was right. He spoke quietly, "As soon as the morning comes... I'm going to tell Michael what you're up to."

"Fine, go ahead. What do you think that will accomplish?"

"He'll... He'll throw you out of the kingdom."

Jean-Luc laughed under his breath as he sat back down. "Hector, are you listening to yourself? Do you really think Michael de Bolbec would throw me out of this kingdom?"

Hector hit the bars with his hands. He knew Jean-Luc was correct and that there was no viable option for stopping him at this point. He stuck his index finger through the bars as he spoke harshly, "Mark my words, Beast. I will do everything in my power to break you, and if you ever get what you are hoping for, I will do everything in my efforts to stop you."

Jean-Luc smiled at his enemy, "Have a good night, Hector. Sleep well."

With one last angry hiss, Hector stormed out of the dungeon.

❧ ❦

Belle awoke from her dream. She looked around, steadying herself, making sure it was just a dream. It was the middle of the night. She could hear rain coming down outside. She breathed deeply, trying to calm herself. A lit candle was still burning beside her bed, giving her a faint glow of light.

Her recurring dream had returned. It had been a week since she'd last had it. It was the same as always. She would enter the Winter Ball and greet the people as she passed through the crowds. When she arrived at the dance floor, she would realize that something was not right, and she would flee. She would always wake up startled and have to take a few moments to calm her nerves.

It seemed interesting that the last few instances she could remember a few differences in her dream. This time in particular she remembered that her dress was different each time. Recollecting on it, Belle knew that the differences were not just subtle patterns or tints of colors, but major changes in the style and color of the garments. She wondered if there were any hidden meanings in this difference.

Belle threw her covers off and walked toward the window. The rain was beating on the window. She found it soothing. It looked as if it was going to let up sometime soon. Looking out to the mountains, she thought of the Northern Ruins. Even though the raid on the ruins was less than two weeks ago, with everything that had occurred, it seemed like months. She remembered how naive she was in thinking that they would rid themselves of the Savage at that time.

Her nerves started to settle and she thought it was time to head back to bed. She walked back to her bed and gently slid under the covers. Laying her head down on her pillow, she fell asleep.

CHAPTER 12

$\mathcal{A}$ week went by and the kingdom of Mendolon was still at peace. The people continued to assume the Savage was caught. Belle and Hector ordered the townspeople to continue to set watchmen around the villages, but for the most part the people went back to their lives as normal. King Sebastian had still not returned. Hector had twice been in contact with him since he left. He had warned Sebastian not to return to the kingdom since the Savage was possibly still at large. Even with Sebastian gone, the people's spirit was not dampened. The markets stayed open later than usual, and the people continued to purchase gifts and various items.

Currently around the kingdom there was much excitement with the Winter Ball occurring tonight. The castle was decorated beautifully and many preparations had already had been made for the grand occasion. Belle and Jean-Luc had met every day to discuss the event. Jean-Luc wanted to know all the specifics about what to wear and what dances he would need to know. Belle, on the other hand, was concerned more about having a beast at the ball. She had told many of the nobles and high ranking officials that he would be present. She warned Jean-Luc that there would be some that would disapprove of him being at the ball, even if he did save Michael's life.

It was the middle of the afternoon, and Belle was in one of her dressing rooms of the castle getting her hair done. Three teenage servant girls were attending to her. Two were working on her hair while another was doing her nails. She was dressed in an exquisite light purple ballroom gown. The royal seamstress had spent several months sewing it in anticipation of this event. The servant girls thought it was one of the most beautiful dresses they'd ever seen.

"Oh, Belle, you're going to look absolutely gorgeous," said the girl filing her nails. "I can't wait to see you out there tonight."

"I wish I had brown hair like you, Belle," another one of the girls said. "It is so beautiful."

Belle smiled at the girl's compliment, "Well, maybe one of these years I can do your hair and nails, and you can attend the ball."

The girl laughed in return, "Oh, don't be silly. The Winter Ball would never be the same without you. The people are going to love you and your dress."

Belle loved these girls and had such a good relationship with them. She instructed them to call her by her first name and told them they were always welcome to approach her if they needed anything. Belle wanted them to know that they weren't there just to serve her and the dignitaries. She wanted them to feel like they were a part of the kingdom.

They continued to laugh and talk for another half an hour. Belle greatly enjoyed these moments. It was definitely different than any conversation she would have with any of the nobles later that night. The banter took a definite turn when one of the girls asked about Jean-Luc. "Belle, there are many rumors about the beast going to the ball. What is he like? I've never met a beast before."

Belle looked at her reflection in the mirror as she thought about how to respond, "Well, he's thin, wears glasses... His name is Jean-Luc."

The girls continued with their work as they listened. "I mean more... what is he really like? Are you afraid of him?"

Belle smiled a little at the girl's curiosity. "Jean-Luc is... he is..." Belle struggled with the exact words to say. "Jean-Luc is smart, mysterious, and musical. He loves his violin and is usually playing it when I see him.

The girls worked in silence for a few moments while they tried to imagine the personality of the beast. The girl filing her nails stopped briefly and looked at Belle, "Your Majesty..."

"Please, call me Belle."

"I'm sorry, Belle..." she said, looking down at her feet. She hesitated briefly before speaking, "Is there anything to be afraid of? I've heard people say beasts are very frightening."

Belle could sense the fear in the girl's voice. She reached over and put her hand on the young girl's arm, trying to reassure her. "No. I would say there is nothing to be afraid of. He is nothing like the rumors you've heard."

One of the girls fixing her hair spoke up, "What is his personality like? Hopefully he's not like the boys our age."

Belle couldn't help but laugh at the young girl's comment. "No... no, I would not say he's like that. Jean-Luc is very kind in his own sort of way. He's well thought out and seems to be very intentional at everything he does. He doesn't act rashly and is not quick tempered.

"Sounds like a gentleman," one of the girls chimed in.

Belle thought for just a moment before answering. "Yes... yes, I would call him a gentleman," she said with a smile.

❧❦

Belle walked down the steps of the dungeon. She held up her dress a little to make sure it didn't drag against the floor. Jean-Luc had requested that she meet him at his cell. He wanted to have the pleasure of escorting her to the ball. Currently she wondered if this was a good idea. The spiral staircase down to the dungeon was difficult to maneuver in her ballroom gown.

She reached the bottom of the steps. Everything was quiet. The injured beast had been moved to the prison facility east of the castle. Now only Jean-Luc remained in the dungeon. She watched her steps closely as she made her way to the end of the hallway. Reaching the front of the cell, she found Jean-Luc standing close to the bars anticipating her arrival. He was dressed in an exquisite dark purple coat with a white shirt. His hair was pulled back, and his mane was cut short. There was no mistaking he was a beast, but Belle was surprised at how much like a man he looked.

"Good evening, Your Highness," he said politely, holding out a flower.

"Good evening," Belle returned. She gently reached through the prison bars, grabbing the flower. She held it to her nose and took in the aroma. It was a red rose, her favorite. Some of the merchants of the markets would have them imported from countries across the southern seas. Belle knew this was an exceptional gift for this time of year.

"Might I add, that you look absolutely beautiful tonight, Belle," Jean-Luc said sincerely.

"Thanks, Jean-Luc. Where did you get this flower?"

Jean-Luc shrugged his shoulders, "I have my resources."

Belle smiled. "It was Bernard... wasn't it?"

Jean-Luc laughed. "Of course, he truly is a nice fellow."

Belle took the key from her hand and unlocked Jean-Luc's cell. She opened the door for him as he stepped out. He couldn't help but smile at the rare chance to get out of his prison. "We'd better be going. Many of the guests have already arrived. We don't want to be too much longer."

"It would be an honor," Jean-Luc said, excited to get to the ball. Jean-Luc escorted Belle out of the dungeon. The ballroom of the castle was located on the north side of the castle and as was the custom, the princess was supposed to arrive by carriage. Belle felt it was a little bit of a silly tradition as they could have easily walked, but nevertheless she obliged.

The carriage took a short detour along a few roads by the castle before arriving at the ballroom. Looking out the window, Belle could see many of Mendolon's nobles exiting their carriages and making their way up a long flight of stairs to the ballroom. Their carriage stopped in front as a footman opened the door for the princess to step out. He held out his hand as she stepped onto the ground. Many dignitaries were already present, making their way into the ball. Belle waved at Gideon's wife as she passed by. She blew a kiss in return.

Jean-Luc stepped from the carriage and readjusted his jacket. He felt great and was excited for the evening. "This is most exciting. I'm eager to see what everything will be like."

"Well, stay close to me. Remember there are some who are nervous with you being here."

Jean-Luc smiled as he spoke, "I will be on my best behavior, Your Majesty." He held out his arm for Belle to take hold as they walked up a flight of steps toward the exterior entrance. There were lights and various extravagant decorations lining the stairwell. Mendolon soldiers could be seen everywhere in armor. Hector had ordered most of them to be on duty. The king's knights were invited to attend the ball, and all were present except Michael.

Belle stumbled slightly on a step. Jean-Luc was able to steady her before she completely fell. "Careful, Belle," he commented. "I'd hate to see you twist an ankle before we even make it inside." She simply smiled and rolled her eyes in response.

Reaching the top of the steps, Jean-Luc could see there was a large courtyard in front of the ballroom's entrance. There was a large fountain in the center of the area with a few hundred people on each side, greeting one another and casually talking. He could see a few musicians on the sides along with a table of food. Everyone was dressed in fine attire that looked worthy of people of royalty. He couldn't help but stare as he tried to take it all in. "Belle, I must say, Mendolon truly knows how to conduct a ball."

"Thanks. It has been a tradition for many years. I think each year the royal decorators try to outdo themselves from previous years."

"Well, some year we will have to borrow your decorators to help us plan a Winter Ball like this in Grimdolon."

Belle laughed under her breath. She grabbed his hand, "Let's go ahead and make our way through the crowd. Everyone will expect me inside when the dance begins." Belle made her way through the people, leading Jean-Luc. She smiled and nonchalantly greeted lots of people as she made her way toward the ballroom. Jean-Luc observed a few stares from folks as he passed by. He tried to smile as casually as possible, hoping it would calm some of the onlookers.

Belle was making her way through the crowd when an elderly lady stopped her. "Belle, my dear, it is great to see you."

"Great to see you too," she returned. The two quickly embraced.

Releasing her grip, Belle turned to Jean-Luc, "Jean-Luc, this is my nursemaid, Elise. She helped take care of me when I was a young girl."

"Pleased to meet you," Jean-Luc said, reaching out and grabbing her hand and kissing it.

Elise smiled in return, seemingly not afraid in the least bit of the beast. "I hear you are the one who rescued Michael."

Jean-Luc shrugged his shoulder, "Well, I mustn't take all the credit. Belle and some of the knights were essential parts of the mission as well. We all worked together."

Elise reached over and rubbed Jean-Luc's arm. "Nevertheless, thank you for your service to our kingdom. We owe you a large amount of gratitude."

"Thank you. You are too kind."

Elise turned to face the princess, "Belle, it is truly great to see you. I know the castle is big, but we need to make it a point to see each other more often."

"I agree," returned Belle.

"Take care, my princess," she said, giving Belle one more tight squeeze before saying goodbye one last time. Belle and Jean-Luc continued to make their way through the crowd. Jean-Luc followed close behind as best as he could while Belle greeted guests.

As Belle passed by the people, she thought of her dream. She wondered if this whole event would shed more light on what was occurring in the dream. A part of her wondered if after tonight it would stop. Possibly something would be fulfilled that would cause it to cease altogether. As best as she could she tried to suppress those thoughts. The Winter Ball was a joyous event and she determined in herself not to let anything damper this occasion.

Arriving at the exterior doors to the ballroom, Jean-Luc looked in wonder at the grandeur of the building. It was made mostly of windows with beautiful stone work between the glass holding everything into place. The building was only one floor with a high thirty-foot ceiling. The light from the chandeliers reflected beautifully through the glass.

The tall doors opened and a trumpet blew as Belle slowly entered. There were a few hundred more guests inside, and many standing near the front doors stopped their conversations to view Mendolon's beloved princess enter the ballroom. "Good evening, Your Highness," she heard someone say.

"Good evening to all," she said with a smile to the few dozen guests who stopped to greet her. A few nobles approached her to welcome her and comment on her dress. Jean-Luc stayed close to Belle's side as she made her way through the crowd. Stepping close to a table with food, Jean-Luc grabbed a glass of wine. Taking a sip, he realized how much he missed the taste of wine, even if it was quite a bit different from the kind made in Grimdolon.

Belle continued to greet as many of the people as she could. Jean-Luc could easily see how much the people loved her. He had heard rumors of her love for the people, but it was remarkable to see up close how much she cared for them. Even though some were uncomfortable with him being there, she took great strides to make sure everyone knew he was responsible for saving Michael de Bolbec. He truly admired her for her kindness.

As the evening progressed, the guests began to make their way to the dance floor. The pleasant sounds of string instruments started to play. Jean-Luc turned to Belle. "Your Highness, I know there are many you want to greet, but if you will be so kind, could you spare a moment for a dance?"

Belle smiled, "I guess this was part of the bargain." Jean-Luc held out his hand as she reached for it. They danced around the ballroom as the music played. Some in the crowd began to follow suit. Others in the crowd stood and watched Belle and the beast dance. Most had never seen a beast before, much less seen one dance.

"You seem to have experience dancing," Belle said as they moved around the floor.

"We beasts do have our own celebrations. Nothing this extravagant of course, but we do our best."

"I can tell you've had lessons," Belle said quietly.

"You can thank my father for that. As a little boy, I thought it was rubbish, practicing all this dancing. I guess in the end Father knew what he was doing."

They continued to move around the dance floor as the crowd continued to circle. They laughed and talked casually. Before the ball, Belle thought it might be strange to dance with a beast, but now in the moment nothing of the sort passed her mind. Jean-Luc was such a good dancer that she seemed to forget any concern she once had.

As the music started to cease, Jean-Luc stopped to take a bow. Belle followed suit. As Jean-Luc arose, he could see a man approaching Belle from behind. He seemed to be walking briskly. The man reached out to grab Belle's shoulder. Jean-Luc quickly intercepted his hand and pulled him to the side. "I don't think so," Jean-Luc said calmly. He then bent the man's wrist back, forcing him to one knee. "Sorry to say, my good lad, but she's with me tonight," Jean-Luc said before squeezing his hand tight. Belle could hear the crack of a bone.

"What are you doing? He's just a peasant," Belle said to Jean-Luc, trying to stay calm. She was thankful they were on the edge of the dance floor where not many people were seeing what was transpiring.

"Have mercy, please," the man said as struggled with the pain. Jean-Luc released the man as he fell to the ground, grabbing his hand.

"Be gone," Jean-Luc said to him. The man swiftly got up and ran through the crowd toward the edge of the room. He seemed quite embarrassed.

The music started to play again, and Belle quickly grabbed Jean-Luc for another dance. She was bewildered by that whole exchange and thought the best solution would be to nonchalantly start another dance and act like it didn't happen. She was a little upset at Jean-Luc for making a scene, especially since many of the guests were uncomfortable with him even being there. "Jean-Luc, what was that all about?"

"Just looking out for you, Princess," Jean-Luc said without breaking his focus.

"He's just a simple peasant. He probably just wanted to meet me or give a gift. That was completely uncalled for."

Jean-Luc spun her around so she could see the peasant through the crowd. "Belle, can you see him?" They continued to dance as he spoke.

"Yes, it looks like he might be nursing his wounds."

"Look carefully at his attire. Yes, his coat is worn and made of a cheaper material, giving the look of a peasant. But look at his shirt. The stitching by the collar is intricately designed and seems to have taken much time. Plus, the overall design seems to say that it belonged to a person of royalty."

Belle focused on the man as best as she could. She was a little far away, but she could tell clearly that Jean-Luc was correct about his shirt. It did not belong to an ordinary peasant. He continued, "I know you can't see it from here, but his shoes are made from a fine leather material. They are definitely not the shoes of a peasant, probably just the best he could steal before the evening."

"Are you saying he was a thief?"

"Precisely. I just wanted to make sure he didn't try to steal anything else tonight."

Belle nodded in agreement, now understanding Jean-Luc's reasoning. "Well, in that case. Thank you for protecting me."

"Anytime," Jean-Luc responded nonchalantly.

Belle smiled as they continued to circle around the dance floor. The music changed its tone slightly and became quicker in tempo. Belle was enjoying the evening and seemed to get lost in the fun of everything. They talked and laughed casually as they spun around the dance floor. The troubles of the kingdom seemed to vanish in the enjoyment of the evening. She was so thrilled to see many of the knights and their families enjoying the evening as well.

The princess and Jean-Luc danced on and off for the next half hour. Things seemed to be going well when all of a sudden Jean-Luc's mood changed during a dance. He became more stern, and he looked as if he was contemplating something. "Jean-Luc, what's wrong?" Belle asked.

Jean-Luc looked toward a large window and squinted his eyes. He released one of Belle's hands and readjusted his glasses. "I think it's time to change things up a bit."

Abruptly he moved to the center of the dance floor with Belle. He held his arm up and twirled her before grabbing her waist and dipping her. Many in the crowd took notice. He then picked up the princess by the waist and spun with the music. "Follow my lead," he told Belle as quietly as he could. The crowd was in awe for the next few minutes. Jean-Luc led Belle in one of the most exquisite and difficult dances of Grimdolon. The guests clapped as Jean-Luc executed the moves flawlessly. Belle was amazed at how he led her and how easy he was to follow. Everyone else in the crowd had stopped dancing at this point to watch the beauty and the beast. The kingdom of Mendolon had never seen anything quite like it.

As the music began to slow, Jean-Luc stopped and took a bow toward Belle. Belle reciprocated as the guests clapped in appreciation. Standing back up straight, Jean-Luc smiled to the crowd as he quietly said, "Thank you." Belle clapped with the crowd, amazed at his ability.

The clapping began to quiet and Jean-Luc spoke up to address the crowd, "People of Mendolon, you have been too kind. If I may, I would like to lead the princess in another one of our Grimdolon dances." The crowd began to clap again in excitement. Jean-Luc smiled as he held up his hand to quiet them, "But I must say as it is our tradition, this dance can only be done under the light of the stars." The guests began to speak to one another in excitement, and they began moving outside toward the courtyard.

Everything took a few minutes to get into place. The musicians found a spot where they could easily be heard. The stars were still out and hundreds of candles lit the way on the edge of the courtyard. The temperature was moderately cold, but the people did not seem to mind. The excitement and thrill of the evening seemed to surpass everything else.

The music began to play and Jean-Luc grabbed Belle by the hand. Belle noticed that his attention seemed to be elsewhere. He kept looking toward the sides of the crowd, searching for something. He was not focused on dancing; he simply danced around in a circle around the courtyard. The crowd seemed to notice and began talking amongst themselves. They wondered what was going on.

"Jean-Luc, what is happening?" Belle asked, a little confused by this whole ordeal.

Jean-Luc bit his lip and kept looking toward the crowd. He looked worried as he began to speak. "Belle... I think... I think..."

"Yes, what is it?" she said, worried.

"I think we are about to..." Jean-Luc was interrupted as a massive explosion occurred in the ballroom. The large windows blew out into the crowd as pieces of the front wall fell to the ground. A cloud of dust and debris engulfed the crowd. People began screaming while others ran for their lives. The scene quickly became chaotic as fire blazed from the ballroom.

❧❧

Michael was in his room in the infirmary when he heard the explosion. He was attempting to do push-ups but found the wound in his shoulder blade very tender. Hearing the explosion, he pulled himself to his feet using the bed post as a brace. He slowly walked to his large window and looked outside. There was dust and debris in the air. He could see the smoke rising from the ballroom. Looking through the clouded air, he could see the glow of the fire coming from the building.

Michael wondered how many people were inside. He wondered if Belle or any of the other knights had been harmed. He wondered if the Savage was now attacking the people. Panic started to set in. He looked over at his bed and could see his sword standing against the wall. His legs were still healing from the imprisonment. He knew there was nothing he could do at the moment.

Looking out the window, Michael could feel the anger and the rage growing inside of him. He wanted to protect the people of Mendolon, and he hated anyone who brought such destruction upon them. He wanted to destroy this beast, no matter what it took.

∞∞

Belle began to pick herself up as she had fallen to the ground during the explosion. She couldn't see a thing as dust from the explosion was filling the area. Her hearing began to return and she could hear the screams and sheer panic from the guests of the ball. Standing to her feet, she wondered if she was seriously hurt. Her arm was bleeding slightly from her fall, but she felt no other serious injury.

Turning to her side, she saw Jean-Luc on the ground, grabbing his leg. Apparently, he had injured it during the explosion. Belle ran to him. "Jean-Luc, are you ok?"

"Yeah," he said, squeezing his eyes shut.

"Is there anything you need?" she said urgently.

"I'll be fine. Check on everyone else. Those closer to the building most likely weren't as fortunate."

Belle promptly stood to her feet and ran toward the dilapidated building. The dust in the air started to clear. Most of the guests began to stand to their feet and check on their loved ones. There was screaming everywhere as those that were able began to run from the castle's premises. Many were bleeding, particularly from the glass blown from the windows.

Reaching the building she saw about a dozen people knocked out on the ground. She began checking those closest to her. Thankfully they all seemed to be breathing. From the corner of her eye, she saw a man buried under a slab from the building. He was trying to free himself. Belle ran to the man quickly and with all her might lifted the slab just high enough for the man to slide himself out. "Thank you," he mumbled as he tried to catch his breath.

Gideon ran to the scene carrying a sword. There was great urgency in his voice, "Your Highness, are you hurt?"

"No, I'm fine. What's your assessment of the situation?"

Gideon shook his head, "I've not found any enemies. A few of the knights are checking the crowd for anyone suspicious. The soldiers have the castle under tight security and are watching the exits."

Belle continued to check on the people lying on the ground. "What about the guests?"

Gideon was quick to answer, "Many injuries, but no fatalities found so far. Thankfully, all of the guests had come outside to the courtyard to watch you and Jean-Luc dance."

She looked Gideon square in the eyes as she processed what he just said. Rising to her feet, Belle looked across the courtyard back toward Jean-Luc. He was still on the ground grabbing his leg. Their eyes met. *Jean-Luc brought everyone outside,* she thought to herself, *How did he know there was going to be an explosion?*

CHAPTER 13

$\mathcal{B}$elle slowly walked down the steps toward the dungeon. Five days had passed since the Winter Ball. The kingdom was in an all-out panic. All commerce had stopped. The markets were closed, and there was talk among some of the townspeople of moving across the southern sea. Soldiers were dispersed among the villages of Mendolon. Everyone in the land was to keep watch for any potential information leading to the capture of the Savage or any of his allies.

King Sebastian was still in hiding. After the ball, Hector had met with him privately along a northern road and advised him not to return. The king spoke of war with Grimdolon. Hector advised him otherwise since the Savage was currently crippling all their resources and personnel. The citizens of Mendolon also saw his absence as a sign of the kingdom heading toward complete disorder. Going to battle with their neighboring kingdom was not possible.

The attack at the Winter Ball had left Belle completely dejected. She felt inadequate as both a princess and a knight of Mendolon. Hopelessness consumed her. Once again, she saw no end to the Savage's reign of terror. The people of Mendolon had suffered enough. She longed for peace and tranquility in the kingdom.

Belle watched her step closely as everything was completely dark. The torches hadn't been routinely lit the last few days as every available man was put on watch for the Savage. Jean-Luc's lantern at the end of the hallway was the only light in the whole dungeon.

She reached the bottom of the steps and slowly approached Jean-Luc's cell. She hadn't seen him since the explosion at the Winter Ball. He had sustained a leg injury in the blast and was now walking with a cane while his leg healed. After the explosion she was able to take him and all the other injured citizens directly to the castle's infirmary. Jean-Luc refused to be cared for but instead requested to be brought directly back to his cell. With all of Belle's duties in helping to disperse troops around Mendolon and caring for the injured, she hadn't had an opportunity to visit him since the attack.

Stepping in front of Jean-Luc's cell, she found him peacefully eating his supper. He looked comfortable. Seeing Belle in front of the cell, he paused briefly and looked up at her. He smiled as he spoke, "Good evening, Belle."

She said nothing in response. She quietly took a seat on the chair in front of his cell. She looked over at his plate and could see he was eating a meal of bread and ground beef. Jean-Luc could tell she was examining his plate, "Strange meals Bernard brings me sometimes," he paused briefly, "but I mustn't complain. You have treated me very well since I've been here." They sat in silence for a while, searching for something to say. Belle struggled to know what to think. Many emotions filled her heart and mind.

After finishing his meal, Jean-Luc shrugged his shoulders, "Belle, I'm sorry our evening together turned out..." he paused, searching for words, "turned out... rather unpleasant."

"When did you know there was going to be an attack?" she said, seemingly ignoring his statement.

Jean-Luc looked off to the side as he shook his head, "I had a feeling early on that he might try to attack the Winter Ball."

"Is that why you wanted to attend?"

Jean-Luc looked directly at Belle and spoke sincerely, "Honestly... I was hoping I was wrong. I was truly having a pleasant evening. How many times in life does one get an opportunity to escort the princess of Mendolon to a royal ball?"

"How did you know there would be an explosion?" Belle asked directly, seemingly not interested in the small talk at the moment.

Jean-Luc nodded his head, readjusting his glasses before speaking. "I noticed irregularities among the guests, and particularly among the peasants. Like I said at the ball, I first noticed it in the thief who approached you. There were clues in his demeanor and clothing that tipped me off to the true identity of some of those in attendance. I then watched the edges of the room and could see a coordinated effort to attack the ball. Men seemed to be getting into position for some sort of attack."

"Is that why you had everyone follow us outside?"

Jean-Luc closed his eyes as he spoke, "Precisely... I just wished I could've warned everyone sooner, but I feared no one would believe me if I spoke outright of an attack."

Belle brushed the hair out of her eyes as she looked to the side. She felt tears beginning to well up in her eyes as she thought back to the night of the attack. The screaming of the injured haunted her.

"How many were killed in the explosion?" Jean-Luc inquired.

With both hands she wiped the tears from her eyes as she tried to gather herself. She took a deep breath before she spoke, "As of right now, none. A couple of the servants are in dire condition." Jean-Luc rubbed his chin as he listened intently to Belle. He was thankful for news of no fatalities. Belle continued, "Thankfully everyone followed us outside, including the servants. Your Grimdolon dance was enough to bring everyone outside."

"How many were injured?"

"Many. I don't know for sure, but I know it was at least a few hundred. Many of the injuries were quite substantial too."

Jean-Luc slammed his fist against his table as he stood to his feet. He was trying to stay calm. Belle was caught off guard as she'd never seen such emotion from him. He paced just a little before calmly sitting back in his chair. "I truly wish I could've seen everything sooner. The Savage is giving me a number of surprises. He's not who I thought he was."

"How so?" Belle asked, puzzled.

Jean-Luc took off his glasses and rubbed his fingers against his eyes as he spoke, "When I first came to Mendolon, I thought the beast, Remy, who we found in the tunnels, was Dominique Delano. Now after examining all the evidence, it is clear that the identity of the Savage is a lot more complicated."

"Do you have any idea who he really is?"

Jean-Luc ran his fingers through his hair, "I have some ideas, but the overall picture is not yet clear. Even my perception of things has been clouded. I need more evidence. I need to widen my gaze just a bit more."

Belle leaned back in her chair. The feeling of hopelessness kept growing. She was discouraged knowing that Jean-Luc did not have all the answers. She did not know what the next move would be. Gideon and Hector were at a loss, and Michael wasn't yet fully mended. She felt a huge weight on her. She longed for answers, "Jean-Luc... what do you... I mean should we... I think..." The princess wasn't sure what to say or ask. She covered her face as the tears began to roll down her cheek.

Jean-Luc stepped closer to the bars of his cell. He felt compassion for the princess of Mendolon. He looked at her with great sincerity. He felt it was now time to test her true honesty with him. He spoke softly, "Belle, why are you here?"

"Why do you think?" she spoke somewhat angrily. "We need to catch this beast. He's raising havoc in the kingdom and..."

Jean-Luc raised his hand to stop her. "Belle... no... why are you really here?"

She shook her head as she was frustrated, "Jean-Luc... I... I..."

He spoke quietly and intently, "Belle, why are you here?"

Belle hesitated. The tears kept falling. She wiped her eyes one last time before looking at Jean-Luc. She spoke truthfully, "Because I'm scared, Jean-Luc. I'm scared for the people of Mendolon. I'm scared the Savage is going to strike again. I'm scared that the kingdom will never be the same. I'm just scared."

"And why are you *here*?"

She brushed her hair out of her face again as she spoke quietly, "Because I'm scared and ... this is the only place in the whole kingdom where I feel safe." Jean-Luc nodded, knowing she was telling the truth. He was thankful for her honesty. He had worked hard to get to this point. She was now trusting him.

They sat in silence for a few minutes. Belle no longer felt the need to search for answers from Jean-Luc. She needed a friend to sit with and talk to. She felt safe with Jean-Luc; both physically and emotionally. Especially with her father gone, others in the kingdom looked to her for answers. She truly felt no obligation being with Jean-Luc.

A few minutes passed before Jean-Luc broke the silence. "Belle, tell me about yourself. What would you desire to do if the kingdom was safe?"

Belle shook her head, "I don't know... I would love to finish my training so that..."

"No, Belle," Jean-Luc interrupted. "I mean apart from all of this; apart from your duties as princess. Where would you go? What would you do on a quiet day?"

Belle bit her lip, just slightly, as she thought about what to say. "I don't know... I used to play the harp... sing on occasion. Sometimes, I like to go the southernmost village and listen to their chorale. They have wonderful voices."

"Do you sing yourself?"

"No... just to myself. I've never had a voice quite worthy of performances."

"I'm sure your humility surpasses your ability."

"Thanks," she said, playing with the end of her long brown hair.

Jean-Luc continued, "What else, Your Highness? What keeps you up at night?"

She shrugged her shoulders, "I like to read on occasion, but I wouldn't say it keeps me up at night."

"Oh... and why's that?"

"Honestly, I haven't slept well the past year."

"Do the images of the dragon still haunt you? I hear he had you in his grip before Michael came to the rescue."

"No... the dragon doesn't haunt me. He never did. I believe Michael took care of him permanently."

"Then what is it, Belle?" Jean-Luc asked, leaning forward, hungry for answers.

Belle looked down at her hands and casually twisted a purple flowered ring on her hand. She wondered how much more she should say. Michael's warning of not fully trusting Jean-Luc came to the forefront of her thoughts. She would hate to say much more and then see it somehow used against her.

Jean-Luc could tell she was contemplating how much to say. He knew there was something clearly on her mind. "Tell me... what is it, Belle?"

Belle looked up at the beast. She hesitated just a little before speaking. "I have a recurring dream that comes at least weekly. It's unsettling. It makes it hard to fall back asleep once it wakens me."

"And what is the nature of it?" Jean-Luc asked curiously.

Belle spoke slowly, "I'm at a ball. At first I thought it was the Winter Ball, but now I'm not so sure. I enter the ball and am greeted by the guests. I walk slowly to the middle of the room. I'm dressed elegantly in a royal gown. People compliment my dress and wish me well as I make my way through the crowd." Belle hesitated.

"Yes, go on," Jean-Luc said quietly.

"I make my way to the center of floor, when I suddenly feel very out of place. I know I shouldn't be there so I become distraught and leave the ball abruptly. The guests seem disappointed and urge me to stay."

"Do you think this dream was some type of warning for the Savage's attack?"

Belle shook her head, "No... it's hard to explain, but somehow I think this dream is bigger than the attack."

Jean-Luc squinted his eyes as he focused in on Belle, "Then why do you feel out of place at the ball?"

Belle didn't think she should say anything more. She rose to her feet. "I think I should be going. Hector is going..."

"Belle," Jean-Luc said abruptly. "Please... why do you feel out of place at the ball?"

Belle sat back down, realizing she had already said too much, but knowing there was no turning back. "I'm not myself. I'm someone else, and I know I shouldn't be there. I feel... unwelcomed."

Jean Luc nodded inquisitively as he listened. "Can you explain more?"

"I don't know. The rest of the dream becomes unclear. Something is stopping me from remembering."

Jean-Luc stood to his feet and began pacing the front of his cell. This new bit of information from Belle was quite intriguing. *Open your eyes*, he kept telling himself. He felt as if he was in a room with boxes with locked hinges, each containing a secret waiting to be revealed. He wondered which one to pursue first.

Belle continued, "What are you thinking, Jean-Luc?"

He turned to face her. "All of this is quite interesting. I'm going to need your help, Belle."

"Ok," she said, somewhat confused.

"The ruins north of the kingdom… I'm going to need you to explore them further."

She stood to her feet, "But Michael searched most of the ruins before finding the Savage. He said there wasn't much of consequence besides the upper room where we caught the beast. I don't think there is anything left to be found."

"Was anyone else with Michael while he searched the castle?"

"Well… no, but I'm sure he was thorough in his search and…"

"Don't you think it's a good idea to have another set of eyes exploring the castle? Remember, at the time Michael was not particularly looking for clues. He was looking for the Savage himself."

"Jean-Luc," Belle was bewildered at this point. "Jean-Luc, I don't know what I'm going to be looking for. Michael said there was nothing else of consequence. We found everything."

"Your Majesty," Jean-Luc spoke calmly. "I'm telling you, everything that you know will be challenged. How you perceive things doesn't always correspond to reality."

Belle was getting frustrated at this point, "You keep saying that… but what does it mean? Do you want me to question everything… to become a skeptic about everything I see and think?"

"No... no," Jean-Luc said, staying patient. "I just want you to know for sure what you believe and know to be true. I want you to realize that your initial perception isn't always correct. Sometimes one needs to explore deeper to discover the greater truths about reality as well as the world beyond. I want you to think through what you perceive and what you believe. I want you to ask questions, explore, and find the truth. It will set you free."

Belle looked squarely at Jean-Luc, not breaking her focus. A part of her wanted to ignore this suggestion by Jean-Luc, knowing that this was the riddles Michael warned her of. The urge to walk away was strong, but in the end she knew she couldn't let this suggestion go unexplored. Jean-Luc was responsible for Michael's rescue as well as saving the guests at the ball. She owed it to him to chase this idea.

"I'll wait till morning, then I'll set out with a few soldiers, and ..."

"No, leave tonight. Go alone. You will need to be completely undistracted. Take Gideon or Bernard if you think you need protection, but I think the Savage has begun his master plan. He is setting up for his final attack, and he won't be watching the route north."

"I just don't understand, Jean-Luc. I don't see where all this is going. I don't see how this will end."

Jean-Luc sat down comfortably in his chair. He did not take his eyes off Belle as he spoke, "Belle, all things will be made clear in time. You said you liked to read. Well, imagine this ordeal with the Savage is a book you are reading. I will simply tell you that you are headed for a surprise ending, and not even I know how it will all end."

Belle stood in silence, looking at Jean-Luc. Her mind was clouded. She was not sure what else needed to be said. "Ok, I will leave at once for the ruins. I'll report back in the morning at sunrise."

CHAPTER 14

$\mathcal{T}$he journey to the Northern Ruins proved to be a difficult one. Belle took a more hidden route through the mountain trails. Snow was falling. She was on horseback, wearing a cloak and hood to protect her from the inclement weather. The princess was alone as she had immediately departed. It was about a two-hour ride on horseback to the ruins, and she had already gone most of the way. So far she had seen or heard no one.

Her conversation with Jean-Luc kept playing through her mind. Belle wondered if there was something she was missing in the conversation. She knew he was holding back answers to many of the questions that she had. A part of her also wondered what was the true purpose of this excursion. *What is it I'm looking for?* Belle thought to herself. *How can I widen my gaze? Further open my eyes?*

She arrived at the ruins. The doors of the front gate were still standing open. Belle rode through without stopping. A lone deer was grazing to her left at the far end of the courtyard. Seeing Belle, it stopped briefly to gaze on the princess. Approaching the front doors of the old castle, Belle dismounted and tied her horse to a nearby post. She pulled off her hood and looked around the courtyard. The fresh coat of snow had added a layer of tranquil beauty to the area. Everything was quiet. There was no sign of anyone.

Belle patted her horse gently on the shoulders. "Stay here, boy... I'll be back shortly," she said quietly. She pulled on the front doors of the castle and found they opened easily. A small patch of snow fell from the door and landed on Belle's head. She gently brushed it to the side and entered the castle.

Nothing had changed since she was last there. There were cracks along the walls and ceiling that let in a little moonlight, but overall it was very dark. There were torn tapestries along the wall and on the floor. A few dilapidated rugs lined the walkways. She found it hard to imagine that it was once a majestic palace.

She made her way toward the stairwell leading to the tower where Michael had first encountered the Savage. *If only we could've been here a couple weeks earlier,* she thought to herself. *I wonder if we could've stopped everything then.* The stairwell was dark but light enough for her to see her way up. She watched each step carefully as some of the steps were broken.

Arriving at the top of the steps, she entered the Savage's study. Everything looked the same as they had left it. She and Michael had gone over everything in the room very thoroughly the night of the attack. This is where they had found the layout for Mendolon's castle along with the routine of the knights. The room was mostly empty as all the books and items had been removed.

Belle looked at some of the bookcases along the wall. As an avid reader, she had read many stories where hidden passages could be found behind bookshelves. She pulled the largest one with all her strength. It came tumbling down with a hard crash. Belle backed away as it fell to the ground. Looking up at the wall, she found it empty. She shook her head in frustration. She knew this was not what she was looking for. She was looking for something unseen the first time; something ordinary that meant more than when first seen. Belle thought about going back to the dungeon where she and Bernard had first rescued the prisoners, but in her heart she knew that too was not what she was looking for. *Where did Michael go before the tower? What did he see?*

❧❧

Michael walked the halls of the castle. It was the middle of the night. He knew he probably wouldn't be seen since most of the knights had been spread out among the far reaches of the kingdom trying to find the Savage. Many of the castle's servants were also gone as some were injured in the Winter Ball attack, while others had quit and moved across the sea. Those who were left were kept on essential daytime tasks. None were left on the night shift.

Michael made his way to the steps leading down to the dungeon. He thought about the night when he was captured, when he brought Belle to this same spot. It was the first time she had met the beast. He slowly made his way down the steps as he was still recovering from his injuries from the Savage.

Reaching the bottom of the steps, he made his way to Jean-Luc's cell. He found the beast asleep with a blanket pulled over him. Michael couldn't see his face because he was facing the wall. "Jean-Luc," he said sternly. "Wake up."

Jean-Luc turned over in his bed to face the one calling out to him. He reached over to a nearby nightstand where his glasses were sitting. He brushed his hair out of his eyes as he put his glasses on. "Michael, it's good to see you out of bed and walking," he paused briefly, pulling off his blanket, "but couldn't this have waited till morning? Citizens of Grimdolon usually like to sleep through the night."

"Jean-Luc, you know why I'm here." Michael looked at him very intently. He would be unmoved.

Jean-Luc looked at him with pity in his eyes. He knew Michael had figured out his true mission. "I'm sorry to say, Michael... I've already made great progress in my plans. You've been very kind, but I don't think you can stop me."

He decided to hold nothing back. "Are you trying to overthrow our kingdom?"

Jean-Luc looked at him with a slight bit of disappointment. "Is that what you believe, Michael? After all this time?"

Michael shook his head and turned to look away from Jean-Luc. A mixture of emotions raced through him. A part of him felt used, knowing this beast was using him to accomplish his own objectives. But another part of him felt grateful for all Jean-Luc had done in helping to catch the Savage, as well as rescuing him from the sewer tunnels. He felt trapped in the middle of Jean-Luc's plans.

Jean-Luc broke the silence, "Michael, I'm sorry. This is nothing personal. You have been more than fair with me and nearly treated me like a guest while I've been in this prison. You are truly an honorable knight."

Michael rubbed the back of his neck in deep contemplation. He paced the dungeon floor just a little before turning and looking directly at the beast. He spoke with great intention in his voice, "Jean-Luc, I will stop you, and I will use all my power and everything in my disposal to do so."

Jean-Luc stood to his feet. He felt sorry for the chief knight of Mendolon. "Michael, you are a person of great power and strength, but I must say in this instance... there is nothing you can do."

Michael stepped closer to the prison bars. "Do you realize what is at stake here, Beast? I am the sworn leader of the knights of Mendolon. I have vowed to protect this kingdom and everything in it. I cannot nor will I hold back."

Jean-Luc stepped closer to Michael. "You can't stop me." His voice was raised at this point, "Have you not put everything together? Do you not yet realize that this is bigger than any feud we might be having?"

"You're bluffing, Beast, I will stop you."

"Listen, Michael, I will tell you why you can't stop me," Jean-Luc said, holding out his index finger and pointing it at Michael. "Go to the castle library. Find out why there was a dragon on the eastern border of Mendolon."

"What? Is this another one of your riddles?" Michael said with a bit of confusion.

"No... no more riddles. No more games. Find out why the dragon was between our kingdoms. It will provide the answers you seek."

Michael was deeply confused by this suggestion by Jean-Luc. He hadn't thought much about the dragon hunt the last few months. Trying to catch the Savage had consumed his mind. He wondered why Jean-Luc wanted him to research the history of the dragon now. He didn't understand what it had to do with anything at present. "Tell me what I'm looking for, Jean-Luc."

The beast nodded his head. He spoke calmly, "Find books on Grimdolon's history. Look from our perspective on why the dragon was there. Many things will become clear."

Michael took a deep breath. His brushed his blond hair out of his eyes. He was frustrated with how this conversation was going. He didn't want to chase any more riddles from Jean-Luc, but in the end he knew that after he saved him from the tunnels, he owed him this much. "Jean-Luc, I will do this... but you must assure me this is not one of your tricks."

Jean-Luc closed his eyes as he spoke softly, "Do as I say and your eyes will be opened."

Michael nodded his head as he turned to leave the dungeon. He was eager to get the answers he sought and ready to get to the bottom of this mystery.

"Oh... Michael," Jean-Luc said, stopping him.

"Yes?"

"I want to assure you of one thing," Jean-Luc said, looking directly into Michael's eyes. "We will catch the Savage... no matter what it takes."

Michael nodded once more as he turned to walk away.

❧❧

Belle checked room after room in the ruins. So far she had found nothing but mice droppings and rusty relics from days past. She wondered if Jean-Luc was mistaken in his suggestion to search these ruins again. Michael had been thorough in searching everything. Surely anything remotely significant was taken back to the castle.

She had been searching the castle for two hours now, and she was beginning to feel the darkness of the castle waning on her. Fear was starting to set in. Belle pulled her sword, just in case she met anything. She was thankful for every window on the wall and every crack on the ceiling that let in any light. As she walked the halls of the castle, she found herself singing to bring comfort to herself. "The dark of night can feel so cold, but do not fear I'm often told. The light of day will be here soon, so just walk in the light of the moon."

The princess arrived at the throne room. The large crack in the ceiling let in light from the moon. She noticed the two dilapidated thrones at the far end of the room. Both were made of metal and were rusted. One even had a dead vine draped over the back of it. Belle thought of the kings and queens of old that used to sit there. She tried to imagine the room filled with guests and nobles of the kingdom. It truly would have been a glorious sight to see.

She moved past the thrones and came to the king's personal living quarters. It was obvious that someone had recently dwelt here. She remembered Michael mentioning that he found where the Savage had been staying. Looking around the room, she saw a bed on one side of the room along with a desk. The desk had various books sitting on it; one caught her eye. It was written in Latin and some of its pages were shredded. She checked the floor and could see more of its pages on the floor.

Reaching down, she picked up a few of the pages and looked through them. Even though the Savage had torn some to pieces, it was obvious the pages were from a once treasured book. It was a book about ancient kings and kingdoms of distant lands. There was one section on a page that had notes written on the side. The section was about the king of an ancient land called Babylon. The king's name was Nebuchadnezzar. Belle's Latin was a little rusty but she was able to translate it in her mind as she read. The great, powerful king, Nebuchadnezzar, was struck by God with madness and turned into a beast. He stayed this way seven years before he was turned back into a man. Belle had heard the story once before as a young girl. She found it to be an interesting story, especially since they had a whole kingdom of beasts living to their east.

A note in the margin caught her eye. The handwriting looked rough and abrasive. It read, "Is there a way to wield this power? How can I use this ability against the people of Mendolon?"

Belle was struck by what she'd just read. This is what the Savage wanted to do. He was trying to obtain this type of power to change the people of Mendolon into beasts. *Was this the magic that the people of Mendolon claimed he had?* she thought to herself. Many questions arose, but she realized this was what she was looking for. She quickly gathered all the loose pages she could find. Running as fast as she could, she left the room. She couldn't get back to her castle fast enough.

⇛⇚

Michael sat in the depths of the Mendolon Library surrounded by books and parchments. Many were covered in dust. A single candle lit his way as he read and studied. The more he read, the more questions arose. Growing up, he had always thought it was strange that a dragon was dwelling between the two lands, and seemingly left alone by King Sebastian and the knights. Searching fervently, he looked for anything that might give him a clue as to how the dragon was related to the Savage and Jean-Luc.

He opened a book entitled *History of Grimdolon Under the Rule of King Bayle*. He read about Bayle's early disputes with a young Sebastian of Mendolon, and how they were on the verge of war. He read that multiple times Bayle tried to appease Sebastian in any way he could, but in the end it was all in vain. According to these books, war was inevitable.

Michael kept reading until he found that Sebastian grew tired of his neighbors to the east and decided to strike the heart of Grimdolon. As he kept reading he found the connection Jean-Luc wanted him to find. Michael couldn't believe what he was reading. It all happened right before the dragon's territory was established. He hit the table with his fist and leaned back in his chair. It was all coming together. *How could I have been so blind?* he thought to himself.

Standing to his feet, he put his hands on his head as he realized the implications of what he had just read. As much as it hurt, he knew he would not be able to stop Jean-Luc.

CHAPTER 15

*I*t was midmorning. Michael, Belle, Gideon, and Hector met in the war room of the castle. Belle said it was urgent. She believed she had new information concerning the plans of the Savage. They all came without delay as they were hungry for answers. Even with the soldiers of Mendolon spread out throughout the kingdom, nothing had been seen or heard from the Savage since his attack at the Winter Ball.

Currently they were all gathered around the circular table ready to hear the news of Belle's discovery. She had met with Jean-Luc that morning to get his opinion on everything before reporting it to the others. She hoped it would be well received. "Thank you all for coming so urgently. I want to relay to everyone my findings from last night."

"Last night? Where were you, Your Highness?" Gideon asked, somewhat puzzled.

"I traveled to the Northern Ruins to..."

Hector quickly interrupted, "What? Under whose authority? Don't you know you could have gotten yourself killed?"

"Hector, relax," Belle said. She hadn't slept all night and wasn't in the mood for an argument with him. "Jean-Luc advised me to explore the ruins one last time before we..."

Hector hit his fist against the table, "Is this what we're going to do? Just keep taking advice from that condescending beast... look where it has gotten us so far. I say we put an end to him, and..."

"Let the princess talk," Michael said, interrupting Hector. Michael was the only one seated. Even though his posture was relaxed, he was close to full strength and complete recovery.

"I checked all the rooms again, searching for anything I might find to help us."

"I thought we cleared the castle fairly well," Gideon said, speaking up.

"We did, but Jean-Luc advised me to look again through the castle for anything that would possibly have significance. I searched every room and came up empty... until I came to the throne room." Michael nodded his head as he listened to the princess. The memories from the raid on the ruins came back to him. He remembered checking the area she spoke of.

Belle continued, "Behind the throne room was his personal quarters. He had a number of books he was reading, all on various topics. In the midst of it all I found a book on the history of ancient kings and kingdoms of distant lands." Gideon and Hector leaned in, anxious for what she would say next. "He was reading about the story of an ancient king named Nebuchadnezzar who was struck with animal madness, and turned into a beast for seven years. On the side of one of the pages, the Savage made notes about this incidence. He asked if he could wield this power and use it for his own evil purposes."

"What, that's impossible! ... Or is it?" Gideon asked, almost scared to let the thought pass through his mind.

"Gideon, I was wondering the same thing too. It seems impossible, but..." Belle paused briefly to collect her thoughts.

"What, princess? Tell us," Hector demanded.

Belle bit her lip and took a deep breath before speaking, "Think about the Savage's followers and those that attacked the knights at the ruins. He had an army of beasts."

"I don't think I'm following you, Belle." Gideon commented.

"Have any of us heard about a troop of beasts passing through the northern lands and into our borders? Have any of you heard news from anywhere about Grimdolon beasts leaving their borders to raise terror in our lands?"

They all thought about what Belle was saying. No one had heard any news from anywhere about beasts leaving Grimdolon and traveling west. Because it was a kingdom of beasts, Grimdolon's borders were usually watched closely. Any news of beasts leaving would quickly spread to surrounding nations. Belle continued, "None of us have heard any reports like that, but what we do know is that the Savage has built up a small army with criminals from our own kingdom. He promises them power and opportunity. He gains their trust and then turns them into his own army. I don't know how he does it but..." She hesitated briefly, "I believe he is somehow possessing the power to transform men into beasts."

"You can't be serious, Belle," Gideon said, trying to object. "It just sounds impossible."

"Impossible?" Hector said with anger. He turned to face Gideon, "It's time you stop doubting this beast's powers. Don't you know he worked in the mines of Grimdolon? It seems he has found some sort of resource that gives him this power. We need to take seriously the magnitude of this threat."

"Have you talked to Jean-Luc about it?" Michael asked. Hearing the name of Jean-Luc, Hector shook his head in frustration.

"I talked to him briefly about it, but I thought it would be good for all of us to hear from him." This statement caught the other three by complete surprise. Belle held out her hand toward a far door, and they all turned to see Jean-Luc emerge from it. He tugged on the top of his red jacket to straighten it and then adjusted his glasses as he made his way to the table. He walked with a slight limp.

"Good morning, everyone," he said with a smile.

"How did you get out?" Hector said through gritted teeth. "Last I checked you were still a prisoner in this kingdom."

Belle held up her hand as she spoke, "Hector, please, I let him out. I want you to hear everything from him."

"No… no… I've waited long enough for this beast to bring us the Savage. I'm done with him. He's no longer going to lead me down a stupid rabbit hole."

"But let's give him a chance," Gideon said. "I want to hear what he has to say."

"Give him a chance? Gideon, do you remember why this beast was in our prison in the first place? Do you remember the dragon hunt, and how the princess was almost killed? I should have recommended this beast be killed as soon as I heard about him. This is preposterous."

"Hector, hear him out," Michael demanded.

"No, I've had it. You keep letting him lead you, but I'm finished with all of this." Hector abruptly turned and left the room. The three knights were sad to see him leave. Even though Hector lost control of his emotions on a regular basis, he was very intelligent and a well-equipped strategist in certain areas of battle. Belle thought about pleading with him to stay, but in the end she knew it would be in vain. He slammed the door hard behind him as he left.

The four sat in silence for a few moments before Jean-Luc spoke up, "Maybe he was just a little hungry. I sometimes get a little irritable when I haven't eaten anything in the morning."

"Beast, what do you know about this power the Savage possesses?" Michael asked, seemingly ignoring Jean-Luc's statement about Hector.

Jean-Luc ran his fingers through the bottom of his mane. He thought about how to exactly respond to Michael's question. He looked into Michael's eyes, wondering if he found anything in his research. He wondered how much Michael now knew. "Michael, it is not a question of what I think. I don't know if you would believe if I told you the truth."

"Jean-Luc, no more games," Gideon interrupted.

"Yes, I'm going to tell you honestly and clearly." Jean-Luc briefly looked over at Michael and saw him nod. He knew that Michael believed him. He continued, "I think you are actually asking the wrong question. I think instead of asking if he can turn people into beasts, I would instead be asking where he is going to use this supposed power."

"Where is that?" Gideon asked.

Jean-Luc leaned forward in his seat. "Think about it. How has he used this 'power' so far?"

"Criminals, thieves, those that are seeking to break the law."

"So listen to me, where is the next obvious place he will strike?"

Gideon's eyes got wide as he thought of the answer to the question, "The kingdom's prison east of the castle."

Jean-Luc nodded his head, "Precisely."

Michael rose to his feet, "We will leave at once. Belle, find Bernard. Gideon, get our weapons ready. We will catch this beast before he strikes."

❧

Jean-Luc stepped back into his cell as Belle closed the door behind him. He turned to face her, "Belle, I would advise you to reconsider. I do believe I can help you on this mission."

She brushed her hair out of her eyes. "I know... but I don't know how the townspeople would react if they saw you walking around freely. After the attack at the Winter Ball, some have suspicions that you were somehow connected."

"Belle," he looked at her sincerely. "Most know those rumors are improbable."

She nodded slightly. "I know, but I do think the best thing for our situation is to keep you here while the knights explore the prison."

Jean-Luc took a deep breath, giving up the fight. "I see... you're probably right. I'd hate to stir up any more suspicion."

The princess smiled back at the beast behind the bars of the cell. She was grateful that he understood. "Thanks for your help this morning. I'll come back right away and report to you what we find."

"I look forward to it," Jean-Luc said, returning the smile. He watched as Belle turned to leave the castle dungeon. He stepped closer to the bars to watch her ascend the steps, making sure she was out of sight.

Knowing he was alone, Jean-Luc slowly walked over to his bed and sat down. He looked around the dungeon one last time, double checking that he was alone. He heard no footsteps. He knew he was safe. Looking down at his left hand, he released his grip on the object he held. It was the key to his cell. He had stolen it from Belle when they were in the war room. He was thankful no one saw him take it.

He tried to think of his next move. *I wonder how everything will play out,* he thought to himself. *Finality feels so close now. I cannot fail... no... I will not fail.* He closed his eyes as he tried to settle his nerves.

❧

Belle, Michael, Gideon, and Bernard made their way to Mendolon's main prison. They were on horseback as Michael led the way. All were dressed in their respective armor. Mendolon was unique to other neighboring kingdoms in that they kept most of their prisoners away from the castle. King Sebastian had many people captured over time and wanted them staying away from the castle. The prison was located a few miles east of the castle. Gideon and Bernard especially knew the way well as they had recently taken the prisoners from the tunnels there. It could hold over two hundred men. At this point, it was well over half full. Most were common criminals, some were prisoners from other kingdoms, and others were sympathizers to the Savage.

Arriving at the prison structure, Michael jumped off his horse and quickly tied him to a tree. The other three knights followed suit. The prison was a cold, gray building that contained two hundred small cells for prisoners, along with a kitchen, and a few other miscellaneous storage rooms. In front a small wall established a courtyard for the prisoners where they were occasionally let out for exercise. The dungeon usually had ten soldiers on duty to guard it. One knight was assigned yearly to lead the soldiers who guarded it.

The four knights approached a soldier seated by the front gates of the wall. "Greetings," Michael said sternly. "We are here on official business of Mendolon, and we..." Michael stopped in his tracks. He noticed the soldier looked nervous with his hand on his sword. He was sweating and pale.

Michael dropped to one knee and was face to face with the guard. He spoke softly, but with conviction. "What is happening?" he asked the soldier.

He was young, probably no older than nineteen. He was breathing intensely. The soldier shook as he tried to speak, "H...He...H...He."

"Michael, what happened to him?" Belle asked, hungry for answers.

"Shh... relax," Michael urged the young man. "Can you tell us what's happening in there?"

"He ... he was here. He came last night with a band of followers. They clouded our vision. A band of beasts struck, killing most of our men." Belle, Gideon, and Bernard pulled their swords thinking the Savage was inside.

"You say... he was here."

The soldier nodded his head and spoke very quietly so the other three knights could not hear, "Yes, that's right. He left this morning with a few of his followers. They... They told me not to tell anyone what I saw. They threatened my family."

Michael continued, looking right into the man's eyes. "I'm going to need you to open those doors behind you."

The soldier shook his head, "But he said if I opened the door, he would kill me."

Michael turned briefly to look at the three knights behind him. He then turned back to face the young soldier, "What's your name?"

"Amis," he said, shaking.

"Amis, I'm going to send you away with the three behind me. They are going to make sure he doesn't come for you."

Belle, Gideon, and Bernard were confused by this last statement by Michael. He rose to his feet and turned to face them. "I'm going need you three to head back to the castle right away."

"What? We can't. Not if the Savage is in there," Gideon objected.

"Well, that's the problem. The Savage isn't in there."

"Then... who's in there?" Bernard asked.

"Just some of his followers and probably the released prisoners."

"How do you know this?" Belle questioned.

"By listening to what Amis just said. I'm thinking the Savage came and took over this dungeon last night. He wanted us to come here so he could enter the castle and attack. It's a diversion. You have to get back right away."

"What about you?" Belle asked urgently.

"I'll do my best to make sure these prisoners aren't released into the castle. I'll create a distraction so their eyes are focused on me. You, Gideon, and Bernard can face the Savage without fear of an army of his followers entering the castle."

Bernard quickly objected, "Don't even think about it. I'm staying with you, Michael. You can't do this alone."

"Bernard, after the attack on my house, I know what I'm up against. I'll be ready for anything..."

"It's out of the question. I'm coming with you."

Michael knew there was no sense arguing with Bernard at this point. Time was of the essence. "Ok... stay close to me, and do as I say." Michael turned back to Amis. "Open the door." He ordered the soldier.

Amis slowly got up from his post and approached a large lever on his left. Bernard walked over to help, realizing that the young soldier in his present condition would not have enough strength to pull it down.

As the doors began to open, Belle grabbed Michael's arm. He turned to face her. "Michael, are you sure you are ready for this? Are you sure you're completely healed?"

Michael looked down at Belle's hand on his forearm. "I'm ready, Belle, and I know this is what needs to be done."

"But... but," Belle objected, "What if there's too many of them?"

"There's no time. We have to act now."

Belle wasn't sure what to say. She had been anxious for her friend and partner to return to full strength. She didn't want anything to happen to him. "What if he's turned them all to beasts? What if you can't escape?"

Michael looked directly into her eyes, "If this is the price of freedom for the people of Mendolon, then I'm ready to pay it."

Belle knew there was no use going any further in the conversation. They had had to act fast. "Goodbye, Michael," she said, reaching up and embracing him. He put his arm around her, returning the embrace.

They released each other as the doors began to open. The hinges strained, making a loud groaning sound. Michael quickly ran back to his horse and grabbed a shield he brought with him. Gideon and Belle along with Amis ran to their horses and untied them before mounting. Belle pulled Amis onto her horse with her.

"Be careful," Michael said, giving one last note of caution. "I'm not sure what the Savage is exactly planning... be on your guard at all costs."

"We will, and you likewise," Gideon said, riding off on his horse. Belle followed close behind him. She looked over her shoulder and looked at Michael one last time before he was out of her sight.

"Bernard, are you ready?" Michael asked his fellow knight. Bernard nodded slightly as he pulled his sword. He felt his nerves beginning to take over.

The courtyard was quiet as Michael and Bernard walked through it. It was about thirty yards in length and width. It was empty. They heard or saw no one. The ground was barren as there wasn't much snow. It consisted of mud with a few patches of dead grass scattered on the ground. Michael held his shield with one hand and kept the other hand close to his belt of daggers. He was ready to pull one in an instant.

They approached the doors to the dungeon. There were two small wooden doors with gold rings for opening them. "Open up the doors," Michael said to Bernard.

"Ok," Bernard said with baited breath. Michael held up his shield and pulled a dagger as Bernard reached for the doors. Both men were startled as they heard growling behind them. They quickly turned and looked behind them. They could see no one, but they quickly realized that the courtyard was beginning to fill with a mist.

Michael turned to his fellow knight, "Bernard, it's me they want. I would advise you to head outside and barricade the doors. Be sure no one gets out."

"But... but..."

"Do it, Bernard!" Michael shouted. Bernard quickly left, not wanting to stick around any further.

Michael knew what would be coming soon. He faced it at his house, and he was ready for another fight. He felt fear beginning to creep in, but knew it had to be suppressed. He must not lose.

CHAPTER 16

$\mathcal{T}$he courtyard continued to fill with a heavy mist. Michael held his shield tightly, knowing his vision would soon be completely obstructed. He wondered what he would soon face. He heard the front gates shut and he knew Bernard had safely made it outside. The growls became louder and stronger. He knew a company of beasts were ready to attack.

He heard the sound of bow strings being pulled back. He dropped to one knee and completely hid behind his shield. Arrows began flying by the dozen. The shield clanked with every hit of an arrow. Michael caught sight of a few arrows flying over his head and to his side.

After a few seconds the arrows ceased. Michael stayed behind the shield a little longer just in case a few were still coming. The mist had totally encompassed him, and he had no visual perception of when the next attack was coming. He heard footsteps coming close. He peeked over the top of his shield. Without warning a beast grabbed the top of his shield. Michael pushed the beast off with all his might. He quickly grabbed a dagger off his belt and threw it in the direction of the beast. He heard the beast yell out in pain.

Suddenly another growl came from his left. He blindly threw another in the direction of the growl. As he heard that beast yell out in pain, he heard another beast on his right. He quickly drew his sword and swiped in the direction of the beast. Though he couldn't see where he struck, he knew he had made contact with his enemy.

He was then completely caught off guard by the beast in front pushing him into a wall. His back hit hard against the wall as his sword fell to the ground. The beast grabbed Michael around the neck and lifted him off the ground. Michael tried punching him in the stomach before feeling the handle of a dagger he had implanted. Michael grabbed the handle of the dagger and pushed it further into the beast. The beast screamed out in pain as he released Michael. Back on his feet, Michael spun around and kicked the beast in the face. The beast fell further into the mist, out of Michael's sight.

A few more beasts approached from his left and his right. He quickly threw daggers and braced himself for any further attack that might come his way. He wondered how long this would last. *Will the mist ever clear up?* he thought to himself. *Were most of the prisoners turned into beasts? How many would he need to fight off?*

Another beast approached him from the front. Michael quickly picked up his sword and engaged the beast. The beast grabbed the blade of his sword and then gave him a fierce head-butt. Michael took a step backwards, recovering from the hit. "No fear," he whispered to himself. He grabbed a dagger from his belt and stuck it in the beast, before pulling back his sword and taking a swipe. He wasn't sure where he hit the beast, but he knew he had done substantive damage.

He was caught off guard when he heard a familiar sound in the distance. It was the creaking of the gates. They were opening. He then heard another beast approaching on his right. He threw a dagger in that direction, hoping it would make contact. He thought of Bernard out front, *I hope he's ready for what he may face.*

Michael's mind quickly went back to the task at hand as he could hear beasts approaching from every direction. He whispered to himself, "Stay alert, Michael... no fear."

❧ ❦

Belle and Gideon arrived at the castle. They had dropped off Amis with a soldier who was guarding the markets. The princess ordered him to protect Amis whatever the cost. They made their way through the gates and into the castle's courtyard. Everything was quiet.

Looking to her left, Belle saw a castle guard lying on the ground, completely motionless. She knew the Savage had struck. "Quick, let's get inside." Belle and Gideon went straight through the castle's front door. They found the inside in disarray. Chairs were knocked over. Glass from broken windows was scattered about. It was obvious a fight had occurred.

Looking around the room, Belle found another wounded soldier lying on the ground. She ran to him and found that he was breathing and conscious. "Gideon," she called to her fellow knight. Gideon quickly joined her. They could tell instantly that he was hurt badly. Belle knelt down close to the man.

"What happened?" she asked urgently.

"The Savage came with a few men. They struck before we could realize what was going on," the man said, holding tightly to a wound on the right side of his chest. "They struck me first, and I decided to play dead. I knew we had no chance."

"How many were there?" Gideon asked.

"I guess he had about five men with him," the soldier winced in pain.

"Where is Hector?" Belle asked.

"He... he... was taken to the dungeon, along with another soldier."

Belle couldn't help but think of Jean-Luc. She wondered if the Savage knew that he had helped rescue Michael from his hideout in the tunnels. The Savage somehow knew lots of information about the kingdom and the castle. He had to know at this point Jean-Luc was helping to find him. Belle quickly reached for her bow, fearing the worst. "Gideon, we must hurry. I fear what the Savage has already found."

❧

Bernard heard the gates begin to open. He quickly ran against the door and tried with all his might to keep it from opening. He pushed hard but quickly found that it was in vain. Backing up a few feet, he pulled his sword and held it firmly in one hand, his shield in the other. When the doors began to open a little more he could see a man, a prisoner, squeezing through.

"Stop, proceed no more!" Bernard shouted. The man took no notice of Bernard as he was seizing his opportunity for freedom.

As the man squeezed himself free, he ran from the gate toward Bernard. Bernard lifted his shield and hit the criminal in his upper body, knocking him to the ground. Bernard quickly realized that another man had come through the gates. "Stop!" Bernard yelled as the prisoner ran past him. He turned to see another man freeing himself from the gate. Bernard lifted his shield and struck that man in the head. He fell to the ground unconscious.

Bernard then pointed his sword at another man coming from the gates, but he quickly realized that it was in vain as men began to pour from the prison gates. He engaged a few more of the men before being knocked down by a large prisoner. He fell on his back and quickly rolled sideways to the edge of a wooded area. Fearing for his life, he jumped to his feet, ready to engage his attacker. He looked up and realized that the men weren't ready to fight. Freedom was their first priority.

As the last man ran past Bernard, he looked through the gates. He saw the misty fog in the courtyard. He looked closely as the fog was beginning to thin out. He could see Michael in the mist of it fighting off two beasts with his sword in hand. While he was watching, a beast grabbed Michael from behind and tried to choke him with his forearm. Without hesitation Michael flipped the beast over his shoulders and threw him into another beast in front of him. Michael then jumped back as two other beasts were approaching.

Bernard knew he had no time to waste. He quickly picked up his sword and gripped it firmly. Even though he was filled with fear, he knew he had to help his friend. "For Mendolon!" he yelled as he ran into the dungeon's courtyard. The mist was clearing even more. He could see the beasts attacking Michael. He slashed one on the back as he came near. Bernard turned to his left and fought with another beast.

The beasts were distracted by their new opponent. This gave Michael just enough time to gather himself and go on the offensive. Picking up his shield, he charged toward one beast and knocked him over with the force of the shield. As soon as the beast was on the ground, Michael delivered a forceful blow to his cheek bone. He could hear a loud crack.

Standing up, another beast approached him, trying punch him in his midsection. Michael blocked the punch and delivered his own jab to the beast's stomach. The beast hunched forward as Michael grabbed the back of his head and rammed it into his knee. The beast fell backward, but swiftly tried to get back on his feet. As the beast was looking up, he saw the right boot of Michael coming toward his head.

The impact was significant and the beast fell to the ground unconscious.

Michael looked over to see the last beast holding Bernard against the ground as they fought. Bernard held the beast's arm back as the beast was trying to plunge a knife into his chest. Looking down, Michael saw the handle of a dagger protruding from a fallen beast. Michael quickly reached for the dagger, pulling it from the beast. He promptly threw it toward the beast's hand. He accuracy was flawless as it stuck through the beast's hand. He dropped the knife as he yelled out in pain. Bernard pushed the beast off himself and reached for his sword. The beast was at his mercy.

Bernard was about to strike when Michael yelled out, "Stop!" Bernard halted, but still held the beast at knife point.

Michael walked over to where Bernard was standing. Bernard breathed heavily as blood ran from his head. The beast was on his knees also breathing heavily. Without the mist, he looked much less intimidating. "I want to hear what he has to say," Michael said calmly.

The beast spat in his direction, "I'll never talk to you."

"Beast, I'm in no mood for mindless banter. Start talking now or I'll have Bernard run you through."

The beast snarled in return. "You would never dare, Michael de Bolbec," the beast said condescendingly. "I know who you are, Chief Knight of Mendolon. I know you would never hurt someone at your mercy."

Listening to the beast, Michael could tell there was something different about this beast. In the past he had met beasts from Grimdolon, and he could tell this one was altogether different.

Bernard held his sword closer to the throat of the beast. "Talk, Beast. Did he turn you into the beast too?" The beast looked at Bernard with a somewhat strange look in his eyes. He looked puzzled but somewhat intrigued at Bernard's question.

Michael looked closely at this beast. He could tell something strange was going on. He was curious as to what this beast knew. He turned away from the beast and Bernard, trying to gather his thoughts. He rubbed the back of his neck as he wondered what to do. *What does this beast know? How can I make him talk?* He paced back in the direction of his sword.

He reached down to pick up his weapon, when something caught his eye. It was the beast he had knocked to the ground and punched in the cheekbone. He remembered something peculiar in his scuffle with him. He walked over to the fallen beast in order to get a closer look. Instantly he could tell something was unusual with this beast. He stooped down to get a closer look.

"Michael, what are you doing?" Bernard called out.

A few seconds passed as Michael examined the beast. Bernard started to grow impatient, "Michael... what is it?"

"I'm... I'm not sure," Michael said examining the body closely. He reached out to touch the beast's face. *Something's not right*, he thought to himself.

❧

Belle and Gideon hid in the shadows as they made their way further through the castle. Their weapons were ready in case they were ambushed. They were heading in the direction of the dungeon. Gideon led the way as Belle covered him with her bow. They now stood before two large doors that led into the war room. Gideon pressed his ear against the door. He listened carefully.

"I hear a few men talking," he whispered.

"How many do you think?" Belle asked.

"Not sure. I'd say let's strike fast. If there's too many, let's retreat back through these doors."

Belle nodded in approval. She got her bow ready. Gideon stood in position and grabbed the door handle. Gideon counted slowly, making sure Belle was ready, "One... two... three!"

With great speed Gideon threw open the door as Belle stuck her bow inside. She let an arrow fly at the first man she saw. It penetrated his shoulder. There were five men in the room, and they all seemed caught off guard by what they saw. Without wasting any time, Belle grabbed another arrow and let it fly -- this time into one of the men's legs. He fell to the ground in pain.

A couple of the Savage's men dove behind some of the large wooden chairs, while another grabbed a shield and ran toward Gideon and Belle. His sword was pulled. Belle quickly dropped to the ground and swept his legs out from under him. The man fell to the ground, dropping his sword. Belle stooped down and delivered a hard hit with the handle of her sword. He was unconscious.

Gideon entered the room with his sword drawn. He started fighting the man with an arrow in his arm. The man proved to be no competition as his main fighting arm was injured. Gideon quickly knocked his sword out of his hands before running him through with his own sword.

Belle picked up the shield her opponent had dropped and ran to the other side of the table, looking for the men who hid from her arrows. She was looking to her left when one of the men jumped from her right side with a swipe of his sword. Belle jumped to the side as the sword cut into the large wood table in the center of the room. Belle quickly hit the man with the armor around her forearm. The man fell to the side as Gideon was coming forward to help. Gideon delivered another blow to the man's head, one that seemed to knock him out.

Turning and looking at the steps on the far end of the room, Belle could see a shadowy figure run up the stairwell. She knew it was the Savage. Curiously he had two cloth bags in his hands. She turned and saw Gideon with his back turned, fighting with the last of the Savage's men. She knew this was her chance to face the beast that had been terrorizing the land of Mendolon for too long. She gripped her sword tight as she ran toward the steps.

Belle knew these steps very well as they led to the tower of her bedroom. The Savage would be cornered and trapped once he reached the top. She ran as quickly as she could. The stairs were a little dark as only one of the torches was lit. She considered grabbing it, wondering if she could use it in fighting the Savage. Running past it, she figured it would be more of a liability in fighting him.

She reached the top of the steps and found her bedroom door open. She grabbed her bow along with an arrow and pointed it into the room. Belle slowly entered, knowing there was nowhere else for the beast to be. It was quiet. Looking around the room, she saw no one. It was empty. Taking another look, she did notice that her window was open. She wondered if maybe the Savage was scaling the outside of the tower.

The princess slowly made her way toward the window. Her breathing was heavy. She tried to steady her arm as she was shaking just a little. Fear began to set in. She brushed a few strands of hair out of her face as she proceeded. She wondered how far down the beast could have made it in such a short amount of time. A breeze blew in from the window as she arrived at it. She slowly peeked over the edge of her window sill and saw... no one. *Where could he be?* She thought to herself.

It was without warning that the room began to fill with a mist. Belle tried to run toward her door, but then heard it abruptly shut. She knew that it was too late. She could see that the Savage had been hiding above her in the rafters of her room. He was wearing a black cloak that covered his head and cast a shadow over his face. Before she could shoot an arrow, she saw him jump down into the mist. She lost sight of him. Her perception was diminished.

The Savage let out a heinous laugh as he began to speak, "Ha, ha, ha... You fell right into my trap, Your Highness. I was waiting for this moment. There is no more escape."

"What do you want?" Belle said with fear.

"Hmmm... I want madness in Mendolon. I want chaos. I want the power of fear."

Belle held out her sword. "Show yourself, Beast!" she shouted.

The mist began to clear just slightly as she heard the Savage speak, "As you wish, Your Majesty."

Belle looked around, trying to find him, wondering where he went. "Show yourself!" she shouted again.

It was then without warning that Belle felt a rope around her neck. The Savage was behind her pulling it tight. Belle dropped her bow and grabbed the rope with both hands, trying to give herself a little air. The Savage pulled tighter as he threatened her, "You are going to be my spectacle. The whole kingdom is going to see your death... ha, ha, ha... and they will never recover from the fear that will ensue."

The Savage began pulling her toward her window. She now knew why it was open. She kept trying to fight, but was quickly losing air. Belle dropped to her knees as everything started to become blurry. It was then in that moment that she thought she heard another voice coming from the doorway... the voice of Jean-Luc Pascal.

❦

Gideon entered the dungeon to find Hector imprisoned along with another knight. Both looked to be injured. "Hector," Gideon called out, approaching their cell. "Are you all right?"

"No, of course we're not all right. The Savage has taken over the castle." Hector said, irritated by the question.

"Yes, I know," Gideon responded, finding the right key to open the cell. "Belle and I defeated his men. They were stationed in the war room. They looked like they were planning... or waiting for reinforcements."

"Yes, you fool, the Savage has released the prisoners from the dungeon. They are coming for us. There is no time to lose. We have to seal the front gates. Where is the princess?"

"I'm not sure," Gideon responded. "I think she ran after the Savage while we were fighting."

"Cursed!" Hector snarled angrily, "Open these doors. We must act quickly."

The doors to the cell opened up. Hector and the knight briskly walked out of their cell. Grabbing the keys, Gideon ran further down the dungeon with the keys in his hands.

"Where are you going?" Hector yelled out.

"I'm getting Jean-Luc. I'm sure he can help us in this..." Gideon stopped mid-sentence as he stood in front of Jean-Luc's cell. He was surprised to find the doors open, and Jean-Luc gone.

CHAPTER 17

The Savage loosened his grip on Belle when he saw Jean-Luc. He clinched his teeth at the beast standing in the doorway. "You!" the Savage yelled out in disbelief.

"Release her!" Jean-Luc shouted.

"You're supposed to be injured," the Savage said angrily.

Jean-Luc held out a short blade he had taken from the war room. "Sorry to disappoint you," he said, sarcastically. "I knew you were watching us closely, so I figured I needed to fake an injury to get a step ahead of you." Jean-Luc took a step further into the room. "Now as I was saying... Release her immediately," he said firmly.

The Savage growled through his teeth before speaking, "You can't stop me, you Grimdolon filth. I know who you really are."

Jean-Luc held up his blade and took a step a closer to his enemy, trying to provoke him to a fight. The Savage laughed sinisterly from under his hood. He released Belle completely and pushed her to the ground. As she hit the ground hard, she let out a gasp of air. The world around her was still a blur. The Savage's attention was now fully on Jean-Luc Pascal. He methodically took off his hood to reveal his vicious complexion. He was by no means a typical beast from Grimdolon. He looked to be some type of werewolf with ferocious razor sharp teeth. His eyes were a strong red color that couldn't be missed. The very sight of him had struck fear in the hearts of the people of Mendolon. Jean-Luc, on the other hand, was not intimidated by what he saw.

The Savage had a long thin blade of his own that he quickly unsheathed. As he walked toward Jean-Luc as he spoke menacingly, "This is going to bring me great pleasure putting an end to you."

Jean-Luc braced for an attack, trying to predict his enemy's first move. The Savage quickly sprang toward Jean-Luc, swiping his blade downward. Jean-Luc held up his own blade to block the attack. The Savage then pulled back and quickly took another swipe. Jean-Luc blocked again before moving against the wall. The Savage pointed his blade forward in order to run him through. Jean-Luc quickly rolled off the wall and unto the floor. The Savage turned and took a swipe downward. Jean-Luc swiftly blocked again.

Jean-Luc tightly held his blade as the Savage continued to push down hard against his blade. Jean-Luc groaned as he held his blade. He knew he had to do something quickly. The Savage was overpowering him. In one quick motion he moved his head out of the path of the Savage's sword and released his own blade. The Savage's sword hit hard against the ground. With all his strength Jean-Luc delivered a punch directly into the left eye area of the Savage. The Savage reared back, somewhat stunned from the blow.

Knowing this was his chance to attack, Jean-Luc pushed his enemy off and rolled to deliver another punch. The Savage blocked Jean-Luc's punch, catching it in the palm of his hand. The Savage then delivered a malicious head butt to Jean-Luc. He fell back a little before the Savage delivered a quick punch to his cheekbone. "Aww!" Jean-Luc screamed out in pain.

The Savage quickly jumped on top of Jean-Luc and delivered another blow to the other side of his head. He reared back again to deliver another punch, but Jean-Luc blocked it before it landed. Jean-Luc didn't have time to react before the Savage delivered another punch with his other fist. The Savage was now moving at great speed and was determined not to let go of Jean-Luc before he was lifeless.

Belle was starting to regain her bearings just a little. Her head hurt severely from the lack of oxygen. She could see the two beasts fighting, and Jean-Luc was on the defensive. With the little bit of strength she had, she removed the rope around her neck. She breathed heavily. "Jean-Luc... Jean-Luc," she mumbled, afraid for her friend. She wondered if this would be the last time she would see him.

≪ঞ৯

Michael and Bernard raced on horseback back toward the castle. They knew they had to move quickly. They figured out that many of the released prisoners were on their way to the castle to assist the Savage. Being just a few hundred yards away from the castle, they started to pass many of the prisoners who were running toward the castle. Some they even knocked down as they passed by. "Careful, Bernard!" Michael yelled as a prisoner fell into the path of Bernard's horse. Bernard moved to the side of the road as he raced past.

Seeing a group of prisoners blocking their path, Michael shouted back at Bernard, "Follow me." He quickly turned off the road and took a path north of the castle, going uphill.

"Where are we going?" Bernard shouted back.

"I'm going to cut through the forest, close to where Belle trains."

"Are you sure that will give us enough time before the prisoners reach the castle?"

Michael took a deep breath, hoping his timing was correct. "I guess we'll have to see."

The men raced through the forest as fast as their horses could go. They jumped over fallen logs and ducked under low branches. Bernard was starting to feel a little sick from the rough journey. He had always been prone to motion sickness. Michael remained focused as he knew another fight would ensue when they reached the gate. Out of habit, he found himself checking his daggers. Unfortunately, his belt was empty as he had used all of them on the beasts at the prison. He knew he would be relying solely on his sword in this upcoming fight.

They continued past Belle's training area. Bernard couldn't help but think about training with Belle. He hoped the princess was ok. He was curious as to how she and Gideon were faring inside the castle. After their fight at the prison, he wondered what type of trickery the Savage might be employing. He wouldn't put anything past their enemy at this point.

The castle came into view and the knights could see about a dozen prisoners coming within a few feet of the open gate. Being uphill from the gates, Michael quickly sped down toward it. A couple of the prisoners saw Michael coming toward them and dispersed, not wanting to risk a fight with him.

Reaching the men, Michael jumped off his horse and onto a man, tackling him to the ground. With great speed he leapt back onto his feet. Another prisoner was just past him, entering the gates. Michael grabbed him by the back of his shirt collar and pulled him out of the gates and onto the ground. Another prisoner took a swing at him. He easily dodged the punch before delivering a fierce punch straight to the man's nose. The prisoner clumsily fell to the ground.

A few of the other prisoners approached Michael ready for the fight. Michael pulled his sword and held it out to the men. They all stopped in their tracks, knowing Michael's ability with the sword. Half of the men had previously been captured by him. It was at that time that Bernard arrived, quickly dismounted his horse, and ran to Michael's side.

"What's our plan, Captain?" Bernard asked nervously.

"No fear," Michael answered back, not taking his eyes off the men.

The prisoners began to form a semicircle around the two knights. They had no weapons. Michael figured they were going to try to lead him away from the gate in order to get the others into the castle. He knew he had to keep the men out, no matter what. "I'm sorry, men, but the only way you're getting into the castle is through me," Michael said, undeterred.

The men began to step closer to the two knights. Michael clinched his sword tightly as he looked into the eyes of his attackers. He hoped Bernard would be fine in the midst of this fight.

The prisoners were just a few feet away when Michael heard a loud creaking sound. He glanced behind him to see the doors of gates closing behind him. He looked back at the prisoners and saw they were a little confused. A few rushed toward Michael and Bernard. Michael quickly delivered a fierce kick to the face of one of the prisoners. The man spun and fell to the ground. Michael gathered his bearing and in an instant held up his sword to the next prisoner approaching him. The man stopped instantly. Michael could see the man eyeing the closing gates of the castle. "Don't even think about it," Michael whispered to him.

The creaking of the gates quieted down as the doors shut. The remaining prisoners looked in despair, knowing they were too late. They all looked at each other, wondering what to do next. The man with Michael's sword by his neck began to slowly step back. Michael and Bernard held steady as they wondered what would happen.

It was without warning that one by one the men began to run away from the two knights. They ran in different directions, knowing they had to escape before being put back into prison. Bernard began running toward them. Michael reached out and grabbed his arm. "No, Bernard," he said calmly.

"But I think we can catch a few before they get too far," he said, trying to pull away from Michael's grip.

"Our first priority is the security of those in the castle. Belle and Gideon may be…"

"Michael!" A voice called out from on top of the wall.

He was happy to see Gideon at the top. "Gideon! What's going on inside?"

"You were right. The Savage *is* here. Belle and I defeated a number of his men. I found Hector imprisoned in the dungeon."

Michael was happy to hear a little bit of good news. He was curious for more information. "What of Belle?"

Gideon shook his head, "I'm not sure. I lost her sometime in the fight with the Savage's men. I think she went after him. Hector's looking for her now."

Michael took a deep breath, hoping the princess was okay. He feared for her life.

≈⁓

The Savage continued to strike Jean-Luc as hard as he could. Occasionally Jean-Luc could block one of the punches, but the Savage was relentless. The blows kept coming. Blood ran from Jean-Luc's head as it soaked his fur. The Savage growled as he delivered each punch.

As he began to grow a little tired, he let up from his punches and grabbed Jean-Luc's neck and squeezed it tightly. "You thought you could stop me, Jean-Luc." The Savage snarled as he spoke. "You gave up so much, and now you will die in this forsaken tower." Jean-Luc grabbed the Savage's hands and pulled them away just slightly, giving himself a little bit of air. The Savage grabbed the collar of his red coat and quickly pulled his upper body up and slammed him back down against the floor. His head hit hard.

The world went blurry to Jean-Luc. His strength was giving out. The Savage patiently stood to his feet and delivered a kick to his midsection. He looked to his right a few feet and caught sight of his sword that he dropped earlier in the fight. He smiled as he walked calmly to the spot and picked it up. He was ready to put an end to Jean-Luc.

Belle could see everything transpiring in front of her. She tried to pick herself up, but found she had not fully recovered. She knew that any attempt to fight with the Savage would be in vain. Trying to think of something quick, she looked over to see her bow lying on the ground. She wondered if she had enough strength to fire an arrow. Reaching for it, she picked it up and notched an arrow in the bow string. She slowly rose to her knees.

Jean-Luc looked over at Belle and saw what was transpiring. He knew that any arrow shot would not penetrate deep into the Savage's flesh. Desperately he looked around the room for any solution to defeating the Savage. As the Savage was getting close to Jean-Luc, he spotted something curious beside Belle. It was a cloth bag about a foot in diameter. It looked to be completely filled. Jean-Luc knew it belonged to the Savage, and he knew what was in it. He quickly thought of a plan.

The Savage was now standing over Jean-Luc with his sword in hand. He held it high with the blade pointed down. Jean-Luc knew he had to act fast. He quickly yelled out toward Belle, "Belle, stab the bag with the arrow!" The Savage was caught off guard by Jean-Luc's statement. He looked toward Belle and could see she was right beside his cloth bag.

It took Belle just a moment to process what was occurring. She looked to her side to see the bag lying beside her. "No!" The Savage yelled out. Belle quickly stuck her arrow into the bag and pulled it out. A small hole formed in the bag, and a white powder slowly trickled from it.

Seeing the Savage was distracted, Jean-Luc lifted his foot and kicked the Savage in the stomach. He fell back a few feet, still not taking his eyes off of Belle. "Shoot him, Belle!" Jean-Luc yelled out urgently.

Belle pulled back on the bow string and aimed her arrow. "No... don't do it!" the Savage yelled out, pleading.

Not persuaded by the Savage's plea, Belle released the arrow. It swiftly flew through the air and penetrated the Savage's left thigh. He fell to his knees and screamed out in horror.

Jean-Luc rose to his feet as the Savage moaned and groaned in pain. He grabbed at the arrow and pulled it out. He fell to the ground and started grabbing at his head. His mind seemed to be in pain. Jean-Luc slowly walked over to where he was struggling. He reached down and pulled him up, grabbing something on his head and pulling hard. Jean-Luc then threw him back onto the ground, where he continued to scream.

Belle looked at the decrepit figure on the ground and saw the body of the Savage... but with the face of a man. She looked back up at Jean-Luc a little confused at what was transpiring. He then threw a mask down on the ground close to where the man was struggling. Looking closely at the man, Belle could see that it was the thief that approached her at the Winter Ball.

Taking a deep breath, Jean-Luc spoke confidently, "There never was a Savage... just cheap tricks and manipulation."

"Aww!" The thief groaned as he grabbed at his head.

Jean-Luc continued, "The mist that he used was made from a strong hallucinogenic powder found in the mines of Grimdolon. The same powder that just entered his blood stream." Belle looked over at the cloth bag again to see a little bit of powder coming from the hole in it.

Jean-Luc brushed dust off his clothes as he continued, "I caught a hint of the powder's taste at Michael's house after the attack. Then after examining the cluster of boar's hair on the door frame, I knew that he was altering our perception even more than I first realized. I knew that the fur was not from an authentic Grimdolon beast."

"Help me!" the struggling man yelled out.

Jean-Luc now directed his speech toward their enemy, "The capture of Remy threw me off a little but I quickly realized that he was the only true beast working for you. He was simply brought along as a decoy that could later be disposed of. At the Winter Ball it was even more apparent that you only had hired criminals and thieves, not beasts. The beasts were only the product of hallucinations and these foolish masks." Jean-Luc took a step closer to his enemy before continuing, "The masks your men wore helped to exaggerate the fear in people's minds while also providing protection from the hallucinations." Belle couldn't believe what she was hearing. She didn't know what to think or feel. It was all truly mind boggling.

Jean-Luc cleared his throat as he spoke further, "Now, Dominique, it is great to see you as you truly are. I heard rumors about you in Grimdolon and your plans to prey on the fears of others. I just never figured that you were actually a man."

Dominique Delano rose to his feet. His eyes watered as he pulled his hair and shook from the pain of the substance in his body. Jean-Luc calmly took a step closer to the struggling man. "I'm sorry to have to tell you this, Dominique, but I am no hallucination. I am truly real... not simply a product of perception."

It was then that Jean-Luc took another step toward Dominique and let out the fiercest growl he could. Dominique screamed in fear as the substance in his body was exaggerating everything. He grabbed his ears and stumbled backward, tripping over his own feet. Seeing him trip, Belle reached out to grab him... but it was too late. Dominique fell backwards out of the open window of the tower. He screamed in terror as he fell.

After standing in silence for just a moment, Jean-Luc ran to the window. He looked forty feet down to the ground and saw Mendolon's enemy lying at the bottom of the tower, not moving. It was almost as if he couldn't believe his eyes. For the past six months he had been following clues, looking for answers in the search for this madman, and now it was all complete. The Savage was truly defeated.

He now directed his attention completely to Belle. He slowly walked over to where she was resting. She sat with her head against the wall, still trying to regain her composure. Jean-Luc simply sat down beside her and put his arm around her to comfort her. She rested her head on his shoulder as she was completely exhausted. "Is he gone?" she asked, closing her eyes.

Jean-Luc simply nodded his head before speaking softly, "Yes... he is gone... he is gone."

They both felt like a weight had been lifted off of their shoulders. The Savage had consumed their attention for the last six months and now he was gone. Belle nearly fell asleep, resting on Jean-Luc's shoulder. Feeling a sense of compassion and sympathy for the princess, he gently stroked her soft brown hair. He knew that the others should be informed of the Savage's demise as soon as possible... but for right now he was content to just sit with Belle.

CHAPTER 18

*B*elle walked the markets of Mendolon. It was late in the evening. The sun had set a half hour ago. The markets were filled with children laughing, music playing, and the vast purchasing of foods and gifts. The citizens of the kingdom rejoiced in their newfound freedom. Belle took great pleasure in this sight.

A week had passed since Dominique Delano fell from the tower and any fear of *the Savage* was completely eradicated. Word spread quickly as people soon discovered that the Savage was simply an elaborate scheme from a madman. Any following he had was dispersed. Many of his men along with the escaped prisoners were either hiding throughout the kingdom or trying to escape to distant lands. Many of the knights were commissioned with the task of tracking them down and bringing them back into custody. So far about a third of them had been recaptured.

A group of young girls ran toward Belle, excited to see their princess. The youngest was in front and couldn't have been more than six years old. Approaching Belle, the young girl held up a purple flower for the princess. Belle smiled as she took the flower. It was obviously an artificial imitation as a real flower at this time of the year would have been an expensive gift.

"Thank you so much," Belle said as cheerfully as she could.

The group of girls stood silent and smiled as they were a little too shy to speak at the moment. Belle held the flower up to her nose and pretended to smell it. "Mmm... smells wonderful," Belle said, trying to the make the girls laugh. They giggled slightly at the princess's humor.

Belle then stuck the flower in her hair to show her appreciation. The girls smiled broadly at Belle's gesture. She continued, "Be safe, girls, and again, thank you for the flower."

"Goodbye," the oldest girl said. Each of the girls gave the princess a hug before turning and running back to their parents. Belle appreciated these little moments, and more than ever was thankful that there was peace and safety in Mendolon.

Belle continued to walk the streets as it was starting to get late. She greatly enjoyed the music and the scenery, but her mind kept going back to her castle. She thought of her friend, Jean-Luc Pascal, still locked away deep in the dungeon. She had visited him every day since the fight with Dominique Delano. He had sustained a few injuries in the fight, but was quickly recovering. Belle, Michael, and Gideon had made sure the townspeople knew that a beast from Grimdolon named Jean-Luc was instrumental in defeating the Savage. This helped to greatly lessen any animosity the people of Mendolon had toward Grimdolon to the east.

Belle had hoped Jean-Luc would have been easily released after assisting the knights in defeating the Savage. She felt this was an easy decision and should have happened right away. Unfortunately, Hector was adamantly against it. King Sebastian had not yet arrived back in Mendolon, and Hector wanted to wait for an official word from the king before this prisoner was released. Belle felt this was a great injustice. After all Jean-Luc had done, she thought he should be rewarded, not imprisoned.

The princess looked back at her castle. She felt sadness for her friend sitting all alone in the prison while the people of Mendolon rejoiced and found rest in their freedom. She knew she had to do something. Belle cared for him greatly. He deserved better than this.

⊱⊰

Jean-Luc sat in his cell trying to read a book under lantern light. It was approaching midnight. He found sleep difficult these days as he was greatly distracted amidst everything that had happened. He was thankful Dominque Delano was defeated, but was disappointed in himself that he hadn't stopped him earlier. He wished he would have put some of the clues together sooner, and maybe prevented some of the chaos and loss of life that had ensued.

The beast put down his book and took off his glasses. He rubbed the bridge of his nose as he closed his eyes. He had lived in this cell close to nine months and he had become comfortable in it. He was confident he would be freed soon. He just hoped it would be sooner rather than later. Hopefully by then his last objective could be accomplished. He had no doubt he was on the right path. Things seemed to be going as planned, he just hoped...

Jean-Luc's thoughts were broken as he heard footsteps coming down the steps. He had heard this sound enough to know exactly who it was. He quickly stood to his feet and put on his red coat. He couldn't help but smile as he realized everything was coming together.

The princess of Mendolon came into view. She was dressed in her princess armor and seemed to be in a hurry. "Good evening, Belle. This is a pleasure to see you as it is quite late."

She didn't make eye contact with Jean-Luc, but rather was focused on unlocking the door to his cell. "I'm setting you free, Jean-Luc."

"Your Majesty… are you sure you want to do this? Surely your father hasn't approved this yet."

"I don't care what my father says," Belle said as she opened the door. "It's not right for you to be locked away in this dungeon. Not after all you've done for us."

"But they will know you set me free," Jean-Luc said as he stepped out of his cell.

"Let them do as they will. Come! Follow me. Many of the knights and soldiers are watching the southern routes as the prisoners are trying to escape from Mendolon. We must take the northern road just north of Dragon Waste. We must hurry."

Belle led Jean-Luc out of the castle. Two horses were waiting for them outside the castle gates. Jean-Luc quickly mounted and then turned to Belle behind him. "Belle, you'll have to lead me through these roads. I don't know them well."

Belle grabbed her saddle and quickly mounted. They galloped away under nightfall.

∽᷅᷄᷅

Jean-Luc and Belle rode swiftly into the night. More than two hours passed as they rode over hills and through small valleys. Their horses kept up a steady speed as they continued east. They saw no one as they rode under the cover of darkness. At times Belle had to stop and recollect on which trail to take. She was thankful for the occasional trail sign that helped direct them.

Jean-Luc followed closely behind Belle. The wind blew gently against his face as he rode. It refreshed and awakened him. He was constantly examining the terrain as he rode, trying to get his bearings. The scenery was gorgeous. He hadn't seen much of the outside world the last nine months and now he now found himself more than ever enjoying the scenery. Occasionally Belle would point ahead, instructing him on which direction they were going.

As the border of Grimdolon got close, Jean-Luc's horse passed Belle's. He sped ahead. Belle followed suit. She wondered what was going on. It was then without warning that Jean-Luc turned off to his right on a thin trail Belle could hardly see. They ascended steadily. The horses slowed their pace as they continued to elevate.

They reached the top of a large hill and Jean-Luc's horse came to a stop. He quickly dismounted and tied his horse to a nearby tree. Belle was confused by the ordeal, "Jean-Luc, what are you doing? We are almost over the border."

"I want to show you something, Belle," he said quietly. Belle was a little confused as she dismounted and walked her horse over to a nearby tree opposite to where Jean-Luc was standing.

As she walked over to where Jean-Luc was standing, she took notice of her surroundings. She could see clearly as it was a beautiful night with the stars shining brightly. They were on a grassy plain on the top of this hill. There was a lone apple tree close to Jean-Luc. She could see he was overlooking the kingdom of Grimdolon in the distance. The castle could easily be seen as lights shone out from it. Only a few other lights could be seen as most of the citizens of the land were sleeping.

"Isn't it beautiful?" Jean-Luc said as Belle came close to him.

It took Belle a moment to process what he said. She was still a little confused by this whole ordeal. She gazed across the whole landscape... Jean-Luc was right. It truly was beautiful. Grimdolon looked like such a peaceful, quiet kingdom. The tranquility of it made Belle herself feel at peace. She spoke softly, "Yes, it is, Jean-Luc. It looks wonderful. The castle especially looks magnificent."

One of the branches of the apple tree hung just over Jean-Luc's head. Without much effort he reached up and picked the lowest hanging apple. He turned to her and spoke with nostalgia in his voice, "This is the only Grimdolon apple tree west of the kingdom. I used to come here as a boy with friends and pick apples. My father would, of course, reprimand me severely for coming into this territory."

"How are they able to still grow through the wintertime?" Belle asked curiously.

"They are unlike other fruit as their thick skin causes them to survive nearly all temperatures." Jean-Luc gently tossed the apple in his hand. He smiled briefly, recollecting on the memories he had of coming to this spot and collecting apples. He was happy to be coming home.

It was in that moment that Belle realized that everything was coming to a close. It seemed so sudden. She and Jean-Luc had developed a deep friendship over these last few weeks. They had worked together so closely in trying to catch Dominque Delano and now everything was over. Jean-Luc would leave and she wondered if she'd ever see him again. She was saddened by the thought of it all. She wasn't ready for it to be over.

They stood in silence for a few moments before Jean-Luc turned to her. His thoughts were similar to Belle's. He knew this couldn't be the end. He spoke quietly, "Come with me."

"What?" she said, turning to face him.

"Come with me, Belle. Come see Grimdolon. I want you to see the people, and I want them to see you. Stories and legends of your beauty and virtue have reached our people. I want them to know that the stories were only half the truth."

"Jean-Luc... I... I can't. I must get back before anyone knows we're gone, and..."

"Belle, most likely everyone already knows we're gone. Hector has spies watching the castle just in case any of the escaped prisoners try to attack it. I would imagine they are already looking for us." He paused just a moment before continuing, "Please, Belle, consider what I'm saying. Come with me."

Belle looked down at her feet. She was unsure as to what she should say exactly. She had never been to Grimdolon and the thought of seeing the kingdom resonated in her heart with wonder. She also knew there would be repercussions if her father ever found out she had explored Grimdolon with Jean-Luc. She wished time could stand still.

Looking deeply into Jean-Luc's eyes, she grabbed his hands as she spoke, "Jean-Luc, these last few weeks have been wonderful with you, and…"

"Just say yes," Jean-Luc pleaded.

"I've enjoyed all our times together, and dancing with you at the ball was wonderful. You have truly been a gentleman, far more than I could ask." She paused briefly as she looked out on the kingdom. She smiled as she looked back at Jean-Luc. She had made her decision, "I would love to see Grimdolon with you."

Jean-Luc smiled back. He felt as if all the world was right in that moment. He gently squeezed Belle's hands as he looked deeply into her eyes.

They were suddenly startled by the galloping of horses' hooves. Jean-Luc turned to see Hector leading a brigade of a dozen soldiers on horseback up the hill. The men came close to where they were standing. Belle could see the disappointment in Jean-Luc's face. He was too late.

"There he is!" shouted Hector. "Lock him up."

"Hector, you sure know how to spoil a moment," Jean-Luc said, disappointed.

"Shut up, Beast! We were on to you right away. You ought to know better than trying to trick me by having the princess release you."

"Well, I do believe the princess can make her own decisions."

A couple of soldiers began to approach Jean-Luc. He stepped aside from Belle and shot her a quick smile. Turning back to the men and before anyone could react, Jean-Luc quickly reached for one of the men's swords and unsheathed it. He spun around and held it out in a defensive position toward all the others. Hector's men quickly drew their swords.

"Stop!" Belle yelled, trying to calm the whole situation. "It doesn't have to be like this."

Everyone stood in silence for a few moments before Jean-Luc held up the apple he had picked from the tree. He showed it to the soldiers as he was speaking, "Honestly, it is a long ride back to the castle." He began peeling his apple with the sword. "I figured I ought to peel the skin off this apple. The skin can be most unappealing."

"Enough of this," Hector shouted, "Bernard, get the sword, chain him up."

Bernard stepped forward among the crowd of men. "But sir, don't you think we ought to at least hear what…"

"I said lock him up," Hector said, hissing as he spoke.

"Bernard, you don't have to do this," Belle said, stepping close to Hector, trying to take command.

"Princess, these men listen to me," Hector said, pointing his index finger in her face. "You know the king would not let this beast go free."

Belle put her hand on the hilt of her sword. More than ever she felt like pulling it and challenging Hector. Anger was building in her. She gripped tight on the hilt of her sword.

"I wish you would," Hector said, challenging her.

"Everyone… I believe I'm ready to go," Jean-Luc announced to the crowd, interrupting Belle and Hector's conversation. He walked past the soldiers who first approached him and gently tossed the sword at their feet. He took a bite of his apple.

Belle ran to him, "No, I won't let you go back to that dungeon. You don't deserve this. I want to go with you. I want to see your kingdom."

Jean-Luc turned to face her. He smiled as he spoke to her sincerely, "Belle... it's all right. I don't want to see anything happen to you. I just want to tell you..."

"I said lock him up!" Hector shouted again, pushing a couple of soldiers toward the beast. Jean-Luc didn't put up a fight as the men tied his arms behind his back. The men then pulled him toward a carriage that they had brought. Jean-Luc was then ushered into it and the door was shut behind him.

Upon hearing the door shut, Belle lost control of her emotions. "No, you can't do this. I won't let you do this." She pulled her sword from her side and approached Hector. She was only able to take a few steps when her sword was knocked out of her hand and unto the ground. A couple of soldiers quickly grabbed her arms, restraining her. "No, you can't do this, Hector. I order you to release him. Your authority doesn't matter. You are being a coward."

Hector turned to face Belle. His black hair covered his face. He gritted his teeth in anger. He was tired of this young princess questioning his authority. He was going to show her who was in control. "Lock her up!" he shouted to his men.

"What?" they said, confused.

"I said, lock her up!"

The soldiers stood frozen in silence, not sure what to do. After a moment in silence, one of them spoke up, "But... she's the princess. We can't lock her up."

"I said do it... and do it now!" Hector said with fury.

With great hesitation the men took Belle and slowly walked toward the carriage. The door was open and Belle was placed inside beside Jean-Luc. Upon seeing him, she started crying ever so slightly.

"Well… it is great to see you, Belle, but I must admit I thought our hillside view was a much better place to spend time together."

Belle couldn't help but laugh a little at the irony of Jean-Luc's humor. She loved how he could keep his wit in any situation. She looked into his eyes as she spoke, "Jean-Luc, I'm so sorry this happened. After all you've done for us, all I wanted was to see you freed."

Jean-Luc started to feel the tears form in his eyes. "Thank you, Belle. In all honesty, right now I'm just thankful to have this time with you. I've cherished every moment we've spent together." He paused just briefly before speaking to her again with great sincerity. "I love you, Belle. I truly do. Your kindness and beauty far exceed any of the legends told about you. I'm thankful I got to have you in my life, even if it seemed like it was just for a moment."

Belle rubbed his mane as she looked into his eyes. The tears were falling from her eyes. She slowly leaned forward and laid her forehead on his shoulder before speaking ever so quietly, "I love you too."

Jean-Luc simply leaned forward and kissed her forehead. He was thankful for this moment.

❧❦❧

Michael walked out of the gates of the castle as Hector and his men came riding back to the castle. It was early in the morning. The carriage was in the midst of the company. Seeing Hector, Michael walked straight toward him. "Hector, what is the meaning of this late night escapade?"

Hector stopped his horse and abruptly climbed off, "The beast, Jean-Luc, was caught escaping our kingdom along with the princess, who was committing high treason."

"You can't be serious? You have Belle locked up?"

Hector spoke calmly as he took a step closer to Michael, "Any traitor to the kingdom is a traitor to the king himself, even if it happens to be the king's daughter."

"You have really overstepped your authority this time. You can't arrest Mendolon's princess," Michael said, clearly angry.

Hector gave a mischievous smile as he walked close to the carriage and opened the door. He did not take his eyes off of Michael as two soldiers came and pulled Belle and Jean-Luc from the carriage. Jean-Luc was still in chains. "Don't tell me what I can't do," Hector said directly to Michael.

Bernard emerged from the group and walked to where Michael was standing. "I'm sorry, Michael. I didn't want any part of this. He was determined to capture Jean-Luc, no matter what."

"It's ok, Bernard. I won't let him get away with this."

At that time Gideon stepped through the gates with a small company of knights. A few were carrying torches to light the way. Gideon was rubbing the edges of his mustache, a clear sign of his anxiety. "Hector!" he called out as he approached the group. "My men will take it from here. We have installed chains on the wall of one of the cells. He won't be able to escape this time."

"Gideon!" Michael objected.

"I'm sorry, Michael. He is a fugitive of the kingdom. We cannot take his crimes lightly." The knights grabbed Jean-Luc and Belle and started walking them through the gates toward the castle. Gideon and Bernard's eyes met briefly. Gideon nodded his head briefly. Bernard quickly realized a plan was in motion.

Hector laughed as he walked past Bernard and Michael. The hissing in his voice was obvious as he spoke, "It looks like you've lost this time, Michael de Bolbec. Eventually, you too will do my bidding."

Michael watched as Hector with the soldiers at his side marched through the gates of the outer wall. Michael whispered to Bernard, "We've got to keep him out of the castle." He knew he had to do something quickly. Trying to stop him, he shouted in Hector's direction, "You know something, Hector..." Michael quickly searched for the right words to say, "You're nothing but a coward. That's what you are today and that's all you will ever be." Hector stopped in his tracks and turned to face Michael. He gave him a sinister look as he looked directly at Michael. His anger was rising within him.

Bernard wasn't sure what to do in that moment, but he knew he needed to help Michael keep Hector out of the castle. Not knowing what to say, he spoke up, "And Hector, you... you... you smell bad too." Michael turned to face Bernard, somewhat confused. Looking back at Michael, he simply shrugged his shoulders, hoping that would suffice for any explanation.

Hector pulled on his hair in utter frustration. "That's it!" he yelled as he ran to where Bernard was standing. He tried to reach for Bernard with his long nails. Michael along with the soldiers quickly got between the two men in order to keep them separated. Chaos ensued as Hector was viciously trying to attack Bernard. No swords were pulled, but a few bruises did occur as Hector was trying everything to get to Bernard.

As the scuffle was transpiring outside, Gideon, along with a company of knights, led Jean-Luc and Belle toward the castle dungeon. They already had Jean-Luc's chains off him. "Hurry, we don't have much time," Gideon said as they walked briskly through the castle.

"Gideon, what is going on?" Belle said, confused.

"We can pass Jean-Luc through the castle's port tunnel and toward the sea. There we have a small boat waiting for him, that is, if he knows how to sail."

"I do," Jean-Luc said affirmatively.

"Excellent! We will chain up the beast, Remy, in place of Jean-Luc. It should throw off Hector for a few hours, maybe even a day or two. Jean-Luc, we will need your coat to put on him. If you don't mind parting with it?"

"Gladly," Jean-Luc said, taking off his red coat that he had worn for so long.

"Belle, we will need you to head to your tower where you will need to stay for a few days. For now, it may be the best thing we can do to keep you out of the dungeon."

Belle tried to think of the right words to object to the plan. Just a few hours ago she was dreaming of seeing Grimdolon with Jean-Luc. She wanted to be with him. She didn't want this to be goodbye. *Truly*, she thought, *this cannot be the end.* It was all happening so fast.

Gideon continued, "We must hurry. Knights, escort Jean-Luc out at once. We do not want to be discovered."

"This way," one of the knights instructed as they started to walk away.

"Wait!" Belle yelled out. She quickly ran to where Jean-Luc was standing and threw her arms around him. She held him tight. His arms closed around her. She closed her eyes as she placed her head on his shoulder. The tears began to well up in her eyes. She ran her fingers through his hair. She wasn't sure what else to do or say.

After a few moments Jean-Luc pulled away and looked into her eyes. "Goodbye, Belle," he said softly.

Belle squeezed his hand for as long as she could as he stepped away from her. She watched as he turned and walked down a long hallway, and then eventually out of sight.

CHAPTER 19

$\mathcal{B}$elle stood looking out the window in her room. It was a beautiful day in Mendolon. The sun was shining bright, and the snow was starting to melt. Belle was dressed in her signature purple and white princess dress. She thought about leaving the tower and venturing out into the markets. She could see them in the distance. With her windows open she could faintly hear the sounds of people buying and selling goods.

Three weeks had passed since Jean-Luc departed from her. She missed him greatly. It only took one day for Hector to discover that Jean-Luc had left. He was very upset for a while but a small part of him was actually relieved that Jean-Luc was gone for good from the castle. King Sebastian had still not returned from the north, but when he did Hector planned on keeping Jean-Luc's escape a secret from him for as long as he could. He knew the king would be most displeased finding out Jean-Luc was imprisoned and then escaped. Belle was thankful that Hector didn't try to go after him. She was somewhat comforted knowing that he had most likely made it home safely.

Belle closed her eyes and brushed a strand of hair out of her eyes. Her afternoon fatigue was starting to take over. Sleep had been difficult these last few nights. Her dream was back and it seemed to becoming more and more clear every night. It would still awaken her suddenly during the night. Strangely, she was starting to find it comforting. It was like a faithful friend that was with her, no matter what the circumstance may be.

The princess walked over and sat on the edge of her bed. She wondered if she should take a short nap before heading out into the markets. Her mind was saddened by the thought, knowing that the last time she was in the markets was the day she set Jean-Luc free and tried to help him escape to Grimdolon. How she wished he was still within the castle, waiting for her in the dungeon. She longed to see him.

Looking toward the small table beside her bed, she saw the small cup of medicine that was so often sitting there. She hadn't been taking it the last few days. She picked the cup up and stared at the thick green liquid inside it. Holding the cup, she stood from her bed and walked back toward the window. Belle took one last look at the green liquid before throwing it out as far as she could. She never wanted to see it again. Her father never told her what it was really for. It was a concoction created by Hector and in her heart she truly knew that its purpose was not for her good and well-being. She would not be taking it anymore.

She looked as far out of the window as she could. Thinking of the "medicine" she had just thrown out the window helped her to suddenly build a greater resolve within herself. She was done with living within this castle. So many secrets surrounded her life and she was done acting like they didn't exist. No longer would she ignore them and distract herself. She would get to the bottom of everything. Belle decided she would leave tonight and find answers.

⥌⥏

Jean-Luc sat in his room all alone. The last three weeks he had stayed in isolation. He was spending lots of time deep in thought. Many of his relatives were thrilled to see him again, but they all knew that he was not the same. They knew he had fallen in love with the princess of Mendolon. Many wondered if he would ever be the same.

He heard a knock on his door. "Yes… you may enter."

A young servant named Jonas opened the door and stuck his head in. "Sir, may I bring you something to eat? It's starting to get late."

"No… no thank you," Jean-Luc replied passively.

"But sir, you have barely eaten these last three weeks. Many are worried about you."

Jean-Luc looked down at his feet, taking in Jonas' words. It was true. Upon first arriving, he was excited to see his friends and family again, but as time went on he became more and more depressed, saddened by the fact that he and Belle were apart. He had fallen victim to her beauty and charm. Her beauty and grace had surpassed any expectations he had had about her. She was truly amazing, and he didn't want to live without her.

Jonas continued, "Sir, please will you hear my admonitions? We cannot have you like this. Many are depending on you." Jean-Luc said nothing in response, but just sat rubbing his eyes. His appetite had left long ago, and as a consequence he was much thinner.

Jonas wasn't sure what to say at this point. This had become a common routine the last few nights. He took a deep breath as he slowly turned to leave.

As Jonas opened the door, Jean-Luc spoke up, "Jonas."

"Yes," he said, turning to face Jean-Luc.

"Be sure to let me know right away if she is seen."

Jonas nodded in approval. "Do you really think she will come?"

"I'm not sure, but," he paused just a second, "I must hold on to hope for as long as I can."

❧

Belle hid among the trees in the woods overlooking her training grounds. She thought she heard something, so she quickly ducked to hide. She was dressed in a black hood and cloak. Leaving the castle proved to be surprisingly easy, but she knew knights were patrolling the woods, searching for escaped prisoners. She would take her time escaping to Grimdolon. At all costs she didn't want to be caught.

Waiting a few minutes without hearing anything, she figured all was clear, so she began to make her way through the edge of her training area. She moved slowly, trying to be as quiet as she could be. She was carrying only a small bag under her cloak and a small sword at her side. She wanted to be able to move as quickly as possible.

Belle was just about through the area when a voice spoke out from the darkness, "If you take the northern route, you will most assuredly get caught."

She turned quickly, grabbing the handle of her sword. She was relieved when she saw the man calling to her. She spoke calmly, "Michael, you completely startled me."

"Sorry," he said, stepping from the darkness. He walked close to where she was standing.

"How did you know I would be leaving?"

He shrugged his shoulders. "Gideon, Bernard, and Amis have been the main guards watching the castle at night. I told them to inform me if they ever saw you leaving."

Belle smiled slightly, figuring it was a little too easy to leave. She pulled the hood off her head and brushed her hair out of her eyes. Even though it was hard at the moment, she knew she had to be completely open with Michael. "I'm sorry, Michael, but I have to leave."

Michael looked off to the side as he spoke, "I know. I feared this day would come."

Belle wasn't exactly sure what else to say. She deeply cared for Michael and appreciated who he was. It truly was an honor to work alongside him. "Michael, I just want you to know that you are one of the most honorable men I've ever met. Thank you for always treating me with great respect. I consider it a true honor to call you my friend."

Michael nodded in appreciation of her compliments. "Thank you, Belle, you too. I hope you find what you are looking for."

Belle smiled, thankful that her friend was understanding. She felt tears beginning to swell up in her eyes. Even though she knew her destiny was with Jean-Luc, she would greatly miss Michael. "Please, Michael, take care of Mendolon for me. You are the greatest hope for the kingdom."

"Thank you, Belle," he said softly. "I will never give up. I will continue the work that you started for all of us."

They stood in silence for a moment before Belle spoke up, knowing she needed to be going shortly, "I'm sorry, Michael. I must be going. I hope it isn't too long before we see each other again."

"Yes, I hope the same," Michael said in response. He continued, "Belle, I would advise you to pass by my house. You are welcome to take my horse. I would then encourage you to take a more central route and travel through Dragon Waste. Most of the knights and soldiers have been moved to the perimeters, looking for the escaped prisoners. You should be able to move about with relative ease. You can leave my horse at the former dragon's cave. I will come for him tomorrow."

"Thank you, Michael," she said as she put her hood over her head and began to walk away.

"Oh, one more thing," he said, stopping her in her tracks.

She turned to face him, "Yes?"

He looked straight at her as he spoke confidently, "I do want you to know that I am happy for you, and I am thankful that you will at last have answers to the questions in your life. I truly believe this is your destiny."

Belle smiled at Michael one last time before speaking up. "Goodbye, Michael," she said as she began to walk away.

Michael watched as she walked away into the dark of night. He knew this was the right decision for her, but he would truly miss her being a part of his life. "Goodbye, Belle," he whispered under his breath.

❧❧

Michael entered through a small door on the exterior of the castle. This was his usual entrance at night. He tried to be as quiet as possible. As he shut the door, he was startled by the small light of a candle entering the room. He turned to see that it was Gideon and Bernard. They had seen Belle leave and had informed him. He knew they were anxious for news about her.

"How did it go? Did you find her?" Gideon asked.

"I did. She was passing through her training grounds," Michael responded quietly.

"Well… is she leaving for Grimdolon?" Bernard asked.

Michael took a deep breath, nodding his head. "Yes, she is leaving… and doesn't plan to return."

Gideon and Bernard were shocked at the news, even though they knew it was inevitable. Michael had shared with them the books he had read in the depths of the library. They knew that this truly was the best plan for her. Even though the three men would miss her severely, they knew she had to fulfill her destiny. Leaving Mendolon was exactly what she needed to do.

Bernard shook his head as he seemed greatly rattled by her leaving. Like many, he loved the princess and appreciated everything she stood for. He stepped closer to Michael as he spoke up, "Michael... I just... I mean.... How are we to carry on without her? What... What are we to do now?"

Michael put his hand on Bernard's shoulder, trying to calm him. "Men, I'll tell you what we are to do." He looked at both men as he spoke, "We continue on, fighting for what the princess stood for: Peace, Hope, Love for the Kingdom of Mendolon."

⁂

Belle made her way through the territory known as Dragon Waste. It was the former inhabitance of the dragon. Darkness still encompassed the land as it was the early morning. She had traveled many miles through the night. Michael was right; the interior of the land wasn't thoroughly guarded. Soon after leaving Michael, she had seen a few soldiers traveling on horseback. They were easily adverted as she ducked behind a tree and covered herself with her cloak. The rest of her travels had been uneventful, for which she was grateful. She was thankful Michael loaned her his horse for the journey. He had run hard through the night. She felt a little remorseful leaving him at the former dragon's cave, but she knew Michael would come for him as soon as possible. Even though it was a long journey, she was now thankful to be close to her destination.

Her mind wondered as to what she would find when she entered Grimdolon. She wondered how she would find Jean-Luc. Three weeks ago he had left rather abruptly, just with a simple goodbye. She wondered if he would be expecting her, or if he would be looking out for any news of her coming. She hoped she would not be viewed as a threat by anyone she met. Mendolon was not seen as an ally and she hoped her coming would not be met with suspicion.

Her train of thought was broken by a sudden command in the darkness, "Halt! Who goes there?" the voice said.

Belle looked around to see where it was coming from. She saw no one.

"Who goes there?" the voice shouted again.

Belle took off her hood, trying to show that she wasn't a threat. "I am Princess Belle of Mendolon. I was coming to your kingdom of Grimdolon. I'm looking for the beast called Jean-Luc Pascal."

Belle looked from side to side while a few moments of silence passed. It was then that she saw three Grimdolon warriors emerge from the dark forest. She felt a little worried as one was holding a bow with an arrow pointed toward her. All three were quite a bit larger than Jean-Luc and were dressed in thick armor. They appeared calm as they approached Belle.

Belle continued, "I'm looking for Jean-Luc Pascal. Do you know him?"

The beasts looked at each other, contemplating what to do next. The middle beast lowered his bow and arrow and stepped forward. He spoke quietly, "Come with us."

The beasts led Belle through the eastern side of Dragon Waste. The sun was starting to rise and a faint amount of sunlight was starting to emerge through the trees. Belle was thankful for the light as the road became more and more rocky. Even with the light she stumbled more than once on a loose rock.

No one said anything as they passed through the land. One of the beasts had run on ahead back toward the kingdom after they met Belle. Apparently he had to inform someone of their return. Belle thought possibly it was because additional guards were needed to watch the border. Once the dragon left, Grimdolon had seen the need to secure the border with Mendolon, as the kingdoms were not on friendly terms.

The two beasts seemed focused on the journey. Belle was between the two warriors as they walked through the wooded area. Occasionally, Belle would look back at the beast behind her. They were unfazed by the princess. They seemed to be unmoved by anything around them. She wondered what specifically their orders were and where exactly they were taking her.

Eventually they emerged from the woods and into the kingdom of Grimdolon. The terrain looked dry and rocky. There were a few small houses on the edge, along with the castle in front of them. It looked faintly familiar from the sight she saw a few weeks ago with Jean-Luc. Strangely, a small gathering of beasts was watching as the warriors emerged with the princess. Belle saw male and female beasts, along with a few children. She found herself staring as she had never seen beast children before. They were creatures of beauty.

More beasts emerged from houses and ran to see the princess as she made her way toward the castle. Many pointed and whispered as she walked past them, following the warrior in front of her. She did not feel threatened in the least by anyone or anything she saw. They were creatures of peace.

Coming within a couple hundred yards in front of the castle, the warriors stopped as they stood amongst a company of beasts. In front of her was a small group of seven beasts, four males and three females, all different ages. She stood before them as tears started to swell in their eyes. One of the women held her hands over her eyes as she wept. More beasts started to gather around her, forming a circle around her and the warriors. Belle wondered what she could say to the ones crying. She felt confused by the whole ordeal. She spoke ever so quietly, "Why... Why are crying?" No one said a word as the group of beasts now numbered a few hundred. Belle wondered when this would end.

The quiet of the crowd was interrupted with the sound of a horn. It was loud and majestic. "Make way for the king," a herald shouted. The beasts started to clear the way and an opening emerged in front of the castle... and there in front of her, Belle saw the young king of Grimdolon... Jean-Luc.

For a king, he was dressed simply in a purple coat with a white shirt underneath. His slacks looked to be made of the finest material. A well-polished sword hung by his side. A small crown was on his head. Even though he was noticeably thinner, Belle thought he looked majestic as his mane had grown back in full glory after he had cut it for the Winter ball. Now seen in this light, outside the damp dungeon of Mendolon's castle, he truly looked like a king.

Approaching her, the crowd stood in complete silence. He smiled as he spoke, "Hello, Belle. I am so glad you've come."

Belle was amazed as she looked at the king. She wasn't sure what to say as she gazed at him. "Jean-Luc... you look... you look wonderful."

He laughed slightly under his breath. "Thank you."

Belle looked at the faces of the beasts in the crowd. She wondered if her mind was playing tricks on her. Was everything she was seeing truly real? She didn't know what to think or feel at the moment. "Jean-Luc... is this... is this real? Is this who you really are?"

Jean-Luc looked at the beasts in the crowd as they looked back at him. The beasts were watching their leader closely. It was as if they wondered what he would exactly say at this moment. He adjusted his glasses slightly before speaking, "Belle... This is real. This is who I am." He paused briefly to choose his words correctly, "But I think the real question is not who I am, but rather who are you?"

Belle was stunned by the statement and question, but she knew Jean-Luc was right. The real mystery was her identity. The questions in her life needed answers. She stared directly at Jean-Luc as she spoke, "I... I'm not sure."

Jean-Luc nodded as he stepped closer to Belle. He looked directly at Belle as he spoke, "Belle... close your eyes."

Belle wasn't sure what to do. She just looked at Jean-Luc, trying to figure everything out. Jean-Luc spoke again, this time a little more quietly, "Belle, close your eyes." She closed her eyes, following Jean-Luc's request. He continued, "Now, I want you to focus, and tell me ... what is your dream."

She thought for just a moment, concentrating hard, trying to recollect on every detail. "There is a ball. I enter, dressed as a princess. I greet the guests as they welcome me and comment on my dress. Music plays gently in the background. I make my way to the dance floor."

"Yes, go on," Jean-Luc said patiently.

Belle took a deep breath. This is where it had started to become clearer within the last few weeks. "The guests clear the floor for me to dance. My partner is on the other side of the room coming for me. I think it is Michael, but I can't see him clearly. I begin to realize that I'm not supposed to be there. The guests try to stop me, but I know I must leave. I flee the Ball, worried, confused, wanting more than anything to find answers."

Jean-Luc nodded, knowing things were becoming clearer. "Belle, now, think carefully. Why are you not supposed to be there?"

"I'm not supposed to be there because," she paused briefly as she realized the impact of what she was about to say. "I'm not supposed to be there because... I'm a beast, and I don't belong at the ball." She opened her eyes and looked at Jean-Luc, "I belong in Grimdolon."

Jean-Luc took another step closer to her. "Belle, you are correct. That is who you really are."

Belle didn't take her eyes off Jean-Luc as he reached for her hand. He knew he would be answering a lot of questions all at once. He wanted to be sure he was clear. He continued, "Belle, King Sebastian has been trying to provoke a war with Grimdolon for many years. He wants our land and our mines. Knowing you were pledged to me, the future king, he had you kidnapped not long after you were born. Then with the help of Hector, he developed a 'medicine' from a chemical in our mines that would transform you into a human."

The sun was now in full view. Belle could now see everything clearly. She looked again at the beasts in the crowd. No one seemed surprised as most knew this history. So many questions plagued Belle's mind. She wasn't sure what to ask next, "Why would Sebastian do this?"

"Like I said, he was trying everything to lay claim to our land. Capturing you and turning you into a human was another way for him to try to show his strength over us. He thought that we would surrender once he captured the future queen of the land."

Belle closed her eyes, trying to absorb all the information she was being given. Opening her eyes, she continued to look at the faces in the crowd. Her eyes were then locked with the seven beasts in front of her, particularly the woman crying. She turned to Jean-Luc, "Who are these people?"

Jean-Luc looked at her sincerely, "Belle... this is your family."

"My family?" Belle said, astonished.

"Yes, Belle. You are the youngest daughter of a wealthy merchant." Jean-Luc then pointed to the members of her family. "This is your father and your mother, along with your three brothers and two sisters."

Belle's mother started to cry even stronger. Her hands covered her mouth and nose. Belle couldn't hold back any further. She ran and embraced her family as they all huddled around her. Everyone was crying at this point. Belle squeezed them tightly. Being in their arms felt strangely familiar. It was like she knew this was where she needed to be.

She embraced each member of her family individually before turning to face Jean-Luc. There was one more thing she needed to have answered. She stepped close to him, "Jean-Luc..."

"Yes," he said quietly.

"You are the now the king. You risked everything to come for me. Why did you do it?"

Jean-Luc smiled, knowing this question would come. "Belle, I once heard the story of a distant king, who stepped down from his throne to rescue those that he loved. He even went so far as to give his life for them." Jean-Luc paused just a moment before continuing, "Hearing this story of this righteous king, I knew that I could do no less." Jean-Luc looked off into the distance as he continued, "Once I became king about a year ago, I determined that I would do whatever it took to save the one I love. I would save the one I was destined to be with."

Belle reached up and rubbed his mane as she looked deeply into his eyes. Tears began to form in her eyes. She smiled as she spoke softly, "Thank you, Jean-Luc. Thank you for helping me to see clearly."

EPILOGUE

*H*ector traveled north of Mendolon. It was late at night. He was alone. Word came that King Sebastian was finally coming back to the kingdom, and he wanted to be the first to reach him. Dressed in his green robe, he would be easily recognized, but this did not concern him. He was anxious to update the king on all that had occurred.

He wondered if the king had heard that they had the young king of Grimdolon in their possession. Hector didn't figure out who Jean-Luc was until a week before the Winter Ball. By that point there was nothing he could do. Jean-Luc had proven himself vital in their hunt for the Savage. Without him, Hector feared the Savage and his followers would destroy the kingdom.

The light of a torch was coming toward him down the road. It was King Sebastian among a company of soldiers. The king was on his horse while the soldiers walked beside him. The king's crown gleaned off the torch light as they walked closer. Sebastian looked quite intimidating with his red robe draped over him while riding on his white stallion.

"Good evening, O King," Hector said as they met on the road.

Sebastian stopped his horse and dismounted without addressing Hector. He then turned to one of his soldiers, "Take the reins. I prefer to walk."

The king calmly walked beside Hector as the two headed toward Mendolon. He spoke quietly, "I have heard news that Grimdolon's new king, Bayle's son, was in our possession."

Hector snarled as he spoke in frustration, "I can't believe I didn't see it earlier. That foolish man, Dominque Delano, blinded me."

"Yes," the king replied patiently. "Let this be a warning to us to never again hire a madman that we can't control."

The two men continued their walk to the south. The soldiers were following a few feet behind. Hector looked behind him, making sure no one was listening before he spoke. "King, what are we to do now? The princess has returned to Grimdolon, and the dragon is no longer protecting our border to the east."

Sebastian breathed deeply, "The eastern border is the least of my worries. I only had the dragon dwelling there just in case Grimdolon was to retaliate for us capturing the princess. Right now all those dreaded beasts are busy rejoicing in the return of their princess. I do believe we have some time before they think about starting a war with us."

Hector wondered what their next move would be. For years they had been trying to conquer the land of Grimdolon. After the capture of the princess, Sebastian had made an alliance with the dragons in the north. He was able to manipulate one into living east of Mendolon. He hoped this would further intimidate the beasts of Grimdolon, while also providing protection for the eastern border. Unfortunately for Sebastian, within the last year he soon found out that dragons can't be tamed. He was quite upset when the dragon started striking the edges of Mendolon and the knights had to finally drive him away from the territory. Looking back on it, he truly wished Michael would have just agreed to his original plan of appeasement of the dragon.

Sebastian's latest plan was the hiring of Dominque Delano. His job was to steal a hallucinogenic mineral from the mines of Grimdolon and then use it against the people of Mendolon. Dominque was to impersonate a beast while striking the people. Sebastian's overall goal was to provoke the people of his kingdom against the beasts of Grimdolon and thereby start a war based on the people's anger. But as he came to find, a madman doesn't keep to the plan. Dominque Delano's newfound power consumed him and he decided to strike not just against the citizens of Mendolon but against the king and the kingdom itself. Sebastian and Hector lost control and now they were paying the price for their actions.

Hector continued, "King, my fear is that this whole plan is out of our control. Once the people figure out you kidnapped the princess of Grimdolon, they will never rise up and go to war against the beasts."

Sebastian nodded his head passively. He seemed unmoved by Hector's pleas. He continued walking calmly toward his kingdom. Hector couldn't take the king's silence, "Please, O King, you must take heed to what I'm saying. We will lose if we don't…"

"Calm down, Hector!" he said, interrupting his advisor. "I'm close to persuading our allies in the north to join with us against the beasts."

"What!" Hector couldn't believe what he was hearing. "They'll never join anyone. You can't persuade the dragons in the wars of men!"

Sebastian laughed under his breath before turning to face Hector. "O, believe me, Hector. Once we have the power of dragons on our side, there will be no stopping us. We will gain the whole world."

Hector looked into the eyes of his king. He wasn't sure what to say. Corresponding with dragons was a dangerous thing. They seemed to have their own plans and could easily take over the hearts of men. Fear arose within him. Hector was scared of what the king would do to gain the power of this world. It appeared he would do anything... even if it meant losing his soul.

෴

King Jean-Luc was inside his castle gates, waiting for Belle. A few days had passed since Belle arrived at Grimdolon. Today was going to be the official pronouncement that the princess had been rescued. The citizens of Grimdolon peacefully waited outside the gates, ready to see their new queen. They didn't mind that she was currently a human. They knew the best doctors in Grimdolon were working furiously to figure out a way to transform her back into a beast. Jean-Luc wondered if she would be back to her original form by their wedding in six months.

Jean-Luc tugged at the edges of his purple robe. He was still getting used to it as he had spent many months inside the dungeon of Mendolon, wearing the same few outfits over and over again. Some of the warriors at his side laughed at him, seeing how uncomfortable he was in this new attire. Jean-Luc smiled at their amusement, "It's not easy being king. If you keep laughing, I'm going to make all of you start wearing robes like this." They laughed harder, thrilled that Jean-Luc was back at his rightful place as king.

They were all caught off guard by the sight of Belle approaching them. She was dressed in a new dazzling purple dress made by the best seamstresses in Grimdolon. The dress sparkled as it was made with gems found in the mines. Her crown also shined beautifully as it was made from a rare translucent stone. It reminded Jean-Luc of a beautiful star shining bright in the sky.

She smiled as she approached Jean-Luc. "Hello, Jean-Luc," she said pleasantly.

He was speechless as he gazed at her. She truly was the most beautiful sight he had ever seen. It was as if her outer beauty shined bright and reflected who she was on the inside.

Belle continued with a big smile on her face, "Well, this is truly a first. I can't remember a time when you had nothing to say."

Jean-Luc laughed slightly as he adjusted his glasses, "I can't believe how beautiful you are. When I set out to rescue you, I never dreamed that you would be as wonderful as you are. I can't believe that you will be my bride."

"Thank you," she said softly, grateful for his compliments.

"I remember the first time you said my name. It penetrated deep into my heart, reminding me that I was coming not just to defeat Dominque Delano, but also to save you. The thought that you were pledged to me from birth overwhelmed me. I knew more than ever that all those months spent in the dungeon were truly worth it."

Jean-Luc's young servant, Jonas, interrupted them, "Pardon me, Sire, but the people are waiting."

"Thank you, Jonas." Jean-Luc turned to his men and spoke confidently, "Open the gates. It is time for the people to meet their queen."

The gates of the castle started to open slowly as the warriors pushed them. Belle wondered if she was ready to meet the people of Grimdolon. Especially being a human, she wondered if she would fully be received as their queen. She grabbed Jean-Luc's hand and squeezed tightly. Jean-Luc turned to face her. She spoke softly to him, "Jean-Luc, I'm nervous. I'm not sure what to do. I've never been a queen before."

Jean-Luc smiled as he looked into her eyes, "Have no fear, Belle. Just stay by my side... and I will lead you."

Belle couldn't help but smile back at him as she felt reassured. Jean-Luc had rescued her, saved her. There was nowhere else she wanted to be, other than right by his side. "Thank you, Jean-Luc," she said softly in return.

ABOUT THE AUTHOR

❧ ❧

Tony Myers is a high school youth pastor and fiction author. He enjoys finding creative ways to illustrate and communicate truth. He and his wife, Charity, currently live in Waterloo, Iowa with their three children. He can be contacted through his website, www.tonymyers.net, or through Twitter @ tony1myers.

Also, check out Tony's first two works of fiction, *Singleton* and *Stealing the Magic*. Both are available at most online book distributers.

Stealing the Magic
"Myers delivers a page-turning mystery that grips the reader with its relatable characters and compelling plot. A taut, satisfying story for young suspense lovers and seasoned readers alike."

> \- Pamela Crane, literary judge and author of the award-winning A Secondhand Life

"Stealing the Magic is a thrilling story about a group of college kids who get involved with a strange and mysterious magician. The story is compelling, intense, exciting and keeps you guessing till the very end! Besides being a gripping, action-filled tale; the book communicates good morals and life lessons such as loving your family and being strong in your convictions even when people are telling you otherwise. The book was fun to read and extremely hard to put down! Stealing the Magic captivates readers with excitement and suspense."

> \- Allisa Gartin